HOSTAGE
THREE

HOSTAGE THREE

NICK LAKE

BLOOMSBURY

NEW YORK   LONDON   NEW DELHI   SYDNEY

First published in Great Britain in January 2013 by Bloomsbury Publishing Plc
Published in the United States of America in November 2013
by Bloomsbury Children's Books
www.bloomsbury.com

For information about permission to reproduce selections from this book, write to
Permissions, Bloomsbury Children's Books, 1385 Broadway, New York, New York 10018
Bloomsbury books may be purchased for business or promotional use. For
information on bulk purchases please contact Macmillan Corporate and
Premium Sales Department at specialmarkets@macmillan.com

Library of Congress Cataloging-in-Publication Data
Lake, Nick.
Hostage Three / by Nick Lake. — First U.S. edition.
pages   cm
Summary: Seventeen-year-old Amy, her father, and her stepmother become hostages when
Somalian pirates seize their yacht, but although she builds a bond with one of her captors
it becomes brutally clear that the price of life and its value are two very different things.
ISBN 978-1-61963-123-6 (hardcover) • ISBN 978-1-61963-149-6 (e-book)
[1. Hostages—Fiction. 2. Pirates—Fiction. 3. Survival—Fiction. 4. Yachts—Fiction.
5. Fathers and daughters—Fiction. 6. Adventure and adventurers—Fiction.] I. Title.
PZ7.L15857Hos 2013   [Fic]—dc23   2013002686

Typeset by Hewer Text UK Ltd, Edinburgh
Printed and bound in the U.S.A. by Thomson-Shore Inc., Dexter, Michigan
2 4 6 8 10 9 7 5 3

All papers used by Bloomsbury Publishing, Inc., are natural, recyclable products
made from wood grown in well-managed forests. The manufacturing processes
conform to the environmental regulations of the country of origin.

MAP OF THE *DAISY MAY*'S ROUTE

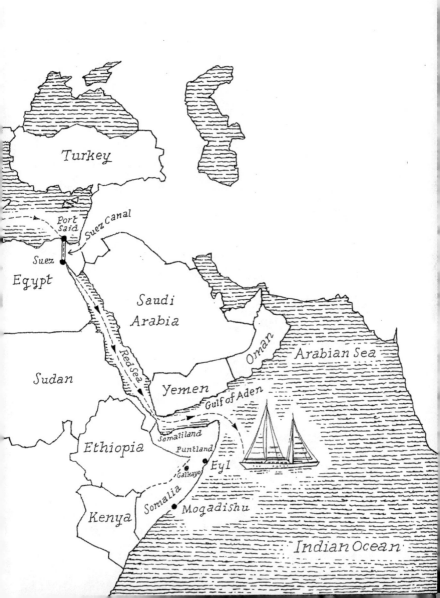

HOSTAGE THREE

THE COAST OF EYL,
PUNTLAND,
SOMALIA

OCTOBER 2008

We stand on the diving platform of our yacht, in the brutal sunlight.

Dad's arm is around my shoulders. I can smell his sweat, the tang of it. This is fairly unusual. In real life, Dad smells of Clinique's moisturiser for men and a casual day for him is taking off his cufflinks. Now he's in a torn, short-sleeved shirt. But then this whole situation is so far from normal it's ridiculous.

There is a gun pointing right at my head.

The pirates are above us, the blazing ball of the sun overhead, frying us all, bleaching the barrel of the gun to a searing, dancing white.

Ahmed, the leader, is shouting about a navy dinghy that's getting too close.

— Turn dinghy around, he says loudly into the VHF handset. Turn around or we shoot hostage.

The dinghy does not turn around. It keeps bouncing over the waves towards us, and I can see navy soldiers in it, uniformed and armed. No one is meant to be armed, I think. That's part of the deal.

I tense up, feel my own shoulders hunch and my knees bend a little, as if someone has tied invisible but powerful string to my extremities and is pulling the ends, sharply, together.

— Don't worry, Amy, says Dad. No one's going to get shot.

— Shut up, Hostage One, says Ahmed.

We have numbers, you see:

My father is Hostage One.

The stepmother is Hostage Two.

I am Hostage Three.

I think this is to make it easier for them if they have to shoot us, though they say it won't happen if everyone follows their orders.

We all watch the dinghy, which is showing no signs at all of stopping. My skin is stinging all over from my sweat and from the loud blasting of the sun.

Ahmed thumbs the VHF handset again.

— Turn around! he shouts. Or hostage die.

At first, I was annoyed that the stepmother came before me, that she was Hostage Two and I was Hostage Three. It seemed typical – her, being more important than me. Standard operating procedure, ever since she came out of a taxi a year and a half ago, drunk from an office party, and into our lives. But that – me being annoyed – was before, before this stopped feeling in any way like an adventure and things started to fall apart. Now the stepmother's place in the hostage hierarchy is the last thing I'm worried about.

And I figured that if things went really badly wrong, she would probably get shot ahead of me.

Our crew also have numbers, but they're standing a little way away. Our family unit is like a force field, keeping the hired help at a distance.

— Stop dinghy, Ahmed says into the radio, or we shoot girl.

Oh, I think. So Hostage Three gets shot first anyway. The way I think this is strangely detached, like it's someone else who's about to get a bullet in the brain.

The dinghy does not turn around. Ahmed keeps his thumb on the *transmit* button.

— Farouz, shoot Hostage Three, he says.

Is that his voice breaking a little?

You don't want to do this, Ahmed, I want to shout to him. I know you don't want to do it. But what if he does? What if he really is prepared to see me die?

And what if Farouz is prepared to do it?

Farouz trains his gun on me, his hand shaking slightly. It's a pistol of some kind, the one he usually wears on his waistband, tied to it with string. I don't know what model it is, what calibre. That's not the kind of thing I'm interested in back in real life, though suddenly it seems terribly important to me, like if I die and don't know what precise model of gun killed me, I might never be able to rest.

— What kind of gun is that, Farouz? I ask.

— Shut up! Shut up! he shouts.

His hand is waving all over the place now, and I think maybe he'd miss anyway. But then Ahmed would shoot me, or one of the others. Ahmed and the other two have AK-47s. That's one of the guns I do know, and only because the terrorists always have them in films.

— Shoot her now, says Ahmed.

The dinghy is about thirty metres away. I can see a sailor on it, binoculars to his eyes. The whole scene is very focused, very sharp; and that's the right word, sharp, because it seems like everything – the waves, the white sail of the yacht, the collar of Dad's shirt – all the things around me would cut me if I reached out and touched them. This feels especially true because in this heat my piercings have turned against me; the sun heats the bolts, and when I touch my face and move them, they scorch my skin.

— Kill her! Ahmed roars.

The stepmother begins to weep.

I stand there, waiting for the bang, but then I think, no, I won't hear it, will I? It's like lightning, a gunshot. Standing here, at the point of impact, I won't be aware of anything. There will be, for me, only energy and violence, and no sound at all.

I close my eyes, and wait to be killed.

My name is Amy Fields.

But the men call me Hostage Three.

THREE AND A HALF MONTHS EARLIER

Parakeets exploded, squawking, out of the tree above me, clattering into the air, wings clapping together with a sound like gunfire.

I jumped, nearly dropping my school bag.

Damn birds, I thought. No one knew where they had come from. Some people said they escaped from a private zoo. Someone else once told me they were brought over for a film shoot at Teddington Studios. They were Himalayan parakeets, which explains why they got on so well here in London, where it's mostly not very warm. You get them all over the city actually, but according to Mom, who knew about all sorts of weird things, we had the biggest flock. You'd be walking down the river path towards Richmond, and they'd be there in the trees, little flashes of green and yellow, making their horrible racket. Mom used to say, the more beautiful the bird, the uglier the sound, which is why nightingales look like tiny brown nothing, and parrots screech fit to wake the dead.

That morning I was on my way to school – my last day of school, in fact. It was my final A-level exam. I was walking across the common to the 65 bus stop, like I did every morning.

School was a girls' college in Surbiton. We lived in Ham, which is in London but is also a little village with a common and a pub and a church. London has grown around it and left it unchanged, like a wedding ring buried in the flesh of someone who got really fat.

Ham means *village* in Old English, apparently – like as in

Buckingham, Cheltenham. Obviously so little happened in Ham, even in the old days, that it was only ever just *Ham*, just a village, absolutely nothing to set it apart. Except that, in a strange way, you could say that even though nothing happens there, it is kind of interesting. I guess because it's been marooned in the past, like a ship that gets separated from land for so long that the people on it end up speaking a slightly different language. So there is something strange about the place, like it comes from a storybook.

For instance, it has a real-life, honest-to-goodness place called Cut-throat Alley, which is a tiny lane that runs down to the Thames. There's also a big patch of woodland between the common, which is where we lived, and the vastness of Richmond Park, and it's called – I swear I'm not making this up – the Wilderness. It actually is wild, too. It looks like the kind of place people get murdered in, on TV shows.

But the weirdest thing is that flock of parakeets.

Wherever they came from, you always saw them around – sitting on power lines, flying across the sky – and if you were like me, you never really got used to it. They were so colourful against the green and brown and grey of London. They made me think: how long does it take before you belong? Those parakeets have been there fifty years, according to some people. At what point do we accept, well, now they're British? I mean, we learned in school that the Romans brought pheasants to Britain a thousand years ago, and now we think of pheasants as the most British thing you can imagine.

I was a bit like those parakeets. I'm half-English, half-American, and I had only been living in England for a few years. I didn't fit in that well, apart from with a couple of girls who I called my friends, Carrie and Esme. They were obsessed with American TV, unlike some of the snobbier kids, so they thought I was great. They would always want me to repeat things because they liked my accent, to learn new expressions from me. But, those two friends aside, I wouldn't say I was popular. So I often looked at those parakeets and wondered how long it would be before I was really British.

My point, my real point, is that if you're one of the few people who've been to Ham, you know what the common looks like, and the houses on it, which means you've already worked out that my dad is mega rich. He worked for one of the investment banks – he ran it, in fact. He's English, whereas Mom was – you guessed it – American. From Arkansas originally, if you can believe that, though she left there when she was eighteen; walked off her parents' farm, all horizontal fields to the horizon, and swapped it for the upright world of New York.

She and Dad met when he was working over there in Manhattan, at the American branch of his firm. I went to school there till I was twelve. Then Dad got the job in London and brought us both over. Mom didn't need to work, of course, but she had this job at a science magazine, which she loved, and so when we moved she transferred to the London office. It's one of those magazines whose name everyone knows, even people who don't know anything about science.

All of which is to say that, in my world, getting thrown out of the school grounds, personally, by the head teacher, was not something that people usually did.

I got on the 65 bus and was sitting on the right-hand side when Esme and Carrie got on, so they didn't notice what I'd done at first. Esme was excited about her parents going away for the weekend – she flung herself into the seat beside me, babbling about it, while Carrie sat down behind, much more carefully, which, to be honest, tells you everything that you need to know about my two best friends.

And when I say best friends, I don't mean I loved them, like they were my soul mates or whatever. They were OK. They just didn't hate me, like most other people.

— They're going for two whole days, Amy, said Esme. Total empty house. Forty-eight-hour party people! She didn't say hello or anything; she wasn't that kind of girl. It's going to be immense, she continued.

— But your snotty brother will be there, too, said Carrie.

— I don't know, I said. I think Jack is kind of hot.

— Ugh, said Esme. Don't perv on my brother.

Carrie pulled a disgusted face and was about to say something, but the reason I could see her pulling a face was that I'd turned round to look at her, so that was when she saw.

Carrie stared at me.

— Oh my god, she said. Your face.

— Amy! Esme shrieked. You're going to get expelled. This is totally incredible.

— It's totally stupid, said Carrie.

I had bolts through my eyebrow, my nose, my bottom lip, my ears, all with little spikes screwed to them. I liked that – I liked the idea of presenting sharp edges to the world.

— They can't expel me, I said. It's my last day.

— Oh, yeah, said Carrie. You don't do French, do you?

French was the last A-level exam – everyone who wasn't doing French was finishing earlier.

— Non, I told her.

— Lucky bitch, she said. She examined my bolts again. What did your dad say?

— Nothing, I said.

— Wow. Your dad's cool.

I shrugged. He wasn't. Actually, he'd probably hate the piercings, but it wasn't like he ever came home from work or paid any attention to me, so he hadn't even noticed. That was the whole point of getting them done, to piss him off, so the fact that he wasn't pissed off made me pissed off.

We went straight to the gym, where the exam was taking place. On the way, though, Miss Fletcher, the drama teacher, stopped us. As always, her glasses were lopsided and her hair made her look like she had been sleeping in a bush. She was looking at my face like it was a snake in her living room.

— Miss Fields, she said, what do you think you're doing?

You know the rules about . . . body decoration. It's an expellable offence.

— It's my last exam! I said. Then I'm out of the school for ever.

— Exactly, said Miss Fletcher. You're still in the school now and the rules are clear. Come on, young lady. We're going to see Mrs Brooks.

Mrs Brooks was the head teacher. I rolled my eyes at Carrie and Esme.

— See you later, I said.

— Er, yeah, see you later, said Carrie. She looked a combination of impressed and worried.

Miss Fletcher waited outside. When I entered Mrs Brooks's carpeted office, her expression changed to sort of sad and patient, like a parent with a wayward child, which I guess was pretty much the situation, the way she saw it.

— Miss Fields, she said. You know that this school has allowed you a lot of compassionate leniency. But you're really pushing it this time.

— It's my last day, I said.

— I know that. And I know that it was your mother's birthday recently, and I know that it's only been two years since, well, you know . . .

I wasn't about to give her the satisfaction of hearing me say anything.

She looked down. I could see the grey at the roots of her blonde hair.

— All right, Mrs Brooks said, still examining the oak desk in

16

front of her. Do the exam. But you leave straight afterwards. No hanging out in the common room. I don't want you setting a precedent.

— Fine by me, I said.

I walked back to the gym on my own. I was, like, two minutes late for the exam, so I had to be quiet as I went to my desk and turned the paper over. I chose the problems I understood the most and filled in my answers in pencil. When I looked up, the big clock on the wall by the monkey ropes said that we had five minutes to go.

Five minutes, and then school was over for ever.

I checked the invigilators. One of them was reading a book, the other was gazing out of the window, hands laced behind his head.

I reached into my pocket, took out a cigarette and put it in my mouth. The girl at the desk next to mine turned and looked at me, her eyes wide. Then I opened my pencil case, got a little box of matches and struck one. I held it to the end of the cigarette, listened to it crackle as I sucked in smoke.

Then I breathed it out, and the invigilators were instantly on their feet, hauling me out of the gym. A few minutes after that Mrs Brooks turned up, and she escorted me off the school premises.

— Very clever, she said, as she marched me to the bus stop. You've made your big statement now. You'll fail this exam automatically, of course.

— What? I said. Are you serious?

— I'm afraid so, she said. You have to understand consequences, Amy. Behaviour like that . . . there has to be a line.

I looked down, silent.

— So, she continued, you've really messed things up now. Do you feel better?

No, I wanted to say. No, I don't.

That last exam, the one where I lit up in the middle of the gym – and, so Esme tells me, went down in school legend – was physics.

This was fitting.

See, in physics we learned about dynamics: the laws about the movement of liquids and air. And there was a time in my life when I thought I knew all about rules and how things unfailingly are. I understood how water is supposed to flow downhill, and air is meant to lose pressure when it's moving fast.

I also understood some other things:

You get wiser as you get older.

Money makes you safe.

People who die are old, like my granny and grandad.

I thought I understood these things, same as I understood that if you keep pouring water into a container it will eventually spill over the top.

But I was wrong.

That night and the next I did the obvious thing: I went out clubbing. The school had called my dad, of course, and he left me, like, a dozen messages about it. He even sent a text. But he didn't bother coming home from work to see me.

His messages were funny.

They started off like:

I'm so disappointed in you.

I thought you knew better.

It's your future and you're throwing it away.

Then they got all like:

I appreciate what you're going through.

Maybe you can resit next year.

Let's talk about it.

I ignored them.

The third night after the exam, I got home late, drunk, in a taxi – the same way that the stepmother came into our lives eighteen months before.

I knew how to climb the stairs so they wouldn't creak. I went to my room and stretched out on my bed, the walls spinning around me. Then I heard murmuring voices. I got up, heavily, and put my ear to the wall. The stepmother was talking.

— . . . getting more self-destructive, I heard her say.

— Mumble, mumble, said my dad.

— But what if . . . what if it's genetic? the stepmother said. Don't you think . . . something, something . . . therapy? I mean, have you seen that stuff in her face?

— Mumble, said my dad. Mumble. Only two A levels. No chance of the Royal Academy now.

I pulled back from the wall like it was a wasp that had stung me. I touched the bolt in my eyebrow. I'm not destroying myself, I thought. I'm marking myself.

But was that true? I knew what I liked about loud music, drinking, smoking: I liked that they made me disappear, even if for a short while.

God, I thought. What if it is genetic? I thought of the scars on Mom's arms and my piercings.

I didn't sleep that night.

I came downstairs in the morning and found the stepmother at the kitchen table, waiting for me. At first I thought she was going to confront me about the night before, but she didn't. Instead, she indicated the chair opposite her.

— Sit down, Amy, she said. I have something to tell you. Your dad wanted to tell you himself, but he had to get into work early for an emergency meeting.

I looked at the table. There were all these maps laid out on it, while Ham Common spread before us, glistening with dew, on the other side of the floor-to-ceiling windows Mom always liked because they brought in the light.

— What? I said, my eyes on the maps. You're sending me away?

— No, said the stepmother, frowning. Remember that yacht? The one your dad mentioned?

I was hungover, and this whole thing was surreal.

— What yacht?

— The *Daisy May*. Don't you remember?

I vaguely recalled Dad going on about some boat, on one of the few evenings when he was around, saying how he might buy it and sail it round the world.

— I guess, I said.

— Well, said the stepmother. He's bought her.

— Bought her? I said, confused.

For an instant, a crazy thought went through my mind – that Dad had bought some other woman. Because you could kind of say that he had bought the stepmother, what with all the Cartier jewellery and Louboutin shoes and stuff.

— The yacht, she said. He bought it.

I sat down. The maps were kind of swimming in front of me. A yacht. OK, that's normal, I thought.

— So? I said, my voice coming out even more sullen than I meant it to. He's always buying things.

I looked her hard in the eye so she would know what I meant, know that I was talking about her. Then I glanced at the Cartier bracelet on her wrist, just in case she hadn't got the message.

— Well, she said, not rising to it. This time he's bought a yacht. By the way, there are bagels keeping warm in the oven. And I bought that cream cheese with chives that you like.

— Thanks, I mumbled.

— Go on, she said. Have one. They're good.

This was the worst thing about the stepmother. I could basically do anything – swear at teachers, take drugs, insult her, go to parties and not come back till the next day – and

21

she would act like nothing had happened. It just made me feel even more awful, which I think was probably her cunning plan all along.

I went and got a bagel from the oven, put it on a plate.

— I don't understand, I said. We're talking about the yacht? The one that was on the web for, like, thirty million pounds?

— That's the one, said the stepmother. It's dry-docked at Southampton. We're going to leave as soon as we find a captain and crew. I mean, if you want to, that is.

— Leave? For where?

— Everywhere.

— Sorry, what are you talking about?

— A trip. Your dad has always wanted to do a round-the-world trip, so that's what we're going to do. Starting in a couple of weeks.

I stared at her. I wanted to think she was joking, but deep down I knew she wasn't. Dad was always mad for boats, though he didn't know how to sail them himself. And way before the Event, too, he was talking about taking me out of school for a year to do some kind of epic trip. Mom always said it was a silly idea, that it would never happen, but then a lot of things Mom said didn't come true. Anyway, I guess after the piercings and the smoking in the gym and all that stuff, he must have got even more into the idea. The stepmother had mentioned therapy, but Dad hated that kind of thing after what happened with Mom, so I think the yacht was his alternative, his idea of a better kind of treatment.

I looked down at the maps. Someone – Dad, I guess – had

drawn little dotted lines on them that went all around the world, across the Atlantic and the Pacific, down to Australia, along the coast of India, the Caribbean. Yes – everywhere.

— Why? I said.

— Why? For a change of scene. You know, a new beginning.

— Are you going to spend the whole day speaking in clichés? I asked.

— Oh, Amy, she said. We thought you'd be excited.

— We? I said. Dad can't even be bothered to be here to tell me himself.

— He wanted to, he just –

— Yeah, yeah. Anyway, I'm not leaving here or leaving my friends to get on a stupid yacht.

— You're not eighteen yet, Amy, said the stepmother. You don't really have a choice.

I held my breath in case it came out in fumes, like a dragon breathing.

— I'll be eighteen in October, I said. Where will we be then? India? Japan? I'll just get off the boat and fly home.

— If that's what you want, said the stepmother blandly.

I took a breath.

— It doesn't matter anyway, I said. Because this is totally not going to happen. Dad will pull out of the trip. You haven't known him long enough to see that. It'll be just like the holiday to Hawaii. And Goa. And the Northern Lights. Just like going to see Santa Claus when I was eight. Oh, no, wait, you weren't around then, were you? And those things never happened. Just like this will NEVER HAPPEN.

23

The stepmother pursed her lipsticked lips and put her hands on the table. She drew in a long breath.

— I'll make coffee, she said.

The thing is, though, I was right. Dad literally did nothing but work. We never even went to the beach house in North Fork any more, like we used to when we lived in New York. I couldn't count the number of trips he had bailed on, like when Mom and I went to Mexico without him, and saw the turtles laying their eggs.

Dad was very high up in a bank that had its logo on every street in London and New York, too, and he was always, always super-busy. Dad had a fortune, yes, but he was also a slave to the business. People noticed Dad – he was handsome, I have to admit, and had this grey hairstyle that you call distinguished. But what you saw when you looked at Dad was something as much like a wolf as a person. What you saw was hunger. For money, for success. It wasn't ruthlessness, not precisely – just hunger. I think a lot of people saw that, and they liked it, and that was why Dad was so good at charming everyone.

At the end of the day, though, it was all about the money and his hunger for the money. No way was Dad going to take a whole year off to go *gallivanting* around the world, which was the kind of word he used a lot when talking about people with less drive than himself.

As it turned out, I was wrong about that, too.

*

A few days later, on Saturday, there was a knock at my door, and then Dad came into the room.

— You really should open your curtains, Amy, he said. It's practically the afternoon.

— Good to see you, too, I said.

He went over to the curtains and threw them open, flooding the room with light.

I blinked, wincing.

— You need clothes, he said.

— I thought I looked quite nice, I replied, looking down at my pyjamas with ducks on them.

— Ha, ha, said Dad. For the trip. You need clothes for the trip.

— The trip?

— You know – the one around the world . . . the yacht.

I stared at him . . . I hadn't actually seen Dad since the cigarette incident. He'd always been at work, and I'd assumed the trip had been forgotten. I hadn't really thought about it since the weird conversation with the stepmother.

— You're seriously going to do that? I said. You're kidding, right?

He frowned.

— No, I'm not kidding. Why would I kid about this?

That was a fair point. Dad wasn't keen on jokes – he felt about them the same way he felt about most things that couldn't be sold.

— But . . . When are we leaving?

— The fifteenth of July.

25

— That's three weeks away!

— I know, he said. That's why you need to buy some stuff.

— How long will it be, the trip?

— Six months, eight months maybe. We're still working out the details of the itinerary.

— But what about your job?

— I'm taking a sabbatical, he said.

— Oh, Jesus. You really are serious, I said.

— Yes, of course. So, I told you, you need clothes. There'll be a range of climates, and we should expect some bad weather at sea. I've made you a list.

He stepped over to my bed, where I was propped up on cushions, watching TV, and handed me a sheet of ruled paper. I looked at the list. There were a lot of things on it. And not just clothes – toiletries, a mosquito net, sunglasses . . .

— Come on, get up, he said. Busy day. I've booked you in for your shots, too.

— Shots? I said.

— Immunisations. Cholera, hepatitis, et cetera. Sarah and I have already had them. Then it's Oxford Street to get the clothes.

Despite myself, I felt a little squirm of excitement in the pit of my belly. Not about the trip – I still didn't believe that was going to happen – but about spending a day with my dad. It had been so long since we'd hung out together – since the Event, I guess.

— OK, I said. Just let me have a shower. What time are we leaving?

— We? he said, baffled.

A falling feeling.

— We . . . me and you. To go shopping. To get the shots. To do everything that you were just talking about.

— Oh, I'm not coming, said Dad. And suddenly I noticed – why hadn't I noticed before? – that he was wearing one of his better suits, that his shoes were shined. I have to go in, he said. A partners' meeting.

Of course, I thought.

He put his hand in his inside jacket pocket, drew something out. He threw it on to the bed at my feet. A black credit card.

— There you go, he said. Knock yourself out. If you see anything you like, anything that's not on the list, get that, too.

I didn't reply because I didn't trust my voice not to go, didn't trust myself not to cry, and that would make me look like such a girl. I just looked down.

When I looked up, he was gone.

We set sail on the fifteenth of July, just like Dad said.

Was I happy to be leaving? I don't know, and that's the truth. It was going to be a year in close confinement with Dad and the stepmother, which didn't sound like a festival of fun. But it wasn't school. And though there wasn't much point in packing the Marlboro Lights – Dad hates smoking – at least there were going to be beaches. Mostly, I think I just didn't care that much about the trip. I didn't have anything better to do. It sounds stupid, but it's true.

And then there was the yacht. It was quite something, and that made it almost worthwhile. Esme would have called it totally a-MAY-zing. Actually, she probably did. After we drove down to Southampton to go aboard, I took a photo of it on my phone and uploaded it to Facebook, and she and Carrie went crazy over it.

It had two sails, which I thought at first were just for show, but which Damian, the captain hired by Dad, said would take us up to a dozen knots when combined with the engine, whatever that meant. It was white and sleek and graceful, despite its size. It looked like a Rolls Royce parked at a broken-down factory against the grey concrete blocks of Southampton. Even the gulls seemed afraid to go near it, to cover it with their droppings.

— This is going to be good, said Dad, as we walked up the gangplank. Some proper time together, as a family.

— Whatever, I said, which was all that little statement merited.

Up top was the bridge, where Damian would steer or drive

or whatever, and a kind of bar or dining-room area with remote-controlled roll-up sides, for eating *al fresco* if you wanted, as the stepmother said with a squeal. Below decks were five en-suite bedrooms, then below those, a cinema room, a games room and access to the diving deck. I already had a Padi licence (I went to *that* kind of school) and Dad had done his scuba-diving qualification in preparation for the trip.

On the diving deck were a lifeboat and a dinghy with an outboard motor – so we could take *sojourns to the shore*. That's the stepmother talking again.

Basically, the only thing the *Daisy May* didn't have was a helipad, and if there'd been a yacht available with one, Dad would have bought it. But the push for this whole crazy idea came from me leaving school, so he had to take what he could get at the time.

What he could get, in addition to the *Daisy May*, was:

Damian, the aforementioned captain. Kind of hot, in an old, Brad Pitt kind of way, with sparkling green eyes and an Irish lilt.

Felipe, the cook. Not hot. Spoke English with a very strong accent. And, as I'd already learned at the cooking auditions Dad had insisted on having, a pretty awesome maker of pancakes.

Tony, the . . . I don't know what you'd call him, really. Guide, maybe, mixed with a bit of security. Not the leader – because that was obviously my dad – but the guy who was meant to know where to go and what to see, and what places to avoid. Dad had worked out some kind of complicated deal when he bought the yacht, and the bank was insuring it. Tony was part of the deal: if Dad wanted to go without him, he would have to pay the insurance himself, and Dad was too smart with money to do that.

In the end, putting Tony on the yacht didn't turn out to be that much of a genius idea on the company's part.

Anyway, Tony was sort of a six where hotness is concerned. Neither hot nor not. He was just one of those men who you see all the time – average height, average weight, hair going grey. He had a touch of a West Country accent, but that was about the most interesting thing you could say for him. For all that, though, he was basically the most powerful person on board, after Dad. I mean, Damian was the captain, but he was just there for the nautical stuff. Tony was there to keep us alive.

First thing I did on board, I went down to my room – Dad insisted on calling it my *berth* – and unpacked my stuff. I had a double bed, a plasma-screen TV with a DVD player and my own bathroom. I put my photo of Mom on my bedside table, the one in the silver frame, where she's pregnant with me, standing by the side of a pool in Greece, laughing, not caring that she's in this green bikini with this absolutely massive stomach.

I put all my stuff away, and that was when I found my violin. It was at the bottom of my biggest suitcase – I had a matching set from Burberry that had appeared in my bedroom at home a week before departure, to go with all the stuff I bought on Dad's credit card. The violin was underneath my clothes, kept safe in its padded case. The breath caught in my throat.

You see, the violin was from Before. I don't know who packed it, my dad or the stepmother, but I guess it was my dad and he should have known better. Just looking at it brought back all these memories, fluttering at me; my memories were moths in the darkness and the violin was a light.

For example, I remembered the private hospital, on the day the Twin Towers fell.

I must have been ten, and my mother was a month or so into a stay in this very expensive place in upstate New York, near Cold Spring. She was getting better – she'd had a few doses of electroshock therapy, which was the only thing that ever did any good – but she'd put on weight since the day she arrived there, seventy pounds, and she was shaking.

I also remembered the previous visit when I was in the dining hall with her and she started screaming for no reason at all, saying that the nurses wanted to poison her.

I know what you're thinking. You're thinking: they don't do shit like electroshock therapy any more. You are wrong.

This was a long time before I knew the terms OCD or Severe Clinical Depression, but, believe me, I knew all about OCD and Severe Clinical Depression.

On September the eleventh, I had brought the violin to the clinic because I was auditioning for a new music school, and Mom said she wanted to hear me play, that it would be *like sunshine in this place*. So we went to her room, which was actually like a suite in a really nice five-star hotel, no matter what she said about how terrible the hospital was, and I played for her. I played one of Paganini's *Caprices*, because that was the kind of little show-off that I was.

While I was playing, Mom smiled. I hadn't seen her smile in weeks, and just seeing that, it was like something opened inside me, and she was right – sunshine was blazing through, lighting up everything.

After that, we went downstairs to the common room. The TV was on. A few people were playing dominoes – I don't know what it is about dominoes and the mentally ill, but they love that game. A few other people were playing cards or chatting. Most of them were watching the TV. That, and drooling and so on. It was super-quiet in there, like a waiting room, but I don't know what the people were waiting for. Themselves, I guess. Waiting for themselves to get better.

Then a few of the more alert people started angling towards the TV. Someone turned the volume up. I saw what was on the screen.

— It's the Twin Towers, Mom said.

But I already knew that. Dad worked only a few blocks away from them, though that day he was on a business trip in Italy, which was why I was visiting Mom on my own. I wasn't completely alone, naturally. Our driver was waiting for me on the gravelled drive, to take me back to our apartment by Central Park.

On screen, one of the towers was in flames. The room was really quiet at this point. Someone on the TV was saying something about a plane hitting the building, which sounded crazy – and that was ironic, given where we were. It was as if the maddest person in there wasn't in the room at all, but on the TV. At the time it seemed like a terrible accident must have happened.

Then, as we were watching, the second plane hit the other tower and exploded. People in the room started screaming and, even at the age of ten, I knew how absurd this was, to be watching something so insane in the hospital, which was all disturbed people and drug addicts. Suddenly Mom also seemed to realise that this was pretty disturbing for a little girl, though actually I was more puzzled than freaked out by the whole thing. She took me by the hand and led me away, back to her room, but she didn't want to hear me play the violin again.

Looking back, I think that was the last time I really *saw* my mom. After 9/11, she was never the same. I think now it must have been the strangeness of it: when she went into what was essentially a mental hospital, the world she left behind was a normal one, in which the Russians and the US had finally stopped trying to nuke each other, the West was safe and rich, and everything was right. Then she came out of there into a scary place, a different world, where people who didn't care about security and cars and mortgages wanted to kill you.

Or maybe that's not true. Maybe the last time she was herself was when she got out of hospital that time, and I came home from school to find that she'd covered my room with those little stars that glow after you turn out the lights.

Not like some people do it – not, like, a few of them on the ceiling. I mean hundreds of them, thousands of them, every-where, on every surface, so that, as she put it, *I would remember that there is magic in the world*. This was the kind of over-the-top thing my mom often came out with. She put them up in my London bedroom, too.

And for ever since then, you turn off the lights in my room and it's like fairyland, like being in an observatory, with the universe all around you. A lot of the time – when Mom was well, I mean – I liked that.

Then she would get ill again, and everything would be terri-ble, and the stars would stop being comforting, would become like a prison instead, a glowing prison holding me inside, reminding me that Mom would always be all around me, would always be the biggest thing in my world, but that she wouldn't always be *with* me.

Mom was often that way. She would give you something amazing. Stars. The universe.

But at some point she would take it away.

The thing about yachts I hadn't realised before: they take a long time to get anywhere. Southampton to the Suez Canal was a month and a half. A month and a half! You could fly around the world, like, thirty times in that time.

The English Channel to Gibraltar was the worst. The sea was really choppy and rough, and for the first week I was just curled up in my en-suite bathroom, making good friends with the toilet. There were times when I would've quite happily strangled my dad for making me do this.

The Med was a bit better. You could see Morocco some-times, this sandy haze to the south, and occasionally little fishing villages, with white roofs sloping down to the sea.

It didn't exactly feel like a holiday. Most days we were far from the coast, just crawling through the water, which has no landmarks so doesn't make you feel like you're moving. It's more like an endless conveyor belt of wetness and foam, unrolling underneath you.

I thought we might see dolphins, but we didn't.

Time warped and stretched, like Play-Doh. It was August already and it was, like, thirty degrees, and I was over my seasickness by then, so I mostly lay on the deck, with my eyes closed. When the sun went down I would go in, read in my room, watch TV, send emails. The yacht wasn't connected to the internet all the time, but the satellite link came online every day at 6 p.m. GMT. Any messages you wrote would be stored up until then to download or send, so I got used to checking my email every evening, to see if my friends had written to me.

Mainly, I just sat in my room at night, because I didn't want to see the stars.

I caught Damian checking me out a couple of times as I lay there in my bikini. It was gross but pleasing at the same time. I mean, I'm not beautiful. I'm aware of that. I have this dirty brown hair, an ordinary face – apart from the bits of metal in it, of course, but I didn't always have those.

What else did I do?

Not much.

I love abstract dance music, mainly dubstep. So I lay there all through the Mediterranean, listening to it cranked up loud, blocking out the world. There's something about music like that: the depth of the bass, the echoes, the disembodied voices. It's sad music, but the sadness is somehow a comforting kind of sadness; it makes me think of the way that seeing city lights across water – the Hudson River in New York, say – can make you feel lonely and warm at the same time.

Mostly, though, that kind of music makes me think of floating in space. Not space with stars, but black space, a cold vacuum, the sounds dispersing all around you. And when there are voices, they're broken, fractured, seeming to come at you like distant singing from the radio of some destroyed spaceship. I know what I love about it: those voices in the darkness, in the deep bass, are like the voices of dead people who you love.

Something else about it I liked: it wasn't classical music. Back when I was young, I listened to that stuff all the time.

Actually, if we're being technical it wasn't classical music but baroque music that I loved – I was a sucker for Bach.

But, after Mom, I didn't listen to it any more.

What with the music, then, and the sunbathing, and the fact that I hadn't really been paying attention to the world around me ever since Mom died, I didn't notice much of anything before the Suez Canal. The days passed, blurred together like squashed boiled sweets left in a warm pocket.

Then one day I happened to open my eyes to look at the sky and I caught a flash of light that I just knew was a reflection from Damian's binoculars.

I don't know why I did what I did next: to turn the tables, I suppose. Make him feel watched. Or like I knew he was watching.

I got up and I went up the short flight of stairs to the bridge. I walked right in there in my bikini. Damian turned round from the wheel, looking surprised and nervous.

— What's up? he asked.

— Nothing, I said. Just bored.

Damian's mouth flapped open a bit. But, to his credit, he got hold of himself pretty quickly. He was still rather pale from all that time in the bridge, out of the sun; his stubble was dark against his skin, like cross-hatching on paper.

— You want to be helpful? he asked.

— Sure, I said. Why not?

He walked towards me and came up really close, and, for a

split second, like when someone in an oncoming car flicks their full beam at you to warn you about something ahead on the road, I thought that this was an unbelievably stupid idea. Then he brushed past me and picked up some papers from the table.

— We're twelve hours from Port Said, Damian said. There's a load of preparation we have to do. Information we have to radio ahead and documents we have to present when we get to the Suez Canal. It'll be much quicker with you helping.

— Oh, OK, I said. Let me just, ah . . .

I backed out of the room, then followed the corridor to my cabin. What could I do? I'd tried to make him feel stupid, but he'd kept his cool and now it was me who looked like an idiot. Jesus! It probably looked like I fancied him or some-thing, when it was him who was the creepy one, with his binoculars.

Anyway, I couldn't back down now – if I'd said I wanted to help, then I had to help. I grabbed a T-shirt and some shorts, put them on and headed back to the bridge.

Damian had pulled up two chairs to the table.

— Right, he said. You find the capacity plan and the regis-tered tonnage from this paperwork. I'll find the engine plan.

— Yeah, I said. Great.

The Suez Canal is weird. You think you're just going to sail through it, but it doesn't work like that. It's more organised, almost like public transport, only you're in your own yacht.

For a start you have to moor in Port Said at the right time, by 19:00 hours the previous evening, or you're not going, simple as that. This is because, Damian told me, it's really busy going south in September. It's to do with currents or winds or something.

Then you have to give all the documents I helped Damian pull together. It was ironic: I was the person who least wanted to be there, but I probably knew more about that yacht than anyone apart from the captain. I think Dad was pretty surprised when the official from the company that was helping us deal with the authorities boarded the yacht in the port and Damian beckoned me over to help talk to him.

In the end, we handed over the following documents to secure our passage through the canal:

Registration certificate.

Cargo manifest.

Crew list.

Ballast declaration.

Declaration of cargo and contents of the yacht's double hull.

Engine room plan.

Registered tonnage.

Capacity plan.

And . . .

. . . a hundred dollar bill.

I don't think Damian would have thought of that on his own. He kind of stood there blankly when the agent still had his hand out, even though we'd presented everything we were meant to present. So I had to nudge him and do that gesture where you rub your fingers together to show some-one needs to be paid.

Anyway, we got the authorisation to go ahead. But that didn't really mean going ahead; it meant joining up with the other ships in our convoy for the next day's crossing. And that didn't really mean day; it meant a crossing at one o'clock in the damn morning.

Still, I have to admit I stayed up for it. It was interesting, so sue me. We were one of only three yachts – all the others were cargo ships of various kinds. There was one that was ridiculous, like a floating city. I swear, the bridge and what-ever else were, like, four storeys off the deck. We went one by one behind an official tug. The *Daisy May* was somewhere in the middle, and in the dark you could just see the lights of the ship in front of us and the one after us.

As we neared the middle of the canal, the sun started to come up. I stood on the deck, wrapped up in jumpers and scarves, shivering, watching. There was flat desert on either side of us, dirty yellow, and we were sailing down this great strip of blue that looked exactly like every canal you've ever seen, only enormous. More than big enough to fit the giant cargo ship that was in front of us. The whole thing was surreal.

We passed some structures on the banks that looked kind of military, which creeped me out, and then it all started to look rather samey – the desert, the canal – so I went back to my cabin and fell asleep pretty much straight away.

*

The next time I went out on deck, we were sailing down the coast of Egypt. That was when I started seeing a proper shore-line as opposed to just empty sea or the monotonous strip of the Suez Canal. What I could see, Damian told me, was the Sinai peninsula. It was all red sand, the leafless tracery of trees whose names I didn't know, mountains dreaming in the background. I thought it was beautiful – it all sort of shimmered in the heat, and the blood colour of the sand was bright against the blue of the sea.

— That's where Moses climbed the mount, said the step-mother, when she came out on deck. She pointed. And where he was supposed to have seen the burning bush, she added, before he came back down with the ten commandments.

— Right, I said.

— No, really, she answered. I climbed Mount Sinai when I was younger. And this is, of course, the Red Sea, that Moses parted.

I looked around me. It was weird to think that those things might have happened close by. I mean, I didn't believe in the parting of the Red Sea, but it was still a story I'd known since I was very young. To think of it happening in a real place, and that place being here, was weird. It was like someone point-ing to the horizon and saying, oh, look, there's Never Never Land.

Sometime after that, Dad called for Damian to cast anchor and lower the diving deck. He'd been looking at some charts or something on the internet, and reckoned that there was an amazing reef right underneath us. He was all for getting out the scuba equipment, but the stepmother said she'd rather snorkel, so the two of them started getting out just masks and flippers and stuff.

— Come on, Amy, Dad said, as he took off his T-shirt. Loosen up a bit. Take those headphones out for once.

I looked at his pasty white skin, at the stepmother beside him, sitting down on the deck to pull on her flippers.

— I don't think so, I said.

— The colours of the coral are going to be amazing, Amy-bear! Dad said.

— Good, I said. Enjoy them. I opened a magazine and plugged my earphones back in.

— Leave her, James, I dimly heard the stepmother saying, and Dad's approaching footsteps stopped. Let her miss out.

Bitch, I thought, closing my eyes, as Dad walked away. Like I cared about missing out. I hadn't even gone to their wedding. They got married at some registry office in Richmond and I went out with my friends and got wasted instead.

Even though I didn't snorkel, I did like the Red Sea. I actually started looking around me from then on, especially after a school of dolphins turned up and followed our yacht for most of a day, jumping into the air, tumbling, the sea sparkling where they splashed it into the sky.

Another weird thing: I started to get why Dad had taken us on this trip. It was to do with the movement when you were on the front deck. You watched the sea coming towards you, endless, and you could turn and see the wake behind. It was like the yacht was moving all the time into the future, always leaving something behind. It was hypnotic. The blue sea, the red land, drifting by.

I understood what the yacht was, then: it wasn't a boat; it was a machine for forgetting the past. I started to like it.

And then came the first time I heard about the pirates.

— We're connected to SSAS, said Tony. He was giving us a security briefing in the cinema room. So if we think we're under attack, he continued, the first thing that will happen is that Damian will hit an emergency button. It's like dialling 999 on a boat – it will tell everyone who matters that we're in trouble.

— Wait, I said. Why would we be in trouble? I'd turned up late, so didn't really know what was going on.

— Pirates, said Tony. From Somalia. There've been a few ships taken this year. But we should be OK. We're not going down the Somali coast – we're just going through a bit of the Gulf of Aden. We'll stay equidistant between Somalia and the Yemen at all times. We'll be a hundred miles from Somalia.

— Oh, right, I said. That's comforting. You didn't mention bloody *pirates*, Dad.

— Actually, said the stepmother, Amy's right. No one said anything about pirates. Why don't we just go another way?

— We can't, said Damian, who was sitting in an armchair at the back. We want to get to southern India before the monsoon season, and that means going this way.

— There are things we can do, Tony said in a reassuring tone. He was standing in front of the screen, and he picked up a remote and pushed a button. A film came up of a little wooden boat, scooting along the waves, men with head-scarves inside it. They were holding guns, one of them shouldering what looked like a bazooka. The film seemed like it was taken from the deck of a larger boat, looking down. As we watched, the pirates' boat came closer, and one of the men inside started reaching out to grab the netting on the side of the bigger boat. The person filming swung down to catch what was happening.

But then a jet of water came from nowhere, hitting the pirate square in the face, making him fall back into the little boat.

— Water cannon, Tony said, pausing the image. We have one on each side of the yacht, for fires. But if pirates come at us, we'll man the cannon and use them to deflect attack.

— You're talking about it like it's going to happen, I said.

— Just being prepared, said Tony. A strong hose can stop pirates boarding. Just watch out for knots in the hose – something like that could make the difference between being taken captive and not. The hoses are powerful when used properly. Mr Fields, I'd ask you to take the starboard side, if that's OK. I'd take portside. Damian would need to stay in the bridge to talk to any navy people, if we can raise them. Once you've got the nozzle in position, just open up and aim the water.

— Oh good, I said. They have bazookas and we have water pistols.

Tony glared at me.

— The point is to stop them getting on board, he said. They won't shoot – we're worth too much alive. As long as we can prevent them from boarding, we'll be OK, hence the water cannon. We'll also trail knotted ropes in our wake from now on. They stop boats from coming up behind us, because they

45

snarl up in the outboards. And we'll run dark from tomorrow night.

— Dark? asked my dad.

— Like in the Blitz, said Tony. No lights at night. All curtains drawn. We don't want to be seen from afar. He pointed to a table, where he'd laid out what looked like rolls of black bin bags, sheets and towels. I'll need everyone's help to block all the windows, please, he said. We don't want any light getting out.

— Of course, if they've got radar, they'll see us anyway, said Damian. Then he winked at me.

— Do pirates have *radar*? asked the stepmother, aghast.

Tony shot Damian a look.

— Some of them do, Tony said in his West Country voice. Some of them . . . They can be quite well equipped.

Dad made a dismissive gesture.

— I've already looked into it, he said. The chances are 0.1%. That's why the big shipping companies still use the lane. Even with the risk of piracy, it works out cheaper to run their shipping this way rather than pay for the extra fuel to go round the Horn of Africa. The ransoms the pirates demand might be high, but the likelihood of coming across them is so infinitesimally small.

— 0.1% is not infinitesimal, said the stepmother. That's one in a thousand.

I sometimes forgot that she worked in Dad's bank as some kind of broker, before he got together with her, so she wasn't completely stupid.

— Well, yes, he admitted. But that's still small. Honestly, dozens of vessels go through the Gulf of Aden every day and don't get taken. The navies of France, Britain and the US are on constant patrol. Besides, we're not a big container ship. From a distance, or on radar, we'll look like a fishing boat or something insignificant.

— Exactly, said Tony. We'll also turn off the AIS.

— AIS? I asked.

— Automatic Information System, Tony explained. It broadcasts our identity, our position, our route, everything about us, by radio to anyone within fifty miles. It tells other ships who we are, basically. If we turn it off, a lot of the pirates simply won't know we're there. And those that do won't know that we're a yacht.

I thought for a moment.

— So that means the navy won't know we're there, either?

Tony frowned.

— Er, no. He paused. But that's OK because we've got the SSAS, like I said. The alarm system. In any case, pirates use small attack boats, which means they're pretty much confined to the coast of Somalia.

— It's not going to happen anyway, said Dad. No chance.

And he was right.

It didn't happen.

Not on the first night.

After the briefing, we all went round and hung stuff up in the windows and portholes – bin bags, cloths, towels, all sorts. We unscrewed the bulbs from the outside lights, the ones that lit up the deck at night.

That night, as we sailed out of the Red Sea and into the Gulf of Aden, we did so in darkness.

It was an odd experience. We couldn't read or watch TV because that might produce glimmers of light, so once we'd had an early dinner, I went to my room and lay on my bed, listening to music in the dark.

When I woke up, it was morning, and my iPod was silent.

We had breakfast on deck. Felipe had made scrambled eggs and croissants to go with the usual cereal and fruit and coffee. It was a beautiful day, the sun a disc of molten metal in the sky, a few scraps of cloud floating overhead. The sea was calm, and there was a slight breeze, so the mainsail was up. Damian said it was always better to use it when we could; it saved us fuel.

After breakfast, I stayed out on deck, just watching the sea, the unending colours of it. Often it was like silver, or steel, flashing in the light. Then it would shift to petrol, all multi-coloured sheen, and then it would be blue, like you think the sea should be, but really only rarely did it look like that. It was properly hot now, too – forty degrees, easy.

Maybe an hour later, I saw something on the horizon, ahead of us. I watched it for a while, until I was sure it was a ship. It looked big, like a tanker or a trawler or something, so I wasn't that worried.

Still, I went inside and up the steps to the bridge. Damian was looking out through the big windows with a pair of binoculars.

— You saw it, too, I said.

— Yep. Looks like a trawler, but I'll give it a wide berth anyway. Good job the sails are up. I can squeeze eleven knots out of her.

— Er, OK.

He smiled.

— Sorry, sailors' habit. You relax. There's no way this is pirates. It's a big old fishing boat, probably Yemeni.

I went back to the deck. Again, the bad thing about yacht travel: it's so slow. It took a good hour before the trawler was close enough for us to see it properly, and then another half an hour for us to skirt around it, keeping the wind behind us, but staying a safe distance away.

Eventually, though, it was in our wake, and then it began dwindling to a speck until, finally, it disappeared completely.

I hadn't realised I was tense until I felt my shoulders loosen. I lay back and picked up a copy of GQ that someone, probably Damian, had left there.

I was about halfway through the magazine when there was a blast from the ship's horn, and I jumped, like, a metre in the air. I ran inside and up to the bridge.

Damian was at the wheel, cursing.

— What is it? asked Tony, who came clattering in behind me.

In my head, tritones were shrieking, like in Bernard Herrmann's score for *Psycho*, when he does D and G sharp together, again and again, to mark the stabs in the shower, so I already knew this was bad because of the discordant music my mind was making – my instincts screaming at me, I guess.

— Dinghies, said Damian. Outboard motors. They came up behind us.

As he spoke, I saw the prow of a little boat appear to our left, just moving into our vision, before falling behind. I thought I caught a glimpse of a man, but then he was gone.

— Fuck, said Tony. The trawler?

— Yeah. Must have been a mother ship.

— A mother ship? I asked. It sounded sci-fi, which was just so incongruous on the bridge of this yacht, in the middle of a desert sea. Inevitably it also made me think of my mother, which wasn't quite so incongruous. For me, the word *mother* isn't one that means anything safe. It has a lot of danger in it already, even before you put the word *ship* after it and use it about pirates.

— I've only heard about them, said Tony. I didn't know if it was a rumour.

— Shit, shit, shit, said Damian, spinning the wheel with a grunt, then pushing the throttle all the way forward.

The yacht lurched, but slowly, and a dinghy came surging up on our left-hand side, containing silhouettes of armed men.

— What's a mother ship? I asked, my voice coming out a bit strangled.

— Pirates live on there for ages, said Tony. It's a big ship with lots of supplies. They keep faster, smaller boats tethered to it. That way, they can go after ships from the middle of the sea, instead of being tied to just the coastline, and –

— Kind of busy here! said Damian.

— Oh, I said.

I felt sick – really, properly nauseous in the pit of my stomach.

— What's going on? Dad said, coming in the door. He was in swimming trunks, his grey chest hair and portly stomach showing. He'd been sunbathing on the rear deck, I guess.

— Looks like pirates, said Tony, surprisingly calm. Head to your hose. I'll go to mine.

— But Sarah, she's sleeping –

— Leave her. Man the hose.

Damian pressed a red button on the console in front of him, then picked up the first of the two satellite phones. He grunted in frustration, put it back down and picked up the other. He dialled a number.

— Yes, Admiral, he said after a pause. This is the civilian yacht *Daisy May*. Our position is . . . 11.93 lat., 44.32 long. We are under attack by pirates. I repeat, we are under attack by pirates.

Just then, the dinghy appeared again, bouncing over the waves as it pulled ahead of us. Three men were on board, each clinging to the sides with one hand.

Dad and Tony back-stepped out of the bridge and ran off. I heard Dad's bare feet slapping on the wooden floor. From the bridge, Damian and I had a good view of the front of the yacht, and a not-so-good view of the sides. But we did see the water from the hose start to spray to the left – is that starboard? It was where we'd just seen the boat, and now we watched it veer away from the stream of water, so much more manoeuvrable than us. That was the moment I first thought that we really, properly might get boarded, when that boat turned so quickly to avoid the hose. It suggested, I don't know, a certain expertise.

Damian spun the yacht's wheel all the way in one direction, and, after a moment, the room lurched to the left. Then he reversed, and I had to grab on to the table.

— What are you doing? I asked.

— Creating wake. So they can't get up behind us.

— I thought the ropes were meant to do that.

— Yes. Well.

The VHF crackled; I guess Tony must have grabbed a handset as he ran:

— Another boat to portside! Four aboard.

Damian picked up the handset in the bridge.

— Roger that. Hose them.

— Shit, Tony said over the radio. He sounded out of breath. There's a knot. Wait . . . OK.

We heard the roar as the water started, and then that was cut off, along with Tony's voice.

— I can't see what's happening, I said.

— Me neither, said Damian. I don't like it. He thumbed the VHF. Mr Fields? Tony?

There was no answer. I couldn't take not being able to see what was happening any more. I ran to the door.

— Amy, what are you –

But I was gone, down the corridor, heading for Dad. When I came out on to the walkway, he was standing there with the hose at his hip, like a gunslinger. For a moment, the sea was still. Then a little wooden skiff came bouncing over the waves towards us. I saw that there was a pirate in it, struggling to manoeuvre a ladder, which he was clearly going to try to hook on to the rail of the yacht.

— Get back to the bridge, Amy! Dad shouted, as he loosed water at them.

The pirates veered away, the ladder bobbing. Then they started to cut in towards us again. I turned and saw a small fire extinguisher set into the wall behind me. Ignoring my dad, I pulled it off its bracket. When the pirate boat came into view below us, I hurled the fire extinguisher at them. I don't know what I was thinking; I guess I was scared, and that got my adrenaline going.

One of the pirates who was waving a machine gun twisted to the side. I saw and heard the fire extinguisher clatter on to the boat beside him, then glance off and splash into the sea.

Oh crap, I thought.

I probably would've tried to grab something else to throw then, but I felt hands on my arms, and someone was dragging me backward. I turned to see Damian, pulling me inside, then back down the corridor. My feet were off the ground – it's weird, but what I felt first was surprise at how strong he was.

— You can't touch me, I said, thinking of him looking at me when I was sunbathing. Only that had been a man looking at a girl. Now he was all business, all urgency; it was like a person made of steel was dragging me.

— Oh yes I can, he said.

— Really? My dad –

— Made me captain, he said. My command, my rules.

— Yeah? You left the wheel.

— We're going back there now.

A moment later, we were in the bridge again. Damian seized the wheel as soon as we entered, started doing his evasive turns. He lifted the VHF with one hand.

— Situation? he said.

— Holding them off for now, Tony said over the noise of the hose. Just . . . Agh, bastards. Get off!

There was a chaotic mix of sounds: whooshes and bangs, cracks, Tony's grunting.

He was still talking when there was a *bang*, not as loud as I would have expected, and a glass spider's web crackled into existence on the window of the bridge, and then, *bang*, another. One of the boats was cutting across our bow, shooting. I saw the headscarved men on board, clinging to the side even as they fired.

— Jesus, said Damian. Down! Get down!

I lay down on the floor, under the console. Damian dialled a number on the satphone again.

— No time to talk, he said into it. They're firing. We're going to surrender. He switched to the VHF. Mr Fields, Tony, drop the hoses. Put up your hands. Don't move. Don't engage. It's not worth it.

— Already done, said my dad, his voice abrupt and weary-sounding over the radio static.

Then we heard someone say something in what I guessed was Somali. I couldn't even tell where the words were in the foreign babble of it; it was just sound running on, sliced up by consonants so hard they stopped the breath. Then the man changed to English and told Dad to take them to the captain.

— Well, said Damian. That's it.

— The engine room, I said, remembering the plans we'd had to submit to the canal authorities. We could hide there.

— Too late, said Damian.

The whole thing had taken maybe two minutes, three at a push. And that's how easy it was for us to be taken captive. Another minute, then Dad came into the bridge, followed by two men in headscarves, one bearded, the other younger, smooth-skinned. The younger one had a pistol tied to the waistband of his too-big chino trousers by a length of multi-coloured string. The older one was holding an AK-47.

— You all right, Amy-bear? Dad said.

I nodded.

— Good. I'm sorry. I tried.

— I know, I said. At that moment, I felt like hugging him, but it didn't seem like the right thing to do in the circumstances. I didn't know if I could move at all, actually. I felt like I was holding a very fragile vase inside me and, if I took a single step, it might break and fall to the floor. I was terrified. I assumed we were going to die.

I'd like to say that I noticed Farouz immediately, that our eyes met and there was instantly some kind of energy between us, but the truth is that I was just aware of two pirates in the room, on our luxury yacht, one of them younger than the other. No, that's not totally true. I noticed his eyes, I remember that. I saw how light they were – true grey, just like mine. I know I did, because I distinctly recall thinking that it was something we had in common, and then thinking, no, that's ridiculous, I don't have anything in common with this man.

— Captain? said the older man, the one with the beard, pointing at Damian with his gun.

— Yes, said Damian.

— You surrender.

— Yes.

— Good. We don't like hurt. Now stop. Stop boat.

Damian hesitated.

— We don't like hurt. But we hurt if you don't stop boat.

Damian reached out and powered down the engine.

— The sail is up, he said. We won't stop completely.

The older pirate turned to the younger one, who said something in their own language. The older one nodded.

— OK. You take down sail, too. Later. He made a gesture to the other pirate.

Just then, Tony was dragged in, followed by Felipe. For a moment I felt bad that I'd forgotten about the cook, but then I looked at Tony properly and I gasped. He was bleeding from his leg, the blood streaking the floor behind him. He was conscious, but his eyes were kind of hooded. One of the pirates who'd dragged him in dropped to one knee, took off his headscarf and pressed it to Tony's wound.

— What the – started Damian, angry.

The older pirate, obviously the leader, held up a hand.

— We sorry, he said. Accident. He . . . The pirate broke off, turned to his younger companion and said something quickly.

— He fired his hose, said the young, beardless man with the grey eyes, and I was amazed by his accent, the smoothness of his speech. That was one thing I did notice from the start.

— The hose caused one of the men's guns to go off, he continued. We apologise. It is not our intention to cause injury. We are really very sorry. The man who shot him will be disciplined and fined.

— Will be . . . ? began Damian, his voice weak – whether from fear or confusion, I don't know.

— Disciplined, repeated the young man. And of course we will treat this man's wounds. For now, though, please, give my boss here a full list of the people on board. Is there anyone not in this room?

— No, said my dad.

I glanced at him. The stepmother, I was thinking. Obviously he didn't want the pirates to know about her.

— OK, said the pirate. OK. Please give me the passenger manifest.

Damian held his palms up.

— I don't have that to hand, he said. I'd have to –

— You are lying, said the young pirate.

I noticed, tangentially, that he was wearing a Rolex. It seemed a surprising thing to see on his wrist. I was pretty sure his baggy trousers, held up with string, were Ralph Lauren, too.

— One more chance, he said. How many people on board?

There was something in his tone that suggested it wouldn't be a good idea to lie to him again. At the same time, I could see his chest muscles under his shirt, and a strong feeling went through me just for a second, like lightning, like electricity.

— One more, Damian said, ignoring Dad, who was glaring at him. This man's wife. She was sleeping in one of the cabins. I guess she's probably awake now, he added, with a nervous laugh.

The leader evidently understood this because he waved at one of the pirates who had brought Tony in and barked out a command. I was thinking to myself that the stepmother must have heard the shots, so she must be hiding or had locked herself in the cabin.

As the pirate left to search for her, the leader said something else to the young man with the impressive English. He nodded back.

— Listen, said Dad. We have around ten thousand dollars in

cash on board, in the safe in my room. We have traveller's cheques. Laptops. The whole yacht is full of valuables. You can have it all. Just, please, leave us in peace.

The leader laughed, said something in Somali.

— He says that you are the valuables, the younger man said. As if to illustrate this, he took the Rolex off his wrist, sneered at it, then threw it in the bin under the table. Ten thousand dollars is not what we have come for. Try ten million, maybe.

— You're insane, said Damian.

The leader shrugged.

— Last month, man in our village get two million.

He nodded to the younger man, the translator, who took a smartphone out of his pocket. I stared at it, amazed, because it was super-expensive, better than my own. But the pirate wasn't looking at me – he flicked something on the screen and held the phone up to each of us in turn, then to the console, then to the front deck of the yacht. Then he turned so that he was facing the leader. Only then, I realised he was filming.

— The time is . . . 12:43, he said, checking a digital readout on the console. We have taken command of the *Daisy May*, a luxury yacht. He turned to Damian. Captain, please confirm our coordinates.

— Uh . . . latitude 11.933263, longitude 44.344254, said Damian.

— Those are our coordinates, continued the pirate. We do not intend to hide. We wish you to know where your people are. If our demands are not met, though, everyone on board will be killed.

The way he said this, it was so casual and business-like, a statement of a fact, simply a consequence.

Oh god, I thought. This is bad. This is really, really bad.

I should have known that before, you're thinking, and I guess I did, but there's knowing something and then there's *knowing* something, and when he said in that cold voice that we would be killed, that was when I truly *knew* the danger.

We were hostages now.

He tapped the screen to stop recording, took out a cable and connected the camera to the laptop on the console that Damian used. I couldn't get over this; there was something so weird about this guy, whose gun was tied on with string, who was barefoot under his trousers, producing a smartphone and then using it, like he did it every day.

— You will tell us the name and email address of this yacht's owners, he said. So that we can send the video.

— I – began my dad, but this time it was Tony who interrupted him.

— It's Goldblatt Bank, he said, his voice strained with pain. I'll give you the address.

Smart, I thought straight away. If the pirates knew it was Dad who owned the yacht, then they would negotiate with him directly. Or they could torture him into revealing how much money he had and giving them all of it. Tony was buying us some time. Dad had clearly twigged this, too, because he was silent, just staring angrily at the pirates.

At that moment, the stepmother was brought in. There were tears running down her cheeks, but she didn't seem harmed.

— There are pirates, she said, her voice breaking. On the yacht! *Pirates*.

Jesus, I thought. I wish it didn't have to be her. I wish my mom could be here instead.

But then I thought, no, I wouldn't want my mom to be in this position, to be in this danger, to be scared like I was.

And did that mean I *did* want the stepmother to feel those things? I wasn't sure.

The only thing I knew?

I didn't want to be on that yacht any more. I mean, obviously I hadn't been concentrating on my future, otherwise I wouldn't have screwed up my A levels, but I wanted to *have* a future.

You have to understand, it wasn't all bad with my mom. The thing that made her terrible was also the thing that made her amazing. So there was my fifteenth birthday, for example. She knew I wanted to go out with my friends in the evening and she was OK with that, so long as I had breakfast with her. Dad was on a business trip somewhere made-up-sounding, like Uzbekistan or something, talking about bank loans.

We were living in London by then. This was a Friday in October, still in term time, so of course I had to go to school after breakfast with Mom. I got up and did the usual, got dressed, did my make-up – not that I ever spent long on it, just put on some eyeliner and mascara, a bit of lipgloss. I don't do lipstick. Then I went downstairs, where Mom was already sitting at the table, which was piled high with croissants and pains aux raisins – my favourite – as well as all kinds of fruit. There was a bottle of champagne, too, which she popped the moment I walked into the room, like she'd been waiting, ready to do that exact thing, and poured into two glasses.

My dad would never let me drink – he hated it – but he wasn't there, so I took the glass that was proffered and sipped it. Bubbles, tasting like croissants smelled, went up my nose.

— Happy birthday, beautiful, she said. Here. I made coffee, too.

— Wow, Mom, I said. You didn't have to. I was confused: it wasn't even like it was my sixteenth or anything. Maybe that should have been my first warning. Maybe she knew she wouldn't be there the next year.

I sat down, and she gave me my present, a sort of shy expression on her face. A small blue box, like the ones jewellery comes in, no fancy logos on it. I had an idea what it was before I opened it. I cracked the box like an oyster and I think I probably screamed. I definitely jumped up and gave Mom a kiss.

— You remembered! I said. Thank you, thank you.

Inside the box was a vintage Chanel watch, the leather of the strap scuffed and the face scratched, the dial an elegant oblong, kind of art deco. I put it on. I'd seen it in an antique shop in Richmond a few months before. I'd loved it at first sight. It wasn't that expensive or anything. I mean, maybe it was. It's hard to know what is and isn't when you grow up with money. You lose perspective. Anyway, something about the watch reached out through the glass of the shop window and tapped me on the shoulder. It was old, yes. But it had charm.

I started to clear up after breakfast but Mom put a hand on my hand.

— You'd better change out of your uniform, she said.

— What?

— Get changed. You're not going to school today.

— I'm not? Where am I going, then?

— You'll have to wait and see.

— What about your work? I asked.

One of the weird things about Mom: she was totally awesome at her job. I don't think anyone there even knew about her being ill, apart from maybe her boss, and only

64

because Mom sometimes had to take time off for appointments and stuff. I could never understand it, the way she was so flawlessly good at that bit of her life. But apparently it's common with people like her. Dad called it *compartmentalisation*. Me, I mostly called it unfair. It wasn't like Mom to just call in sick.

— I took the day off, she said. I've been planning this for a while. She winked and smiled.

— Er, OK.

Mom flapped a hand at me.

— Come on! Get moving.

I started up the stairs.

— Oh, and wear something warm, Mom called after me.

When I came back down, we left the house and started walking. I thought maybe we'd get in the car, which was parked just down the street, but we didn't; we walked right past it. We crossed the common, passed the duck pond, then went along the cycle path by the Wilderness. Eventually we got to Richmond Park and then carried on towards Roehampton along the bridleway.

We walked past the Long Water, along the path that crosses between Ham Gate and Roehampton Gate, the red deer grazing beside us. A stag stood up out of the heather, huge antlers prehistoric against the high-rise apartment blocks.

— Where are we going? I asked. It wasn't like Mom to go for walks for no reason. I mean, she walked, of course she did. She was a person, not a bird, or something. But she didn't do hiking or rambling. She only walked to get somewhere.

— It's a surprise, she said.

She winked at me and led me up the hill towards the Royal Ballet School, where there's a bench that looks out over the ponds, the heather-covered ground, the backdrop of trees, and you can imagine you were in Scotland, or something. When we got to the crest of the hill, I saw something that, if I was in a cheesy old TV show, would have made me blink and take a step back, like, *really?* It was a table, a dining table, with a white cloth on it, set out with this incredible lunch, all on china plates, with wine glasses, everything. I could see a roast chicken, chocolates, salads, cheese, quiches.

— I wasn't sure what you like now, she said. Your taste is always changing.

— I . . . I . . . Jesus, Mom.

— You don't like it.

— Of course I like it, I said. It's amazing!

This is not what I should have said. What I should have said was, I love you. You are amazing. But I didn't, and now I can't.

Still, she was pleased that I liked it, I could tell. And it *was* amazing. It was a bit chilly to be eating outside, I was aware of that, even though it was the kind of thing Mom would never think of. But it didn't matter. There were no people around, apart from a couple of guys on rollerblades who had stopped to stare at the table, which was set about three metres away from the main path. I couldn't work out how she'd done it, how she'd pulled it all off.

— How did –

She held a finger to her lips.

— A magician never reveals her tricks, she said.

So, we sat down and ate this astonishing lunch in the middle of Richmond Park, with all these different foods, and wine, so that by the time I went out with my friends that evening I was already tipsy. That was OK, though, because Mom said she'd pick me up from the pub at 11 p.m. exactly, and I'd better be there, otherwise she was taking back the watch. That was another great thing about Mom: I was way too young to drink, but she was cool about it.

After a while, a park warden turned up in one of those green Land Rovers they have. He parked up and got out.

— I'm sorry, he said. You can't just . . . I mean, the table. You can't do that.

— Oh? said Mom. Funny. We just did.

After that, we had to leave. But that didn't matter because I remembered every minute before they made us go. I remembered eating and drinking while the stags wandered below us, and the sun was shining, and there was a smell of leaves and fire in the autumn air, and birds were calling, and no one ever, ever died.

The pirates gathered all of us on the sofas and armchairs in the cinema room. I was sitting next to Dad and he was holding my hand.

— It's OK, Amy, he whispered. We're worth more alive than dead.

How reassuring, I thought. Then I looked at him.

— Wait, I said. *You*'re worth more alive – you're rich. I'm just your daughter.

— Don't be silly, said Dad. We're all valuable here.

— Are we? Felipe said. I don't have any money.

— That's not the point, said Dad. It's simple economics – if any of us dies, the pirates know they won't get their ransom, no matter who's paying it.

Again, not very reassuring. I still wondered, and I caught Felipe's eye and I could see him wondering, too, was there a point where what Dad said stopped being true?

Say Felipe died. Or Tony. Wouldn't Dad still have to pay to get the rest of us out of here?

But I didn't say anything. I didn't think it would be very good for morale.

I wasn't scared any more, though, not precisely. I was feeling kind of numb. Shock, I suppose. Or maybe it's me. I mean, I'm kind of a numb person. Empty, like a hollow chocolate bunny. I'm not saying that in some, like, self-pitying way. It's true.

Tony was stretched out on the biggest sofa, the leather one. One of the pirates had lifted him up and deposited him there. I wasn't really paying attention to the differences between the pirates at that point – I didn't even know for sure how many there were – but something about this one creeped me out immediately. I saw that he had a red bandanna on, a weak chin and hard eyes. Flat eyes. Dead eyes. The cabin walls had more emotion in them than those eyes.

The younger one came in with a kind of bandage made out of cloth and tied it expertly round Tony's leg. I hoped the bandage was clean – it looked like it was. He gave some sort of order, by the sound of it, to the cold-eyed one, then he left. The other pirate took some kind of chewing tobacco or something – khat, I found out later – and put it in his mouth, began chewing it. He went over to a chair in the corner, sat down and closed his eyes.

After he did so, Tony turned to Damian with a wince.

— Did you alert anyone? he asked softly.

— Yep. The navy and SSAS.

— Good.

— And your leg? Are you in a lot of pain?

— A little, said Tony. But the bullet just scratched the flesh. I was lucky.

— When they get our money and our stuff, they'll leave, right? asked the stepmother.

— I'm afraid not, said Dad.

— Why not?

— They want a ransom.

— Then pay it! Pay whatever they want!

— Yes, said Felipe. Please pay them. I want to go home.

The bandanna pirate's dead eyes flickered open. He grunted,

shook his gun a bit and closed his eyes again. Already I definitely didn't like this one.

— It's not as simple as that, said Tony. There's insurance. The navy. We need to sit tight for a bit. Wait and see what they want.

— For god's sake! said the stepmother. She started to cry again.

I caught Damian's eyes. He smiled thinly, those Irish dimples flicking on like a light.

Shortly after, the leader came in. He indicated his face.

— Ahmed, he said, introducing himself.

I saw now that he had a scar that went all the way from the corner of his left eye to his chin, skirting his mouth. It looked like someone had tried to cut his face in half. But there was some quality about him – his eyes, mainly, which were clever and bright. You could see why he was the leader, is what I'm saying.

Then Ahmed pointed to the younger guy, the English speaker.

— He is Farouz. I am the boss, Farouz is translator. OK?

— OK, said Dad. My name is –

— No. You have no name. You Hostage One. Her, Hostage Two. And her . . .

He went round all of us, gave us our new names. I was Hostage Three, you know that already. At the time it was pretty chilling. I mean that literally: I know it's a cliché, but this cold feeling, fluid, rolled down my back. Because it was obvious why they were giving us numbers. It's much harder to kill someone once you know their name. They went on and numbered Tony, Damian and Felipe. Felipe got the last one, number six, and I was pretty impressed, despite myself, with how the pirates had seen the pecking order, just like that, even knowing that although Damian was the captain, Tony basically outranked him.

— Now, said Ahmed, you take me safe with ten thousand dollar.

— Bring it to you? asked my dad.

— No. You take me.

He gestured with his AK-47 for Dad to go out of the door in front of him. Dad looked at all of us, shrugged and led the way. Ahmed followed him out.

When they had gone, Farouz looked over at Tony. Anger flashed on Farouz's face and he went over to the other pirate, the scary one who was chewing – who had bothered to open his eyes at least since Farouz had arrived. Farouz started shouting at him. I heard the word biyo repeated several times.

The dead-eyed pirate with the red bandanna sighed, got up and left the room. Farouz tapped his foot impatiently. A minute later, the other man came back with a couple of bottles of water. He gave one to Tony and put the others on the glass coffee table, before sitting down again.

— Thank you, said Tony.

— You are welcome, said Farouz. You should have had it sooner, he added, with a glance at the other man, who sneered back at him.

I noticed that. Him being kind, I mean. I was also considering, in some distant part of my mind, the way the other pirate had curled his lip at Farouz, thinking that if the pirates ended up fighting each other, that could be good for us. It's the fact that I was able to think about things like this, strategically, that tells you I was in shock, I guess.

I was in shock, but also hyper-aware. The walls seemed to be pulsing, alive. I was very conscious of the details of everything – the brush strokes on the generic English countryside watercolour on the wall, the flecks in the cream carpet. It was as if someone had suspended the whole room under water, and it acted like a lens, that water, magnifying everything, and at the same time it made the sounds that reached me echoey and far away.

— How long are you going to keep us in here? asked the stepmother.

Farouz looked surprised.

— In this room? I don't know. An hour? We are only searching the boat. Then you are free to do as you wish.

— We can go where we want? asked the stepmother.

— Why not? There are guards everywhere, so you can't escape, but you can move around. You all sleep together in this room, though. OK?

— OK, said Tony, who obviously wanted to show some kind of authority, not that Farouz could care less about that, judging by his expression.

No one said anything for quite a while after that. Finally, Ahmed came back in, Dad behind him. Ahmed was carrying wads of banknotes, and smiling. He threw one of them to Farouz and laughed. Then he jerked his thumb for Farouz and the other guy to head out.

_____, Dead Eyes said in his language, which was all harsh throat sounds and squelchy Ls, and sounded like the person speaking was trying to swallow every second letter as if it were food. Then he laughed long and hard, and left the room.

— What was that? said the stepmother. What did he say?

— Nothing, said Farouz.

And I thought, he's the one with the gun – he doesn't even have to bother with lying.

For all that, though, nothing too scary happened to begin with. True to his word, Farouz let us leave the cinema room later that afternoon.

We went out and on to the rear deck – I think we were all heading towards sunlight without realising it. Seeing the changes that had already taken place on the yacht was weird. One of the pirates was wearing my Superdry hoodie. All of them had on new clothes of some kind – jeans, trainers, even a raincoat. One of them was wearing a parka that the step-mother had bought for Patagonia, which was where we were originally meant to be in six months' time. Somehow, seeing a pirate strutting around a luxury yacht in a parka in thirty-five degree heat made all of them seem a little less intimidating because it was so ridiculous.

Then I remembered the smartphone and the video, and I stopped feeling amused.

It was easier now to get a sense of the numbers. In addition to Ahmed, Farouz and Dead Eyes, we passed two guards in the corridor on the way out to the rear deck. There were three others out on deck by the diving platform, and I guessed more at the front of the yacht. So somewhere around ten pirates, at least, for six of us hostages. No wonder they weren't worried about us escaping.

Men came in and out of the interior of the yacht. All of them, apart from Farouz, were bearded. All of them carried machine guns, apart from Farouz, who had his pistol on that piece of string, and another man, skinny, who carried the bazooka or rocket launcher or whatever it was. The thing looked heavy, but he carried it easily, despite his small frame. As well as guns, the men also had random items. One came out with a laptop – my laptop, I think – which he threw into one of the two little wooden boats. These were tied to the diving platform, to the eyelets where Tony had secured the knotted ropes that were meant to choke the pirates' outboards.

It seemed like a hundred years ago that I'd watched Tony tie those ropes. Now, in their place, the little boats bobbed in our wake, which was gentle at the moment since the engine was off. It was unbelievably hot with only the sail up and no engines running. The heat was like something heavy you wear – a forced embrace, stifling, a fur coat in the height of summer. It pushed at you, not a temperature, but a pressure.

— Excuse me, said Dad. We need water.

One of the pirates looked at him blankly.

— Biyo, I said, pointing to us. Biyo.

Dad looked at me, surprised. But the pirate nodded. He went inside and came back five minutes later with a six-pack of mineral-water bottles, which he set down in front of us, and, bizarrely, my hair straighteners, which went into the little boat. What he thought he was going to do with them, I don't know. Maybe he didn't know what they were for. He was wearing my beige French Connection trench coat, so I guess anything is possible.

Above us, the sun continued to shine. I thought that was incredible, impossible – that simple things like that should carry on being, carry on unfolding, as if nothing had happened. As if we weren't prisoners on our own yacht.

— That's my bloody Prada jumper, said the stepmother, as another guard – or was it one we'd seen before? – walked past.

— Darling, you have to try to . . .

I wasn't really listening to them. I was looking at Dead Eyes, who had just come outside. He spat a black gobbet of khat on to the deck, rolled his head on his shoulders with an audible *crick-crack* of bone against bone. But that wasn't what caught my attention.

He was wearing my watch. My vintage Chanel watch that my mom gave me.

I stood there, and I guess I must have blanched – I mean, my distress must have been obvious – because Dad frowned, then walked over and touched my elbow.

— What is it? he said.

I pointed to the watch.

— It's . . .

But my voice caught, and I couldn't finish. Dad followed my finger, though, and saw the watch. I guess he hadn't completely forgotten about Mom because he tensed, and I felt his fingers grip my arm.

— I see, he said in his I'm-going-to-sort-this-out voice.

— No, Dad, it's OK. I don't –

— Ahmed!

Ahmed had come out on to the rear deck, a cigarette between his lips. He turned to look at Dad.

— Yes?

Dad walked over to where Ahmed stood and spoke to him for a while, his voice low. I thought, oh god, we're all going to die. But I was strangely calm about that, probably because, since the Event, a hidden part of me had secretly wanted to die.

I waited, my mind blank.

But nothing happened. Ahmed didn't even raise his voice or anything.

Then Ahmed faced the other pirates.

— No more steal, he said. We give back. Now. He repeated it in his own language then, I think.

He grabbed the arm of the man passing him, who had the stepmother's pink iPod in his hand. Reluctantly, the pirate handed over the iPod and Ahmed presented it to Dad, sort of solemnly.

— Here, he said.

— Ah, thank you, said Dad.

— Of course. We guests. We not steal no more.

This is the strange effect my dad has on people: he can sometimes charm them into doing what he wants. He chooses the right words, uses this special tone. I guess that's how he ended up so successful, because he pretty much spends his life asking people to give him their money, and counting on the fact that they will.

A sort of pained look crossed Dad's face.

— My daughter . . . he said. She will be safe?

Ahmed actually looked offended.

— We not touch, he said.

— Because if anything happened to her . . .

— We not touch! Ahmed waved a hand angrily to encompass the yacht. This boat, worth nothing. You, worth much. All of you. So we not touch, OK?

— OK, OK, said Dad.

— Girl is precious, said Ahmed. We need her safe to get money.

— Right, said Dad. She's precious to me, too. So that's good. He smiled at Ahmed, used that magic again, and suddenly the two of them were not friends, but something understood. Colleagues.

I smiled at Dad, then. I was proud of him, which was a rare thing.

Then I turned to look for Dead Eyes, to get my watch back, and he was gone.

Soon after we were boarded, the first supplies and reinforcements arrived. We heard the commotion and went outside. It was a relief to be out of the cinema room. It was starting to smell of sweat and was always hot and close, and even though you couldn't see steam rising from all the bodies in there, I couldn't help but imagine it.

On deck, the pirates were waiting. A third little boat was making its way towards the yacht. There was only one man in it, but there were also two goats, and that was a surreal sight, believe me. It was welcome, too, though. There was something awful about being on that yacht in the middle of the ocean, with all that blue blankness stretched out around us. What's the word? Agoraphobia? I think so. And then, at the same time, the opposite thing. Claustrophobia. On the one hand, we were trapped on what was really quite a small boat, with these pirates everywhere. On the other hand, there was nothing but sea and sky around us, right to the horizon.

Thinking about that made me dizzy, so when the little boat appeared, a dot far away that moved slowly closer, it was like we became a bit more anchored somehow. Like the boat was tracing a line that joined us to something else – another ship, land.

What I mean is, I looked at that boat and I didn't only think about the boat; I thought about the place it came from. I thought about land, earth. A beach, or a port. It wasn't just a boat: it was a possibility of another place.

Then, when I saw the goats, I stopped having those kind of philosophical thoughts and I just stared. This guy chugged up to the diving platform, standing by the outboard motor, the goats in front of him, dark-furred and white-bearded, bleating at the low waves. The sun was setting behind him, which just added to the craziness, red lava pouring on to the sea over the horizon, setting it on fire.

It was goats, on a boat, in the middle of the sea. I'll never forget it.

Also on the new wooden boat were boxes of all sorts of stuff. The first two boats had heaps of boxes, too, as it turned out. I guess all this cargo had come from the mother ship, as Tony called it.

There were:

Like, a hundred cartons of cigarettes, at least.

Massive cartons of dried pasta.

A gas stove.

Tins with French writing on them.

Lots of bottles of booze.

Thousands – I mean, thousands – of litres of water in big bottles.

All of these things were in just huge quantities, which I didn't take as a good sign at all. And I could tell from the look on the stepmother's face that she didn't, either. I found out after, from Farouz, that all this stuff came from a French container ship that the pirates had taken the previous month. It was clever, really, to reuse the spoils from a previous mission. Actually, I don't know why I say *really*, because, as I quickly learned, the pirates were very clever indeed. And very organised.

So yeah, it was smart. And it meant, I realised sickly, that they could be here a long time.

Right then, though, I was watching the pirates carting cigarettes – they loved cigarettes – up into the yacht, watching them drive the two goats up on to the deck, where they tethered them.

It was total chaos, as you can imagine. The goats did not want to get on the yacht, and they resisted the pirates' attempts to move them, squealing in a creepily human way and kicking. When one of the goats was finally forced on to the diving platform, it bolted, clattering on its unsteady hooves through the door, into the dining room. One of the pirates had to plunge in after it, and emerged a few minutes later, cursing, bleeding for some reason from his nose, pushing the complaining goat ahead of him. It was a good half an hour before the goats were tied up.

We moved as far away from the animals as we could. Already, one of them had shat on the mahogany slats of the deck. I could smell them, too, that sour, musky smell of animals that feed on grass.

— I make good curry with goats, said Felipe, who up till this point hadn't said very much.

— *Goats?* said the stepmother.

— Yes. It's quite sensible, if you think about it, said Dad. They don't have to worry about meat perishing, and the goats supply milk as well as –

— Oh, shut up, James, said the stepmother.

*

Later that first night, when we were inside, there didn't seem to be any plan, or any sense of what we were meant to do. We asked Farouz if we could go to bed, and he shrugged and walked away, as if it were a matter of total indifference to him what we did. Even when he shrugged, I noticed how he moved kind of liquidly – not graceful, exactly, because that makes him sound like a dancer. More like someone comfortable in his own skin.

That struck me because it was so different to the boys at school, who didn't seem to have settled into their post-puberty bodies yet. The word people always use for that is *gangly*. But a lot of those boys weren't gangly – some of them were pretty bulky, or average size. They just didn't move like they knew their bodies very well. Or it was like their bodies had been made for some other mind to move into. Farouz, though – he moved like his body was a glove and his mind was the hand.

Tony had insisted on going outside to see what was going on, but he needed to lean on Dad's shoulder and Damian's to do so. He wasn't in terrible shape, but he wasn't doing well, either. He had gone quite pale. When we got back to the cinema room and had put him on the couch, I tapped Dad on the shoulder.

— Let's go and see if we can get him some painkillers, I said.

Dad nodded. He told the stepmother to wait with Damian, Felipe and Tony, then we went to look for Ahmed.

On the way, we passed our cabins. I was puzzled to see little paper signs with amounts of money written on them over the doors. I guessed the pirates must have stuck them there:

$500 on the door to my room.

$1,000 on Dad and the stepmother's door.

And, on the door to the bridge, *$5,000*.

I pointed them out to Dad, who splayed his hands out in an I-don't-have-a-clue gesture.

We found Ahmed on the bridge. He was watching the radar screen – I suppose he or Farouz must have known how to turn it back on, because I'd seen Damian surreptitiously turn it off when we were boarded. On it, a pretty big dot, glowing and bleeping, was slowly moving towards us from the east. I thought, that's the navy. And I was glad – it felt like the cavalry were coming to get us, which is pretty stupid in retrospect. You don't send commandos to liberate a yacht when there are men with guns on it. Too much chance of collateral damage, which is a polite way of saying that me and Dad and the stepmother and Damian and Tony and Felipe might get riddled with bullets.

— Hostage One, said Ahmed, when he saw us. Hostage Three. What want?

Ahmed was the only one of the pirates who wasn't wearing our clothes. He'd told them to return our stuff, though this seemed to be a slow process. Instead, he still had on some kind of Somali hooded cloak, a djelleba, apparently, that went down to his knees. He didn't wear shoes, but went barefoot everywhere, his feet surprisingly clean.

— We need painkillers, said Dad. For, ah, Hostage Four.

— Pain?

Dad thought for a moment. Then he mimed pain in his leg,

clutching it and moaning, before going through the motions of swallowing a pill and sighing in exaggerated relief.

— Oh! said Ahmed. OK. We don't have.

— No, that's all right, said Dad. We have.

— You have?

— Yes. In the medical supply cupboard. If we can just take them . . .

I think Dad thought that Ahmed would let us go to the medicine cabinet and take what we wanted. Maybe he had some kind of idea of radioing for help, too, while we were at it. I could see it on his face – the desire to be a hero. But Ahmed wasn't an idiot. He lifted the VHF handset from in front of him and spoke some words into it. Someone gave a reply, and he hung it up.

— OK, he said. You show me.

We led Ahmed back down the corridor, down the steps towards the rear deck. We stopped by a recessed cupboard door in the wall, one you wouldn't notice if you weren't looking for it. This was the medicine cabinet. Mom, being American, would have called it a hurt locker, which seemed like quite a good name for the situation we found ourselves in. Locked up by people who could hurt us.

Dad opened it up and inside were rows of neatly packed first-aid supplies: bottles of pills, bandages, plasters, even hypodermic needles. Dad reached in and took out one of the pill bottles. He checked the label and put it in his pocket. Then, for good measure, he took some iodine, a needle and thread, plus a bandage.

— For? said Ahmed.

— Infection, said Dad. To clean. Yes?

Ahmed nodded. He had a certain expression on his face –
of what? wonder? sadness? both? He raised a calloused hand
and touched the things inside the cupboard, like someone
might touch a holy relic.

— What is it? said Dad.

— Is medicine things, said Ahmed patiently, as if Dad were
stupid.

— No, I mean, what's wrong? Are you OK?

Ahmed shut the cupboard. His brow furrowed in concentration.

— My children . . . when sick, I can give nothing. No medicine. Here, on yacht, is easy.

My stomach did a little flip. He had children? This guy with
the scar on his face, and the AK-47? Well, of course he did.
He must have been forty. Suddenly, and for the first time, I
had a flash of what this yacht must look like to them. To
people with no medicine to give to their children. With no
shoes.

Then Ahmed's face went hard again, like it was clay that
had come out of an oven.

— You tell captain we move tomorrow, he said.

— Move? I asked. I was thinking of the ship on the radar
screen, the steady blip as it got closer; the navy coming to get
us, I hoped.

— Move. To Eyl.

— Where is Eyl? said Dad.

— Is small town. In Puntland. In Somalia.

My heart sank. I'd been longing for land, thinking about the scary feeling of being adrift in wide, open ocean, and how nice it would be to see a beach. But I guess, in my head, it had been a neutral beach, not somewhere that made us even more powerless. Somewhere that we could . . . maybe . . . escape to. I'd been thinking vaguely of Robinson Crusoe, I realised, picturing us swimming away in the night, finding ourselves under palm trees, eating coconuts.

Somalia was not neutral. Somalia was home territory for the pirates. We could swim away, maybe, but not far enough away.

It seemed from the radar like there was a ship coming to rescue us – that was the irony – but we were leaving. Leaving to go to Somalia.

Like I said, the first time the stepmother came home with Dad was after an office party. I have a feeling they thought they had hidden it from me, but I heard them, the giggling under their voices, after the taxi dropped them off at 3 a.m. This was, I don't know, months After. *Way* too soon, anyway.

The next morning, I watched out of the window as she sneaked out, then walked across Ham Common to the 65 bus stop. She was wearing purple high heels, a dark blue dress, and she was pretty. I remember being annoyed that she was pretty.

It wasn't long after that that my dad brought her home for dinner, so I could meet her. He'd mentioned her name a few times already, just casually – stuff she'd said or done at work. She must have been fairly high up, I suppose, for him to be spending time with her, but I never really asked what she did.

When she came, she brought me a CD and some expensive make-up. She stood on the porch and held them out. I didn't even have a CD player, just an iPod. She had blonde hair, and eyes so incredibly pale blue that it was as if you could see right through her head to the sky behind.

— I hope we can be friends, Amy-bear, she said.

I thought, don't use my name like that. I didn't even reach out for the presents until Dad dug his elbow into my ribs and I had to. A CD! It was a joke. She must have thought we were going to be best friends – it was like she got her idea of teenagers out of a magazine.

The whole time over dinner, she kept talking about bands, and TV, and male actors and stuff – to bond with me, I guess. It was just excruciating. And she kept putting her hand on Dad's arm when he made jokes, smiling at him. Like I couldn't see what she was doing – coming into our house, which was basically a mansion, getting her feet inside the door.

In the weeks that followed, Dad started taking down some of the photos of Mom.

And then came the day of the polo.

They weren't married at this point, so she wasn't the step-mother. She was just Dad's girlfriend, Sarah. She was, I don't know, thirty at the most. She phoned up one Saturday, and asked Dad, did he know that there was polo on at Ham Polo Club the next day, and had he ever been?

No, we had never been.

So, on Sunday, she turned up, wearing a big wide-brimmed blue hat with a kind of pouffe thing on it, like she was going to Ascot or something. And we all walked down the path that led from Ham Common to the polo field. I didn't want to go – I couldn't think of anything worse – but Dad made me. To get him back, I was wearing a torn vintage dress and Doc Martens.

Much as I hate to admit it, though, the start wasn't too bad. It was a sunny day, late April, the poppies and daisies out in the verges. We sat on a rug on the grass, on the far side from the stands, because Sarah said that was more like a picnic. I had no idea what was going on in the polo, but it was excit-ing, watching the horses galloping up and down, the men leaning over as they rode, almost to where you thought they would fall off, to hit the ball. We had a hamper, with all sorts of incredible food that Dad had ordered from the deli, and champagne – which Sarah insisted on pouring me a glass of, even though Dad objected. It reminded me of Mom, but in a good way.

I almost liked her in that moment.

But then one of the horses fell. It belonged to the orange and black team, whoever they were. There was no dramatic reason – it was turning, and it went down. I could tell immediately it was bad. The horse's head got kind of stuck under its own neck when it went down, and it took the whole weight of its body. I don't know if I'm just imagining this afterwards, or if I actually heard it, but I think there was a *crack* sound. The polo player managed to jump off just in time, but he hit the ground hard, too, and rolled.

Silence, from the crowd.

For maybe a couple of minutes, I thought the horse might get up. I could feel Dad tensely sitting there beside me. Sarah was clutching her champagne glass so hard her knuckles were going white, and I thought she might smash it. But the horse didn't get up.

Why didn't we leave? I don't know. It was like we were hypnotised, like we had to see it through to the end. None of us said anything for quite a long time.

Then Dad said:

— I think its neck might be broken.

— Why don't they get a vet? I asked.

No one answered.

The horse was kind of twitching. It was awful. One of the most awful things I have ever seen. The polo player was kneeling by it, whispering to it. Then, and it seemed like a long time before this happened, some official-looking people came with a sort of tent-like barrier with hinges, which they erected around the horse. This meant the people from the stands no longer had to look at it. Only, from our angle, we could still see it.

Yet we still didn't leave. We didn't drink any more champagne, and we didn't eat anything, but we didn't leave, either. A voice came over the tannoy, apologising for the delay, saying that the only on-call vet on a Sunday had been called.

— They don't have a vet here? said Dad, incredulous.

I checked my Chanel watch. An hour went past before a Land Rover turned up, with the logo of a vet's surgery in Reigate on its sides, and drove right up on to the polo field. A man with a leather bag got out and went over to the horse. He kneeled down beside it, palpated its neck, looked under its eyelids.

The polo player was young, I realised suddenly. Mainly because another man, who looked like him but older, turned up in a Mercedes, and went to stand with him just outside the barrier. The man put his arms around the guy whose horse had gone down, and I thought, that's his dad.

The vet stood up straight and walked over to them. He talked to the player for a few minutes, and then the player's dad gave him an even bigger hug. It was like watching a play that's being staged far away, where you don't hear the words, but you still know what's going on – the big stuff, anyway.

I looked over at Sarah and saw that she was crying. That was when – and I know this was unfair – I decided I hated her. I mean, it was a *horse*. My mother had died and Sarah was taking her place and she was crying over a *horse*.

The vet went back to his bag, took out a big needle, almost comically big, like something from a sketch show. He injected the horse, and it died.

Finally, it was like the spell was broken.

Dad stood up and silently started packing up the picnic stuff. Sarah helped him, then we walked home.

On the way down the footpath, as we passed Ham House, the old manor, this blonde girl came towards us. She was wearing jodhpurs and swinging a riding helmet in her hand. She asked what all the commotion was about, and we told her about the horse tripping and breaking its neck.

— Who was it? she said, sounding concerned. I mean, the rider.

We described him – dark curly hair, tall.

— Oh no, poor Henry, she said, in a voice that actually didn't sound sorry at all, more brisk and matter of fact. How ghastly. My first gee-gee went the same way.

As we walked away, Dad and I snorted at exactly the same time.

— Gee-gee, he said. Jesus.

— What? said Sarah. I think it's tragic.

I caught Dad's eyes as he rolled them. Because the thing

— My daughter's watch, said Dad. It hasn't been returned to her.

This was the next day.

We'd passed another uncomfortable night, the six of us, sleeping on the sofas and armchairs and on makeshift beds of cushions on the floor in the cinema room. Tony was looking better, though. The stepmother, who turned out to have done some kind of first-aid course – so maybe she wasn't totally useless – had cleaned his wound with iodine, wrapped a fresh bandage around it and given him some painkillers. Codeine, Dad said they were. Powerful. In moments he had fallen asleep.

Now we were out on the deck, and it was less hot because Damian was up on the bridge, and the engines were going again. We were on our way to Eyl, the yacht's movement creating its own breeze. I was relieved it wasn't so punishingly hot. Even now, as I watched, the constant sun was making blazing, dancing diamonds out of the ridges of the sea, and these were shifting so constantly that it seemed like the sea was racing past us, when really it was sluggish, just the very shallow breathing of the tide.

Light moves so fast, it seems totally still, I thought. Water is so slow, it seems to be always moving.

Dad was pressing Ahmed about my watch. Ahmed was spreading his hands out to say, what do you want me to do?

— The watch, it has sentimental value, Dad said. We don't care about the other things so much. They can keep the iPods, the laptops –

— Hey, said the stepmother, and Dad waved at her to shut up.

— But the watch, he went on. My . . . late wife gave it to my daughter. It means a lot.

Ahmed looked pretty confused by all this.

— What?

— The watch, it's not worth money. It's worth . . . Dad touched his chest, over his heart. Feelings.

Ahmed obviously didn't understand. He shouted something to the guard by the main door to below decks – Dead Eyes, the one who had taken my watch. Dead Eyes shouted back, and a minute or so later Farouz appeared.

His hair, which was medium-length and midnight black, kind of wavy, was sticking up at the back, like he'd been asleep. I had an urge to reach out and smooth it down, to feel the structure of the back of his skull. It was so strong, this urge, that I tightened my fist, curling my fingernails into my palm.

Ahmed pointed to Farouz, who was standing there looking a bit confused.

— Tell to him, to Farouz, he said to my dad.

Dad explained again about the sentimental value.

Farouz nodded, his hair still somehow crying out for me to touch it. He turned to Ahmed and translated. Ahmed did, like, an *ah* with his mouth, only with no sound. He turned to Dad.

— Who has?

Dad pointed at Dead Eyes, who was slouching sullenly against the railings.

94

Ahmed shouted something at him.

Dead Eyes shouted back.

— He says he does not have, Ahmed said with a shrug.

It was naive of me, I know, but I was shocked by this out-and-out lie. I stared at Dead Eyes.

— But he does, I said. Even to myself I sounded petulant, like a little girl. He took the watch. I saw him wearing it.

— Sorry, said Ahmed. I fine him. OK?

This was the second time they'd mentioned fining people.

— What do you mean, fine? said Dad.

Now Ahmed had to look patient, like it was Dad who was the idiot.

— I take from his . . . He looked at Farouz.

— Share, said Farouz. Ahmed will deduct the value of the watch from Mohammed's share of the ransom.

— But the value of the watch is sentimental, Dad said again.

Farouz raised his hands.

— Ahmed cannot deduct sentiments, he said.

— Christ, said Dad. What do I care about his share? It's not even his money! You're stealing it from . . . from the owners of the yacht.

There was a droning noise from above and somewhere to the north. Ahmed and Farouz looked up. The other pirates, too. As we watched, a black speck on the horizon slowly turned into a toy helicopter, which then turned into a real helicopter, black and serious-looking. It swung in low, flying over the yacht, and I saw military markings on the side, the glare of someone – maybe? – looking out with binoculars.

One of the pirates fired up at it, the retort of the gun shockingly loud, but the helicopter just pulled higher, did another, quick sweep of the yacht, then started to fly away.

— Rescue! They're going to rescue us! said the stepmother.

— No, said Dad. They're just checking. Just doing a recce. They still can't risk anything.

The helicopter *was* something, though, even if the pirates seemed supremely unbothered by it. They didn't even comment on it, just went back to whatever they were doing before.

— So, said Ahmed. I fine him. We forget. OK?

— No, said Dad, it's not OK, it's –

— Dad, I said. Let it go, yeah?

I started to walk back inside. But something struck me then.

— Those numbers on the doors, I said, turning to Farouz. Are those fines, too?

—Yes, he said, all matter of fact, like it was the most natural thing in the world. Everyone was stealing from the cabins. Your father asked Ahmed to stop it, so Ahmed decided to charge anyone who went into the rooms.

— So if someone goes into my dad's cabin, it costs them a thousand dollars? I asked.

—Yes. This is normal. Also, the man who shot your friend –

— Tony.

— Not Tony! Farouz's eyes blazed. It was the first time I'd seen him angry, and I took a step back instinctively. Hostage Four. The man who shot Hostage Four, he loses ten thousand dollars.

As hostages on the *Daisy May*, we entered a weird kind of time warp. Really, I couldn't tell you exactly how long we sailed for – five days? a week? – because I don't know. I do know it took quite a few days to get to the Somali coast. But when you're in a situation like that, it's so easy to start losing track of what day it is, whether it's the weekend or not. It all becomes one endless day of worry.

We got used to the prayers, that was one thing. The first morning, when one of the guys started singing – Ahmed, I think – I woke up and saw by Tony's digital watch that it was only 5 a.m. and I couldn't believe it. This voice in the darkness, going, *Allahu akbar, Allahu akbar* . . . It was like a reminder in the middle of the night, some kind of alarm you set, so you didn't forget: you have been boarded by Somali pirates.

The first time I saw them, one afternoon, laying out their little rugs and kneeling down, I was surprised because I thought they'd be facing east. I mentioned it to Tony later, and he looked at me like I was stupid and said that Mecca was basically north of where we were, and only a little bit east.

One time, Damian came down to the cinema room and said that a call had just come through on the satellite phone when he was with Ahmed, who had been telling him where to sail to. Damian had answered because Ahmed didn't seem bothered, and it was the navy on the other end! They said they were following us, that they knew where we were, that we should hang tight.

— Ahmed heard the whole thing, said Damian, back in the cinema room. Afterwards Ahmed took the phone from me and said to the navy, don't call again. We call. Then he hung up. The whole time he was calm. It was like he just didn't care.

Something turned inside me, like an eel, in the dark crannies of my mind.

— Why wouldn't – I started to say.

— Think about it, said Tony. What are the navy going to do? The pirates have hostages. That automatically makes all the navy's guns useless.

It was a sobering thought.

Finally, we saw land. It was a little like Egypt, but also more wild, more . . . ancient-seeming.

— Ku soo dhawaada Somaliland, Ahmed said, as the beach grew towards us. Welcome to Somalia.

There was an arc of sand, with many small wooden boats lying on it, toppled over, looking strange and wrong out of water, like toys discarded by a giant. Behind the shore were dunes, and then rocks rising to mountains, a thousand shades of red that, as the sun moved behind clouds, shifted colours, became shimmering rainbows.

And between the sand and the mountains . . .

— Eyl, Ahmed said, with a grin.

I wasn't sure why he was so proud. All I could see, apart from sand, were some shacks, a single pickup truck, a wizened tree, a few goats tethered here and there. Some of the town was hidden by the dunes or the rocks, but it still wasn't an impressive sight.

— For fishing? I said, pointing to the dozens of beached little boats.

Ahmed laughed and pointed behind me.

I turned. We were on the front deck, so I had an uninterrupted view down the coast, and that meant I could see the tanker at anchor a mile or so away and the container ship even further along.

— For supplies, he said. From town.

I stared. The little boats were for shuttling supplies to the yacht. And there were other ships here, being held hostage. We weren't alone. Somehow that made it even more scary. It was like piracy was the industry of this town.

We realised how true that was in the following days. It became impossible to keep track of the guards because the motor boats were coming and going all the time, relieving shifts, bringing more food.

At this point, we were still eating the yacht's food and Felipe was making it. The pirates ate pasta, only pasta, for every meal. One of them would fire up the gas stove and they would boil it for hours, with stuff from the tins they had brought aboard. It looked gross.

Oh – and the coffee! I have to tell you about the coffee.

I think it was, like, the third day before we reached Eyl that we saw them do it. I was taking Tony for a walk outside, along the walkway that led between the two decks. He was moving more freely all the time. We happened to go past the galley porthole, and some movement caught our eyes. Inside, a pirate was squatting by a big washing-up bowl. He unscrewed the lid from a tin of coffee – the writing on it was Arabic, which made me think it wasn't ours. He tipped the whole tin into the washing-up bowl, then straightened up and went to the store cupboard. He came back with a packet of sugar – a fricking kilo of sugar – and poured that in, too. Then he carried the bowl over to the tap and poured cold water into it.

— What the – said Tony.

The pirate took a metal cup that was tied to his waistband and dipped it into the hideous concoction, then sipped. He seemed pleased because he left the galley with the bowl.

— Jesus, I said.

— Yeah, said Tony. We must make sure Felipe never sees this.

I laughed. Felipe treated the galley like it was his castle. He hated the pirates going in there, though he knew he had no choice. And he hated that they had taken away his knives and would only give them back if there was a guard to watch over him.

— Well, said Tony. At least we can hope that they'll give themselves heart attacks from a caffeine overdose.

They didn't, of course. But they did drink a massive bowlful of that stuff every day. You never saw a pirate who wasn't smoking or chewing khat or drinking their so-called coffee. The corridors and decks became spotted with splats of black

I didn't mean to see the stars.

I couldn't sleep, that's all. It's not like we were totally under lock and key, even now that we were moored by Eyl. We were free to come and go as we pleased, though not to leave the boat, of course. If we did, what were we going to do? Swim to the Somali coast? The idea was absurd.

So they didn't watch us every moment of every day, is what I'm saying.

One night, soon after we reached the coast, I left the cinema room and went out on to the front deck. I thought maybe the fresh air would make me sleepier. It was stupid of me, really. I'd spent so many months not looking up at the sky, not even thinking about what was up there when the sun went down, deliberately not thinking about it to spite my mother with her stupid stardust reference and her belief that I could see her in the stars, that you'd think I would have been more careful. I suppose that's what getting kidnapped does to your concentration.

There were three sunloungers on the deck. They seemed ludicrous now, out of place, like a swimming pool in a war zone. I stood by one and looked down at the dark sea.

Except it wasn't dark.

Below me, the water was on fire, glowing with blue phosphorescence. At that moment I split exactly in two, like a walnut out of its shell, and one half of me was silently gasping at the beauty of it, while the other half of me thought, even when I look down I'm seeing goddamn stars.

I turned around, dizzy, and lay on a sunlounger, stretched out on my back, eyes closed, so as not to look up. I sighed.

There was a noise, the kind of noise you can't describe, but that you know is a person moving. I sat up a bit and turned. Then a shadow to the right peeled away from the darkness and came towards me.

It was the young one, the English speaker, Farouz. He stood a little way away from me. I could see the silhouette of his gun. He lit a cigarette, and the cherry sparked, a little star on the yacht, though not as bright as the ones above. Smoke drifted up, and his cheek curved just so. My mind took a snapshot – the way minds sometimes do – that I can call back and picture even now: the precise angle of his head, the curlicues of smoke.

— You like the stars? he said. His voice was soft.

He couldn't have known that this was a difficult question. Actually, I was feeling pretty choked up about Mom and really didn't want to speak to him. I had an urge to get up and leave, but – my manners kicking in – I was worried that would be rude. I was aware, at the same time, of the preposterousness of this. Of worrying about offending a pirate, someone who was holding me hostage, basically threatening to kill me if he didn't get money.

Also, I was scared that if I didn't speak to him, he might hurt me. So . . .

— I wasn't looking at the stars. I was just sitting, I said.

— Look, then, he told me. He pointed up.

I was a tiger, trapped by spears on all sides. I looked down, mumbled:

— No, sorry, I . . .

He smiled at me.

— I won't hurt you, he said. Please, look. They are beautiful.

What could I do?

I looked up.

Above me, glittering, were billions of stars. I had never seen anything like it in my whole entire life; it must have been the lack of light pollution, I suppose. Part of me wanted to go back inside, to leave the young pirate there with no explanation at all, to hide from the pain that was lighting into flame inside me; and part of me couldn't move a muscle, was locked there, on the sunlounger, staring.

There were stars I had never even imagined existed – in between the stars that I was used to, the ones I used to look at with Mom, sitting in our back garden, a blanket wrapped around us. I could see the Milky Way, not like a pale splash on the sky, but like I'd seen it in a slide show of space photography: a great white cloud, flecked with blue, billowing with fire, stretching across the heavens. All around it, in the blackness, sparkled the universe.

Mom taught me all the stars. So from the deck of the *Daisy May*, sitting on that sunlounger, I could see Ursa Major, of course – you see it all year in the northern hemisphere, which just about still included us. But also Aquarius, Capricorn, Pisces – the autumn constellations.

For a moment, I couldn't speak. I was afraid the words would break apart in my mouth, like a Communion wafer, and tell him from the crumbling of my voice what I was feeling.

Then.

— There are more here than where I live, I said finally.

— No, he replied. There is the same number. But you see fewer at home because of the street lights.

His English was very precise, like he was reading from a book. Maybe it wasn't exactly like I'm saying it, maybe he wasn't so grammatical and he sometimes had to search for a word, but I'm not going to apologise for that. If I said his words like he sounded them, it would make it seem like he was simple, someone you could feel condescending about. But he wasn't, and you can't. He was smart – much smarter than me.

— Yes, I know that, I said, a little bit annoyed. I'm not an idiot, I added. Then I *felt* like an idiot for saying something so childish.

I saw him shrug. He took a drag on his cigarette.

— I have heard, he said after a moment, that sailors used to navigate by reading the stars. I wonder how they did it.

— You don't know? But you're a sailor.

— Why a sailor?

I didn't really understand him.

— You have boats, I said. You're on a boat now.

He laughed.

— You are on a boat. Do you know how to sail it?

— Well, no, but –

— But? I went to school in Mogadishu and in Puntland. To high school, you understand. I read books. I was going to be a professor, like my father. I don't know about boats.

— So why did you become a pirate?

106

He stepped a little closer to me, and I could see his features now, in the gloom.

— Are you joking? he said. I think you are joking.

— No, I –

— There is no school any more. There are no professors. There is no father. The rebels came and took most of it away. Then the Muslim fundamentalists took the rest. The Al-Shabaab.

— You're not Muslim?

Another laugh.

— Of course I am, but not like them. People like that . . . Do you remember 9/11? When those buildings were destroyed in New York?

You have no idea, I thought. But I just nodded.

— There were people here who celebrated when that happened, Farouz said. Laughing in the street. They said it was the start of a war between Islam and the West. They were happy about that. Me, I was afraid. Because I thought they were right. It was the start of a war. But now . . . Now the war is not just against the West. They kill their own people, the Al-Shabaab.

I don't know why, but I felt sorry for him then and I wanted to show him something, like my mom used to show me. I pointed up at the stars from where I sat on the sunlounger.

— See the Plough? I said. Ursa Major, it's also called. Follow the right-hand side of it upward. Trace a straight line. Above it, that single star, the bright one? That's the North Star. Wherever you are, if you aim at that star, you're going north.

He followed my eyes and my finger, then he smiled broadly; I could see his teeth white in the darkness. I noticed that he had long eyelashes – longer than mine, and I'm a girl. He stubbed out his cigarette butt against the wall of the dining area.

— Thank you, he said. That is good to know. You are wrong, though. It is not the Plough. It is the Camel.

— Camel? I don't see . . .

— No?

Then he was sitting on the sunlounger next to me, kind of perching on the edge of it. His skin was hot; I could feel it, like a furnace in the night. My heart lurched at the sudden closeness. He raised his own finger, traced a line.

— See? That is the rump. The hump. And the head at the other end.

I saw it. A camel, sitting down. Maybe not very obvious, but who says that the Plough really looks like a plough? Or a bear, like the Greeks thought?

— Oh, right, I said. But it hasn't got a tail.

— No, he said. The tail was pulled off. He said this like it was the most normal thing to say, ever.

— The tail was pulled off? By who?

— By a hungry man.

I sat up properly. This was a weird conversation when it started, and it was getting weirder.

— What do you mean, by a hungry man?

He put his gun down on the cushion beside us, still attached by its string. For half a moment, I thought maybe

I could pick it up, turn it on him. But what would I do then? No way would I pull the trigger. For all I knew the safety was on, anyway, and I wouldn't know how to turn it off. And there were others like him inside, ready to kill Dad and the stepmother. I didn't want that. I didn't want anyone else to die.

When I looked up from the gun to his face, he was holding my gaze with his – and that was what it felt like, a hold, like I couldn't turn away even if I wanted to. He glanced at the gun and back at me. Then he smiled, and I didn't know what it meant, that smile, whether he was indulging my little fantasy, amused by it, or whether he was telling me that I wouldn't have a chance, that I would be dead before I could pick it up. For the sake of my sanity, I decided to assume the former.

— All our stories are about hunger, he said.

— Er, right, I said. Why? I still wanted to go inside, but there was something about him, something about the quiet measured way he spoke, that made me stay where I was.

— It's a desert country, he said. There has always been famine.

— I see, I said. So because of that, someone pulled off the tail of the camel in the sky? I caught the sarcasm in my own voice and felt a little ashamed. It's not like famine is a big joke; it was just that he kept saying these things that sounded like a pretentious voice-over on a documentary in his overly correct English. There has always been famine – like that, you know?

— It's not that simple, he said. You want me to tell you, really?

No, I wanted to say. No, I want you to leave me alone. But he seemed quite gentle, surprisingly, and it wasn't like I had anywhere else to go.

— Er . . . yeah, all right, I said.

— OK, he said. The sky camel. He indicated the constellation again with his hand. So, this was the fault of the Warsangheli tribe. There was a terrible famine, and kids were dying, old people, too. This happened all the time, but this particular famine was bad. There was no rain, never. The cattle died. Men hunted hyenas and ate them. I don't know if . . . Is there an animal in your country that is dirty to eat?

— Some people don't eat pigs.

— I don't eat pigs. I am Muslim, remember? But the hyena, it's more of a bad creature. A pig is just a pig – it doesn't care about you. We don't eat them because Allah says not to. But a hyena, it's a cruel animal. We call them all sorts of names: the night walker, the corpse eater, the unfaithful, the child stealer.

— Child stealer?

— Yes. They used to attack children if the children were on their own. At night.

— Oh, I said.

I wondered what that must be like, to live in a place where there were animals that could kill you. I'd never really thought about it before.

110

— It must have been terrifying, I said. But that was a long time ago? I added. It's safe now, right?

He stared at me without speaking for a long moment, his brow furrowed. I didn't know where to look; I felt embarrassed, though I didn't know why. I understand now what his silence was saying, but he didn't say it out loud, not then. He was saying that there are other things that can take away your children, even now that the hyenas are mostly gone:

Other people.

Then, though, I just looked back, oblivious, and eventually he turned again to the Camel in the night sky.

— The people ate the hyenas, he said, which, if you were from here, you would know is a sign of their starvation. Everywhere the beirda trees were stripped of fruit. Hungry parents fed on the flesh of their dead children. And so the Warsangheli held a clan meeting. They asked for people to suggest a way to save the clan. One old man stood up. He said that they had eaten all the cattle and the zebras and the hyenas. But there were animals that were untouched – the animals that live in the sky, like the great camel.

But the constellations are sacred. If we eat the sky camel, said some of the men, then worse things might happen than drought.

Farouz made a graceful gesture intended, I guess, to give the idea of sacredness or – what's the word? – sanctity. Even his gestures were different – his body spoke in a foreign language, too. He moved in another tongue, and sometimes he would say one thing with his mouth and seem to say another with his hands, which was strange to me.

— Are you listening? asked Farouz.

— Oh, yes. Sorry, I said.

And I *was* sorry, because I really was listening, or I wanted to listen, anyway. It was such a relief to be talking to someone roughly my age, and someone who wasn't my dad or Damian or the stepmother. All of a sudden I was aware of how lonely I'd been on this trip, listening to my music, doing nothing but doing it alone.

— OK, he went on.

There is nothing worse than drought, said another of the men of the tribe, in reply to the man who said they should not eat the sky camel. Soon there will be no clan at all, and then what use will it be to have sacred things? Better to eat them and survive.

The next day, the whole clan, those who were still alive, moved to the Al Medu mountains. They organised themselves into a giant human tower, so that they could reach the heavens. The entire clan, everyone, was part of this big tower. And the man at the top found that he could touch the ceiling of the world, where the stars are. The night sky was cold, and the people in the tower began to tremble as the wind blew through their clothes.

The camel of stars was sitting in its usual position. The man at the top reached out and caught hold of the camel's tail. I've got him, he called down.

He's got him, the others called, until even the people right at the bottom, standing on the mountain, knew that the camel had been captured.

Except, then, one of the men lower down remembered that he had left his basket at home. He realised that he would not be able to take a piece of the meat home to his family because he had no container to put it in. Quickly he left his place and began to climb down the tower.

This was a mistake, because when he left, the tower began to topple, and then it collapsed, everyone in it tumbling down, down, down to the mountains. The man at the top was desperate. He took out his machete and chopped at the tail, thinking that he could just take that one piece with him. The camel, feeling this, bellowed and ran, its tail severing from its body as it went.

I shivered, listening to Farouz, and in my head it wasn't the tribe falling, but my mother, spiralling down through blackness, the stars above her. In religion classes at school, they were always talking about the Fall, and that's how it was for me, with my mother; it was in capitals, always. The Event. The Fall.

— Are you OK? asked Farouz.

— Yes, I said. Just cold.

It *was* cold, actually – when the sun went down, it was amazing how quick the heat leached out of the air.

Farouz nodded, taking off his jacket and putting it around my shoulders, almost distractedly – or maybe he was just looking away so that the gesture didn't seem awkward, overfamiliar.

— But then the people below the top man were gone, Farouz said, and he was falling, too, holding the tail. Some people say that he is still falling, still clinging to his tail, because he was so high up when he fell.

Farouz pointed to the Camel with the tip of the cigarette he had just lit.

— That is why the Camel has no tail, he said.

He got up as if to leave. But just before he reached the door, he turned and held something out. It sparkled in the moon- and starlight, and for a moment, a crazy moment, I thought he was giving me a star. But then he drew closer and I saw that it was my watch, my Chanel watch.

— Here, he said.

I took the watch and, as I did so, our fingers brushed against each other. This happens all the time in life – when you take the change for your coffee, when someone hands you your bag in a club. But this wasn't like that. It was like our skins spoke to each other.

Farouz touching my hand, and other people touching my hand: these things were the same like water and vodka are the same, appearing identical, hitting your insides in a totally different way.

I stood there, dumbstruck, for a moment.

— How did you – I started to ask.

— It doesn't matter. But do not wear it. Do not let Moham- med see it. He is . . . he has a powerful family. He would like to be boss instead of Ahmed. We must be careful. You must keep it hidden.

— I will, I said. Thank you. Thank you so –

But he was already gone.

*

The next day, I sort of pathetically moped around, thinking about Farouz.

I thought:

Does he like me?

Does he fancy me?

Is it just me who feels this, like, static in the air when he's there?

I imagine you've wondered similar things, too, though maybe not about pirates, for which you should be grateful.

The thing was, I just couldn't believe it, that he could be interested in me. I've said it already – I'm not attractive. My only unusual feature, which I shared with my mother, is my grey eyes. They're truly grey, a rare colour. Like the sea, my dad always used to say.

Of course, looks aren't everything – true beauty is on the inside and all that crap – but it's not like I'm an interesting person, either. You have to understand, and it's worth getting this out of the way: I know I'm telling you this story, but it's the story that's interesting, not me. I don't have charming personality quirks. I don't have any hobbies to speak of. I don't paint or make clothes or write a blog or even particularly like shopping. I don't own a phone in the shape of a hamburger or have an invisible friend.

The only interesting thing about me used to be that I was very good at playing the violin, and I stopped doing that.

In fact, ever since the Event, I've tried to stop being a person at all. I don't have opinions. I don't get angry any more. I have no goals or ambitions. I just am.

Besides, even before that, Mom had enough personality quirks for both of us. You know when someone says they're a little bit OCD just because they like things to be tidy? I used to think I'd like to bring those people round to my house to show them what OCD really looks like. People forget that it's *Obsessive* Compulsive Disorder. They just get hung up on the Compulsive part, think it's all about counting things and turning the light off three times and keeping things clean. Believe me, my mom did that stuff. The lights did have to go off three times, the oven had to be checked twice before bed, the fridge, too – to make sure it was on, then to make sure it was closed. This is the kind of thing that, on a TV show, might be endearing.

But there's the Obsessive part, too – the part that made her afraid of bad luck and contamination. The part that made her wash her hands any time someone shook hands with her, and throw away food if someone else touched it, refuse food if someone else handed it to her.

I saw my mom on her hands and knees in the kitchen, scrubbing the floor with wire wool until her fingers bled. I've seen her with a chopping knife, carving great big slashes in her arm because I'd been naughty and she'd said something mean about me to a friend and she thought god would take me away from her as punishment. I had to call an ambulance that time, and years later she still had silvery scars all over her forearm.

I saw her screaming, I mean really screaming, pulling out her hair, because we had to go to a family party and she didn't know what to wear.

116

I saw her lie in bed for three days in a row, crying.

I saw her tell Dad she would kill him, she would gut him in his sleep, because he wouldn't turn the car around, three hours from home, so she could check the dials on the oven.

I saw all those things, so I've always been happy to just be me quietly, to not be quirky. I'm also one of those people who prefers hanging out with other people to doing stuff on my own, who would rather go out clubbing than listen to music on my own. Not that going clubbing worked out particularly well, which is another reason the head teacher had reached the end of her tether with me. Looking back, I had too many late nights in the East End, with bass-heavy dance music making the floors shake, the sonic boom plugging me straight into the speakers.

On the yacht, there was no escape from myself, and it wasn't like there were any distractions. I was just stuck there with my own ordinariness, like a prisoner in my own skin, wondering, all the time, if Farouz might have feelings for me.

Never wondering what it might mean if he did. How I might pay, like in a cautionary fairytale, to get what I wished for.

Every second day, the pirates let us have showers. I was glad when it came round the next time because I was feeling really sweaty and horrible. I went first, then the stepmother went after me and said not to expect to see her for an hour or maybe more. I thought it would be less than that – the heating came from solar panels, and it didn't last that long.

As she washed, I went out on to the rear deck. I was surprised to see Dad there, sitting on the diving platform so that his feet were in the water, a glass of something dark in his hand, with grainy bits floating in it.

Normally, I avoided my dad, but I guess I was feeling a bit guilty about last night and Farouz, even though nothing had happened, so I walked up to him. My shadow fell over him.

— Is that what I think it is? I asked.

— What do you think it is?

— The coffee, I said, that the pirates make. Half coffee, half sugar. Lukewarm water.

For some reason, something softened in Dad's face, tension slackening from muscles.

— Yep, he said. When in Rome. He raised the glass to Ahmed, who was strolling above us, gun in hand, and Ahmed saluted back.

The way my dad makes friends, it's weird, I'm telling you. But I didn't say that.

All I said was:

— Ugh, Dad, gross.

I sat down beside him, kicking off my sandals as I did so. He was wearing shorts, and I could see his legs disappearing into the clear warm water – or, rather, not disappearing, but starting again at a certain point on his calves, at a slightly different

118

angle, so that by immersing his legs partly in the water it looked like they were very slightly broken, dog-legged around the joint of the sea's surface.

I put my feet in the water, and they, too, jagged off from me at an angle. I was startled by the silkiness of the water, the coolness of it. Funny, how simple your desires become sometimes, like when there's stifling hot air wrapping you up, restricting you.

Heat → Cold. That's all your body wants, and it's enough.

— This is good, I said. Refreshing.

— Yes, said Dad.

I closed my eyes. The pirates had the engine going to power the computer or something. It made a kind of counterpoint with the sound of the waves, the tone similar but the rhythm different, like baroque music. I stopped that thought before it led me to my violin.

That was when I caught a whiff from Dad's drink.

— Oh my god, Dad, I said.

— What?

— That's not just coffee.

Dad looked at the glass in his hand as if someone else had just put it there.

— No, he said. I don't suppose it is.

— But you hate drinking!

— Do I?

— When Mom drank, when I drink . . .

— I hate my daughter drinking. You're seventeen.

— Nearly eighteen!

Dad sighed.

— I don't want to discuss it, Amy, he said in his and-that's-final voice.

— No way, no. You don't get out of this that easily –

— I lost my job, Amy-bear.

I turned to him so fast I nearly made him spill the drink. There was more coldness in me now, more than the water was giving me. I looked at him. Still handsome. Silver hair. Crow's feet, but still those green eyes: sharp, clever eyes, always moving. Which goes to show what you can't always see from people's eyes, because Mom's grey eyes were always still, and her mind never was.

— You're kidding, right? I said.

— Absolutely not.

— But . . . I said. *Why?*

He took a breath.

— The financial system is in trouble, he said. It's been in the news a bit. But it's going to get much worse. Our bank . . . we took some risks. And I was . . . I guess you could say I was the one who took most of them.

I watched the shifting sea, digesting this.

— What kind of risks? I asked. Are you . . . I mean, would the police –

— No! said Dad hurriedly. Nothing like that. It was only stuff other banks were doing, too. Mortgage derivatives, essentially. Collateralised Debt Obligations, they're called. We bought them and sold them. Now they've gone bad.

— Derivatives like in calculus? I asked.

I knew about those from school. The derivative of $x^2 + 4x = 2x + 4$.

— No, said Dad. Something else. Derivatives are financial products based on mortgages. The wrong ones, as it turns out. He met my eyes. We fucked up, basically.

— So the bank is going to, what, go bankrupt?

— Probably not. They'll sell it to someone else. But some of us . . . Decisions were made, Amy. Now they're cleaning house.

— What do you mean, *they*? You're . . . whoever you are. Managing Director of Investment, or whatever. You're in charge.

— Not any more.

— Oh, I said.

This was a new calculus, it seemed: the derivative of mortgages = losing your job.

Part of me wanted to reach out, to hold his hand, but I didn't. He'd never once been there for me after Mom died. He was always working. Now he'd been fired, was I supposed to be there for him?

— You said the company was insuring the yacht, I said. That's how come Tony is here.

— They are, Amy. It's complicated. I have share options, you see. They've made me redundant, but they can't afford for me to die.

— Right, I said. Cheery.

— Hmm, said Dad. So that's my secret. Anyway, what about you? Your A levels, will you retake them?

— We're being held hostage, Dad. In case you haven't noticed.

— I know that, said Dad. But we have to stay positive.

— Do we? Who says?

— I don't know. Me.

— Oh, well, in that case . . .

Dad stretched his back, frustrated.

— Look, just answer the question, he said. About your A levels.

— No, I said.

— Well, that's really mature –

— No, I won't retake them, I said. I was thinking of getting a job. In a bar, maybe.

Dad sighed.

— What, that's not good enough for you? I said. I felt anger kindle inside me, just like a fire sparking in my chest.

— No, I'm just not sure that –

— That you want your daughter doing a menial job, like a poor person?

Dad took a long breath.

— My parents were upholsterers, Amy.

— Exactly. And now you're rich, and you have rich, famous friends. How embarrassing it would be for you if your daughter was just a barmaid!

— I don't care what other people think, said Dad. I'm thinking about you. About your fulfilment. What about five years down the line, if you're still behind a bar? You have a talent, Amy. For the violin. You should use it. You could still enter the Menuhin as a senior.

— Don't tell me what to do.

— I'm just saying. Look at me. I spent half my life in that bank. And now I wonder what I did all that time. That's why I wanted to get away, to buy the yacht, to see new places.

— So that's what this was about, then? I said, that spark inside me flaring now, like a gas stove being lit. If I could have put my hand down my throat and into my lungs at that moment, it would have come out on fire.

— Amy.

— So this has nothing to do with fucking spending time as a family, I said, talking over him. You just got canned by the bank and needed something to do.

Dad physically recoiled. Something lizard-like happened with his eyes; they went all hooded and guilty.

— No, he said. It's not like that.

— Anyway, what did you do, *really*? I said. What does it mean, a mortgage derivative? Did you steal people's money? Their houses?

— No! We took some risks. We bought some mortgages from another company who actually lent the money to the homeowners. Then we packaged them up in a great big pool of money, and we sold them to other people as an investment. That's all. In retrospect, it wasn't very intelligent, because now the homeowners have stopped repaying their mortgages, so we can't pay the interest. And we bought them in the first place with money that wasn't . . . that wasn't absolutely, in the final analysis, necessarily ours.

— Jesus, I said. You're a pirate. No wonder you're such good buddies with Ahmed.

— Amy. I'm a managing director of a very respected, multi-national –

— Were a managing director.

— Sorry?

— Were. A managing director. You were.

— Yes.

Silence. And I stood up, slid my sandals back on, slimy with seawater.

— Enjoy your vodka, I said. Or whatever that is.

Dad watched the sea. He didn't look up as I walked away. Just then, the stepmother came out, with a sun hat on.

— Hot water bloody ran out, she said. Couldn't even do my conditioner.

Damian was standing in the corridor when I walked back from the toilet the next evening.

— You want to watch yourself, he said.

— I'm sorry?

— You and that boy. It'll end in tears.

— I don't see what –

— It has to do with me?

God, I hated it when Damian finished my sentences – it was something he was always doing.

— Yeah, I said – a bit lamely.

— Of course you don't. Because you're a teenage girl.

I wanted to say, it didn't stop you ogling my bikini. But I didn't because there was already a weird tension in the air.

I just said:

— And you're a bloody sailor. You don't get to tell me what to do.

He rolled his eyes. I mean, he actually rolled his eyes in kind of an exaggerated way; I'd never seen anyone do that before.

— It's not just you who'll get hurt if something goes wrong, he said.

— Nothing's going to go wrong because nothing's happening, I said. And as I said it, I wondered if it was true.

— Good, he said, and walked away.

That really pissed me off because it gave him the last word, which made it seem like he had won.

I went down to the front deck again, secretly hoping that Farouz might be there.

And you know what?

He was.

— Farouz, I said, and then instantly blushed, because the way your mouth shapes his name when you speak it means that the second syllable comes out long and slow – Farooooouz – like a sigh.

Try it now.

See?

His name, it has longing built into it.

— Hostage Three, Farouz said, returning my greeting, not seeming to notice my embarrassment. He was smoking, obviously, his gun dangling from his trousers – only these were new trousers: Armani jeans, Dad's. Most of our electrical goods, the blatantly valuable stuff, had been given back by now, but the pirates were still dressed in our clothes.

I took a deep breath. If I was going to get killed, I wanted at least one of the people who killed me to know my name.

— Amy, I said. Not Hostage Three. Amy.

Farouz was silent for a long time. Then he said:

— Amy. That is pretty.

Letting out my breath, I sat down on a sunlounger. It was the first time, I think, that I felt any hope that I might survive this. He knew my name. Surely that would make him hesitate before pulling the trigger?

— So, Amy, he said. What is it like to be rich? There was an edge in his voice I hadn't heard before. He blew out smoke, and it curled around the horns of Capricorn.

— It's . . . I don't know.

I had to be careful what I said because of Tony claiming that the bank owned the yacht. But still, it had to be obvious we were well off – I guess the pirates assumed we were paying passengers or something. And in the back of my mind, I was wondering: are we still rich?

But I was sure we were. I knew enough about how corporate finance worked to know that Dad wouldn't have left without a massive golden parachute, or whatever they were called.

— I think it's not money that makes people happy, I said. It's not the most important thing, not like family, friends, that kind of stuff. Birthday parties. Sometimes I think I would rather swap my life with someone who had nothing but a farm, some chickens to look after, a view of the sea . . . That sounds sappy, I said. I should shut up.

I shut up.

We were both facing the sea, which was black, but glimmered with starlight, so we weren't really looking at each other. That was sort of disconcerting and liberating at the same time.

— Money is important in Somalia, he said slowly. When you have no medicine, no food, no water, money is important.

— Of course, I –

— We cannot swap our lives with anyone. Half of what you said, I do not even understand. Do you see? You, you can think: oh, my life might be better if this, or if that. It is not even possible to think this in Somalia, because there is nothing that is better.

His voice was cold, older than him. I didn't know how old he was at the time – seventeen? eighteen? – but his voice was a hundred years old.

And you know what? I thought I did understand him, at least a bit.

I also felt stupid and clumsy, like I had woken up and accidentally put on a body that was too big for me, like wearing someone else's clothes, a body that was heavy and awkward around my bones.

— I'm sorry, I said. I didn't mean . . . I just mean, bad things happen to rich people, too.

— And what has happened to you that is bad? he asked. There was a challenge in his voice.

— Give me one of those, I said, pointing to his cigarette.

He raised his eyebrows, but handed me one. He gave his own, for me to light it from. When I did, the tobacco fizzing and popping as it caught, I drew the smoke down deep into my lungs, and it was as if it were spreading through me, making me into smoke, my body made of air and particles now, instead of solid flesh.

I breathed out, sending myself, my particles, into the night air.

Then, weirdly, I told him.

But when I started, I faltered immediately.

— I – I began. Then I broke off. I mean . . . I – ah.

— It's OK, said Farouz. I was being . . . nosy?

— Yes, nosy, I said.

— Sorry.

— No. Well, I mean, yes, the word is nosy. But you weren't being nosy.

— Oh.

I took a breath.

— My mother . . . she . . .

He was looking right into my eyes, and it didn't feel odd that he was doing that.

— Your mother, she is not on the yacht, he said gently.

— No, I said.

— That woman, with the red fingernails. She is your stepmother.

— Yes.

— I understand, said Farouz.

— No, you don't, I said. Because there were things I hadn't told anyone. Things I hadn't even told my father.

Farouz held the railing, looking down at the sea. He didn't press me.

— One day Mom called me when I was meant to be in class, I said. This was in London, in Surbiton, where I went to school. I wasn't meant to answer my cell, but it was a free lesson and I was hanging out in the common room, so I did. At the time, Mom was happy. She was on some new antidepressants, which were working quite well, and a new antipsychotic that seemed

129

to make her finally believe that god wasn't out to punish her for being a bad person.

— I'm sorry? said Farouz.

— It doesn't matter, I said. It's not important.

— OK, said Farouz. He didn't say anything more, he just kept looking at me, like he knew the story wasn't over.

— She told me that if anything happened to her, I should look after my dad. My voice was catching – this was the part I hadn't told my dad about, hadn't told anyone about. I told her nothing was going to happen to her, I said. She told me again, if anything happened to her, I should look after my dad.

Farouz nodded slowly.

— She was sick? he said.

— Yes, I said. She was sick. In here. I touched the side of my head, in what I figured was a universal gesture.

— I see, said Farouz.

I held the railing, my hands pale next to his dark ones on the smooth metal.

— My mom went to work after speaking to me, I said. She went to the roof. She stood on the roof. And . . . and . . .

Farouz touched my hand, and it was warm, his fingers were warm.

— I see, he said. I see. It's OK. I see. You don't have to say.

I nodded. I took my hand away. The sea was so black beneath us it looked like a hole in existence.

I was seeing someone falling through that blackness, from the stars, down to the earth.

*

When my mother rang me on my phone at school, I was play-ing Bach's *Chaconne* in my head, imagining the movement of my fingers. It was the virtuoso piece I was going to play if I got to the finals of the Menuhin Competition, which is this really big deal contest I'd been selected for – one of twenty-two chosen in the world. As soon as I answered and heard her tone, the music stopped. It never started again, not really.

The whole time my mother was speaking, I was looking at the coffee machine in the common room. It was a Gaggia, because that's the kind of school I went to. It had a scratch on its right-hand side and a two-nozzle espresso system. It was silver. Behind it was a window with a hand-shaped smear on it and, on the other side of the glass, a chestnut tree, with a girl juggling brightly coloured balls underneath it. There was one cup of coffee, half full and cold, on the formica table. Just to my right, there was a single chip in the formica.

There was a pigeon strutting on the windowsill. It was 11.16 a.m., according to the clock on the microwave next to the Gaggia coffee machine – and the microwave was a Samsung, with a tomato stain on the inside of the glass, most of the buttons worn away, apart from the one that said *360 watts*.

I still can't *not* see those things; I can't forget them. And ever since, I can't look at a Gaggia coffee machine in a café, or a Samsung anything, without seeing what happened next. It's, like, you know when you see your own phone, or your own coat? It's just a phone. It's just a coat. It's an object; it doesn't mean anything. But because it's yours, there's a kind of glow that it has. It has meaning, a link, a

131

then hit the ground, and was taken to hospital by ambulance, where they gave her 5.7 litres of blood, and tried to set her broken ribs and collarbone and leg and hip, tried to restart her heart three times using a combination of palpitations and shocks at increasing voltages – I saw the medical report, it was on my dad's desk, and now I can't ever, not ever, forget it – until, eventually, they had to give up, after the defibrillators kicked for the final time and, at precisely 14:01 and 45 seconds on the 22nd of July 2006, according to Dr Hafaz, who signed the certificate with a semi-legible scrawl, she died.

Farouz didn't speak for ages. I thought I could see him frowning in the dark.

— Oh no, I said. Your religion. You probably think people who commit suicide go to hell, or something. I'm sorry.

I don't really know why I was apologising, though – out of politeness, I guess.

He sucked in air through his teeth. Then he reached out and touched my hand.

— I think that a person who commits suicide is leaving hell, not entering it, he said.

At that moment, the moon came out from behind some clouds, and I turned and met his eyes. I looked down, broke the gaze.

— I have a brother, he said, taking back his hand.

I looked at him. What he had just said, it was like . . . It was like it didn't follow on from what I had said, but at the same time it did. Straight away I thought, his brother is dead. And then I found myself thinking, I hope he isn't. But I was pretty sure I was right.

— Older? I guessed. I could tell from the slightly awed tone in his voice, which I was sure he wasn't aware of.

— Yes. He is in prison.

— What for? I asked. Oh, I thought. So not dead then.

— For this. For being a coast guard.

— A coast guard? I asked.

— That is what we are. You call us pirates. We call ourselves coast guards. We, here, we are the South Central Coast Guard.

I snorted.

— You think it's funny? he asked. The people here, they used to be fishermen. Do you know what happened to them?

— No.

— Fishing vessels from your country, from other countries in the West, they came and fished in our waters after the government collapsed, in 1991. There was no one to stop them. So our fishermen took guns and went to attack them, to stop them stealing our fish. There were a lot of guns because of the war. Then the fishing boats began to have navy escorts, and we could not do anything against them. So we stole ships instead. That is how we began.

My mind was reeling. It hadn't even occurred to me that these men had a story of their own, that they were anything but thieves, pure and simple.

— OK, I said. So you and your brother are coast guards.

— Well, no. I am, but he isn't, actually. He did one of those hollow laughs.

— Then why –

— Why is he in prison? In Somalia, we have a saying. *If you cannot catch a thief, you catch his brother.*

— Right . . .

— Well, he is my brother. He was riding in the wrong car, in Galkayo, where we live. An expensive car, belonging to a friend of ours, who is like me, but older, more successful. In Galkayo, if you have a sweet ride, or you have bought yourself a big crib, then the police, they –

— I'm sorry. A *crib*?

— That's not the right word? You know, a house.

— I know the word. It's just, it's something American gangsters say.

He shrugged.

— Sometimes I watch MTV, he said. I pick things up.

I felt embarrassed, then, like I shouldn't have said anything.

— So they pulled your brother over, I said, to try to get back to the subject.

— Yes. And they decided he was a pirate because he was in a nice car with a pirate. So they threw him in jail and they told me I must pay fifty thousand dollars to get him out. Of course, the pirate who was in the car with him could pay this money himself, so he is already free, but my brother is still in there.

— Wait. Where did they think you were going to get fifty thousand dollars?

— From this. From hostages.

I was pretty confused by this point.

— So the police know you're a pirate?

— Yes. Of course.

— Then why not arrest you?

He sighed.

— I told you. Do you not understand anything? You don't catch the thief, you catch his brother. I am useful to this crew, to the South Central Coast Guard. I speak good English. My brother does not. So it is me they need. It is me who must work, who must pay.

There was a tightening in his voice, as if someone were wrapping a wire around each word, strangling it.

— I'm sorry, I said, though I still didn't really understand anything properly.

He lit a cigarette, smiled in the light of it.

— I will earn a lot more than fifty thousand dollars from this one, he said. I hope so, anyway. I will free my brother. And then he and I will leave this country. Go to Egypt, maybe.

We talked for a while longer, but it was late, and I guessed my dad would be worrying about me, so I got up to go back inside. Farouz stood up, too.

— I have to stay out here, he said. To guard.

— I know, I said. I . . . Thank you for my watch. Thank you for showing me the stars.

Oh god, what a lame thing to say. How cheesy. And so ridiculous, like something out of a Disney movie, when here I was with a Somali pirate, someone from a completely different world, who might as well have been an alien.

But he didn't seem to think it was odd.

— You're welcome, he said. He shook my hand and electricity poured into me, practically crackled blue and sparked in the air.

Then he lit another cigarette and turned away.

— I'm on guard duty, he said.

And he left, and the electricity left with him, like someone had pulled the plug on the world.

I wasn't angry with my mom, not exactly. I'm not angry even now. What I'm saying is, I understood what she did. She was miserable, and she ended it. I suppose I respected her choice.

There was only one note, and it was for me. It was under my pillow that night, after the hospital. After the waiting room. After the little bag they gave us, that had her wedding ring in it – the one I wear on my ring finger, and who cares that I look engaged – but not her handbag and purse, with the baby photo of me in it, because those were covered in blood (contaminated, the hospital secretary said) and they had to be burned (incinerated).

I never told my dad about the note. I never told him about the phone call, either. Can you blame me? It would basically be like telling him that I killed her, that I was so colossally stupid that I didn't get it when she said what she was going to do.

The note under my pillow said:

We are stardust.

My hand clenched, scrunching up the note. My breathing was loud in my chest. Everything seemed very bright.

In my head, I was on the beach in North Fork with Mom. I was little – I don't know, nine, maybe. She was pointing up at the stars. The North Fork is a bit like the Hamptons, but less pretentious, or so Dad says. He bought the house soon after he got his first big promotion. It's near a little town called Greenport, where there's a marina, lots of antique shops and

138

a few bars and restaurants – Emilio's, where we used to go for pizza; the Sound View, where we would sit and watch the ocean, eating crab and lobster.

Mainly, you go to the North Fork for the views. At our end of it, the far end, it's a narrow strip of land. Farmland, mostly: corn and pumpkins, which people sell in season from carts by the road; wine; grapes. And on either side is the sea, framed by impossibly long beaches, sparkling in the sun, or glowering grey in the rain or gloom. The land is flat and there are dunes, seabirds, tufts of grass. It's beautiful.

Especially at night – there are so few lights compared to New York, compared to anywhere, really, and it makes the stars pop out of the blackness.

— We're made out of those, said Mom to nine-year-old me, pointing to the stars. Did you know that?

— Huh?

— Stardust. We're made of it.

— No, we're not, I said, because I had been learning things at school. We're made out of DMA.

— DNA, Mom corrected. And that's right, yes. But I'm talking about smaller than that. You've got to go back to the big bang. What happened then? There was a big explosion that threw carbon atoms, bits of matter, all over the place. Some of them made stars. Some of them made moons. And some of them made us.

— We're made out of the same thing as stars?

— Yes, honey. On the particle level.

— Wow, the nine-year-old me said.

— And when our star dies, she said – the sun, I mean – when it goes supernova, we'll all be broken down to carbon again, and we'll go floating around the universe. Then everyone who ever lived will be together, just drifting, in little pieces. And eventually, they might form a new star. You and I, even if our bodies die, we might end up in the same star together, one day.

I wasn't really paying attention to that then.

— The sun's going to *die*? I said. When?

I was scared now. Looking back, it was pretty messed up, what my mom was saying to me; it wasn't the kind of thing parents are meant to tell their young children. And it should have set off all kinds of alarm bells. But I was a kid; if I heard bells, I didn't know they were alarm bells. I was like a Blitz baby who thinks that an air-raid siren is a nightly lullaby.

— No, baby, sorry, she said. I didn't mean to scare you. The sun won't die for a long time, like a billion years from now.

— Oh, OK.

— But the point is, when we die, it won't be the end. The atoms live for ever. You and I, we could be made of bits of dinosaur.

— Dinosaur?

— Yeah. You and me, we could have the same T-rex in us.

I put my hands up, bared my teeth, roared. Mom fake-squealed. I chased her down the beach, giggling, giving out my roar.

*

Back in my room, six years later, after I found the note, I sat down on the bed, my head swimming.

I knew what she was trying to say. That the two of us would end up in a star together, one day.

How dare she? I thought.

That night, and my dad never asked why, I took down all the little glow-in-the-dark stars from my room and I took them into the back garden and I fucking doused them in lighter fluid and I fucking burned them.

— Tell me about your family.

— I don't have a family. Only Abdirashid. My brother.

— OK, tell me about your brother.

— I have already told you. He is in prison.

— I know that! I mean, tell me about before. About growing up.

Farouz pursed his lips. We were sitting on a sunlounger. Me with my iPod and earphones on my lap, so I could say I'd been listening to music, if anyone asked.

— I went to school because of an imam, he said.

— An imam?

— Like a priest. Of Islam.

— Oh, OK.

— This imam, he was the head teacher of a charity school, in Galkayo. That is where my brother and I ended up, after my parents were killed.

— Your parents were –

— That is a different story, he said, cutting me off. Galkayo is in Puntland. We are not from Puntland, my brother and I. We are from Mogadishu. So it was difficult for us at first. The dialect is different. The people did not like refugees. The first year, we lived on the street. We begged for food. We walked to get water from wells. Sometimes, we caught rats.

— Jesus, I said.

He shrugged.

— A rat is better than dying. My brother, too, used to go off places. I don't know what he did. Maybe I do know what he did, actually. But, anyway, he went away, and when he came back he would have small amounts of money, and we would eat well for a day or two. That was good. Always, when my brother left me, it was the same place I had to wait for him, a little shop that sold fruit and snacks. Now, that same shop sends supplies to pirates here in Eyl. I know the owner – he is quite a rich man.

Farouz paused, seeming to examine the sea. I could hear it tap, tap, tapping against the yacht.

— Every day I waited at that shop for my brother, he said. Until one day, I stood up and walked away. I don't remember thinking, I can't bear this any more. Nothing like that. It was just something I did. I walked around Galkayo for many hours. In those days there were no big houses, because the piracy had not really started, or it had not started being so profitable. And no big cars on the road. Just shacks, mainly, and mosques, and some small houses.

After a while, I came to a low building and heard the voices of children from inside, chanting. I looked in the window. They were sitting there, with textbooks in front of them. It was a school! I had not realised until that moment that I missed school. I know Abdirashid didn't. He was always in trouble when we went to school in Mogadishu. His grades were terrible. My parents were always saying to him, why can't you be more like Farouz? And I thought that was funny because I wanted to be more like Abdirashid.

— So the school, I said, they let you in?

— Not just like that! he laughed. The first day, I merely

peered in the window. And when I came back to the little shop, Abdirashid beat me and told me never to run away again. But of course I did, the very next day. I went back to the little school every day, and I stood by the window, listening to what was being said inside.

— And then the imam saw you and asked you to come in?

— No!

Farouz lit a cigarette, drew in a deep breath of smoke, and it was like the stars were burning up into vapour, then entering his lungs; like he was sucking the stars from the sky.

— No? I asked.

— No, of course not. What happened was, I knew what Abdirashid was doing by then. So the next time I saw the imam, the one who taught the class with the window by which I would stand, I went up to him on the street. I told him that I would go to bed with him if I could enter his lessons. I told him I would do whatever he wanted.

— Fuck, I said.

— Yes, that, too.

I met his eyes. There was no indication at all that he was joking.

— Jesus, Farouz, I said.

I wanted to make this conversation stop, but it was like a car whose brakes have gone. I looked down.

— What happened with the imam? I asked eventually. What did he say? Did you . . . did you go to bed with him?

— No. The imam did not want to, said Farouz.

I smiled.

— Does this make you happy? You should not be. Instead I had to be that man's slave. I had to clean his house, cook his food, every day. And of course Abdirashid beat me when he found out, except by then I was going to school, so it was too late to stop me.

— Cleaning for the imam doesn't sound as bad as –

— As going to bed with him? No, that would have been easier. Have you ever scrubbed floors until your hands bleed?

I thought of Mom doing just that, and for no good reason.

— No, I said.

— No. So you cannot understand. And then . . . Well, I went to school. It is not a very interesting part of the story, though I enjoyed learning. Abdirashid made friends with some coast guards. He went to bars with them, drank, took drugs. He even went on a mission once. But something went wrong, I don't know what. An argument with another pirate, maybe. Or maybe he hurt someone. Anyway, he never went again.

— So how did you end up with them? I asked.

— They came to my school, said Farouz, when I was sixteen. Not my brother's friends. Different ones. To look for people like me. Crazy, isn't it?

— And the imam let them?

— Oh, they said they had reformed. They came to talk about how children should not get into piracy. They asked which of us was clever, which of us could speak English, and they made it sound like they were just interested in the school, like they wanted to donate some of their money

145

to help the imam. They did, in fact – I think Amir, who is now our sponsor, actually gave them a hundred thousand dollars. Then Amir stood at the front of the class. He is tall. He is handsome. People like him. He said, if something is dirty, wash it. If something is filthy, wash it with bleach. I am filthy, Allah, he said. Wash me with bleach. Forgive me for my sins.

— Wow, I said.

— Yes. The imams do not like pirates, but they like it when we ask for forgiveness. So the imam and the other people from the school, they loved Amir when he said this. Anyway, afterwards, when I was leaving the school, the pirates stopped me – the coast guards, I mean. They knew that I was the best at English because the imam had told them about a prize I had won. We know how you can make millions, they said to me when the imam was gone. How to get you and your brother a house.

You know my brother? I asked.

We know everyone, they said. So that was it – that was how I joined the South Central Coast Guard. For a few years it was OK. I mean, I was just a guard. I didn't make much money, but it was better than before. Then my brother got arrested, and I was stuck with them. I had to earn the money for them, to get him out.

— Wait, I said, catching the allusion in his voice. Are you saying the South Central Coast Guard arrested him?

— No. The police did. But did they pay the police to do it? Of course.

— Wow, I said, sounding like a moron because that was the second time I had said that word in as many minutes. So you're working to free your brother, and the people who put your brother in prison in the first place are the people you're working for?

Farouz thought for a moment.

— Yes, he said.

Then he dropped his cigarette, crushed it under his heel, and the darkness rushed in at us, like hyenas.

People like Carrie and Esme asked me, after the Event: were there any signs? With my mom, I mean. And I wanted to say to them: well, of course there were signs. She was depressed. She had OCD. But I know that's not quite what they meant. They wanted to know whether there was anything that, in the words of the counsellor I saw briefly at school, *made manifest her intentions*.

There was, of course, the phone call. The one where she told me. But I didn't talk to anyone about that. Instead I told them about this other time.

It was the summer holidays one year Before. Dad was working, as usual, but Mom wanted to go away, so she got some complementary tickets from her magazine, review tickets, for a new luxury eco-hotel on the east coast of Mexico. The idea was, we'd go and see some Mayan temples, hang out on the beach, and then Mom would write an article about it when we got back.

— Let your father miss out, said Mom. We'll have fun, just me and my Amy.

And we did do that. We had a great time, actually: the hotel was all little wooden huts by the sea, no electric lights, no TV, so it was just us and the palm trees, the birds, the shushing of the waves. Pretty magical, really. We had massages, swam, read books.

We took the bus to Chichen Itza and saw the pyramid there, where people used to have their hearts cut out on top and then their bodies got thrown down the steps. We clapped our hands at the face of it, and the sound came back, hissing and chattering – like a rattlesnake, the guide told us, like the snake god carved on to the sides of the pyramid.

Most evenings, we ate in our room. But there was also this restaurant right on the sea, ten minutes' walk down the beach from our hotel. One night, we had both finished the books we were reading and were at kind of a loose end. We went to the lobby of the hotel, and there was this mom and kid that we had sort of made friends with, though I don't remember their names.

Anyway, the mom said to us:

— Why don't you come turtle watching? They're supposed to be laying this time of year.

— Laying? said Mom.

— Their eggs, on the beach.

— Oh, yeah, Mom, we should totally do that! I said. I'd watched a documentary with the giant turtles crawling up on to the sand to bury their eggs. I thought it would be amazing to see that in real life.

— You're going now? asked Mom.

— No, said the kid, who was about ten – cute, with freckles and an encyclopedia or something always in his hand. We're having dinner first, he said. Then the turtle watching starts at midnight. It's the best time.

— Till what time? I asked.

The boy shrugged.

— Till we see one.

— 3 a.m., said the mom. That's when they give up, apparently, if no turtles have come.

— And we have to remember where they put the eggs, said the boy, so that people can dig them up and put them in a safe place to hatch. Otherwise robbers steal them.

— They're valuable in Chinese medicine, said the woman, who had a few piercings in her ears and a little tattoo of a fat Buddha on her inner arm.

Mom looked at me.

— We'll pass, she said. Sounds fun, though!

What she meant by this was: it sounds absolutely godawful, and I'd rather eat my own sick than sit on a beach doing nothing until three in the morning. Mom was all about physics and stars; she didn't have a lot of patience for anything that involved animals – she used to talk about how crazy the British were, with their sanctuaries for donkeys, when it was people in need who deserved sanctuary. She could get pretty evangelical about it. I told the mom and her boy that it sounded really nice, but we had planned to go out for dinner instead, so I could get Mom out of there quickly, before she said anything embarrassing about wasting time on digging up turtle eggs, when there were people being blown up in Baghdad, or whatever.

So now that we'd told the mom and her boy that we were going for dinner, we sort of had to. We walked down the beach to the restaurant, where we'd been before, so we knew that it did an amazing puerco pibil, which is a bit like a really slow-cooked pork belly, except it comes served in palm leaves. We sat at a table overlooking the sea, our toes in the sand. We ate our dinner, and Mom let me have a couple of Coronas, which came to the table glistening, cold in the heat of the night, lime wedges shoved into their necks.

Above, the stars were a blanket of brightness across the sky. Nothing like in Somalia, but still impressive, and of course I hadn't been to Somalia then, so I didn't have that to compare it to. As we sat down, Mom pointed up.

— Watch that patch, she said. The Perseid cluster.

— Why?

— Just watch.

So, all through dinner, I kept glancing up at the swathe of star blanket that Mom had told me to watch, wondering what I was meant to be seeing. Then, just as I was finishing my second beer, it happened: a shooting star flared across the sky, sudden as a firework. Then another, and another, little flickers of angled light, like arrows of white fire.

— Shooting stars! I said.

— Meteors, actually, said Mom. The Mayans measured time using the stars, you know. It's how they knew when to plant things, how to orientate their buildings.

— Right, I said.

— Prehistoric European peoples, too.

— Yeah, I said. Like Stonehenge. Where the sun rises through the entrance at the summer equinox.

— Summer solstice, said Mom.

— Oh, yeah.

— But it's not just that, said Mom, who had that faraway look now. Did you know, Amy, that Taurus used to set, in

Neolithic times, at the precise point on the horizon where the sun went down on the spring equinox?

— No, I said. But, then, I generally didn't know the things she knew. Mom had, like, three PhDs. Dad said she was the smartest person he'd ever met, and he was pretty damn smart himself – he did something very complicated to do with computer modelling of weather at MIT, which is how he got the job in the bank in the first place.

— Well, said Mom, it's true. The sun would set right on Taurus just that one day of the year. A lot of people think that's how bull sacrifices started: people looked up at the sky, just as spring was about to start, and they saw the sun killing a giant bull made of stars. Then things started to grow again. So they figured that to bring the warm weather back, bulls had to die.

— Obviously, I said a little sarcastically. But they didn't really think it was a bull in the sky, did they?

— Oh, I think they did, said Mom. Another interesting thing, she said, as if she were talking to herself, is that most cultures see a bull. The same as most cultures see a hunter for Orion. But neither of those constellations actually look much like what they're meant to be, like a bull, or a hunter with a bow and arrow. I mean, it doesn't make sense that people see the same things when the so-called images are so abstract. There's a theory that these stories of the stars, and the shapes they made, started in Africa, when all humans lived there. Then, when people dispersed, they took the stories with them. So before writing and religion came along, nearly everyone in the world looked up at the night sky and saw a bull there, riding.

I leaned back in my plastic chair. It was a weird thought, that people used to look up at the stars and see stories they really believed were true. Orion, the hunter, chasing a swan. An eagle. A bull being murdered by the sun.

If I could go back in time, I'd say to Mom, well, I know someone from Africa, and he thinks the Great Bear is a camel, so, you know. But I can't.

— Of course, said Mom, the earth's orbit varies over time. Taurus stopped setting in that place at that time. And religion moved on.

— People forgot about the stars, I said.

— No, said Mom. They didn't. Think of the wise men, how they found Jesus.

— Oh, yeah, I said.

That was what happened during dinner. I'm telling you so you get a sense of my mom, the kinds of things that interested her, but the important thing is what happened afterwards. We were walking back along the beach, hand in hand. Mom was carrying our flip-flops. We were on the hard-packed sand, close to the shore, where the water had firmed it up, darkened it. The moon was huge and round, lighting up a path along the sea towards us that looked like we could walk down it, over the water, to somewhere else.

At the back of my mind, I was thinking of the turtles, so something snagged on my attention when we were passing some big rocks in the surf. I glanced at the rocks. Then one of them moved.

— Mom, turtles! I said, and I pointed.

We stopped.

— Oh, yes, she said.

Close by there was a dune with some grass on it, so we went and sat down. We watched as the turtles crawled slowly up through the white froth of the waves on to the sand. Neither of us said anything, even though this must have taken maybe fifteen minutes. Then another half hour passed, with the turtles moving up the beach. There were two of them, each one as big as a coffee table, leaving smooth trails in the sand behind them. Their flippers swept at the sand, dragging the shells upwards. Their great hooded eyes looked around for danger. The way their mouths were set, it was almost as if they were smiling.

It's like we've been chosen, I remember thinking. Like we've been selected to see this, and it means something. I knew it was a silly thing to think, but I thought it anyway.

We'd chosen our dune well because one of the turtles stopped just below us and started digging its hole. We were practically holding our breath the whole time. We saw the turtle position herself, and then the eggs coming out, miraculously smooth and white, like a magic trick, and falling into the hole. After that, the turtle turned around, ponderous, and filled in the space with sand to keep the eggs safe.

Then, very slowly, it crawled back down to the sea, closely followed by the other one. We kept our eyes on them as they sank into the water, before finally disappearing. There was something about the whole scene – the moon, the giant turtles, the beach where you couldn't see any modern buildings or lights – that was utterly magical and old, really old, like we were seeing something ancient and powerful. And we were, I suppose: turtles must have been coming up to lay eggs on that beach for tens of thousands of years.

— Holy shit, said Mom.

It was the first time I'd heard her so excited about anything to do with nature or animals. Usually it was only the stars, or music, that got her like that.

— Yeah, I said.

— We should tell the turtle preservation people, she said. Let them know where the eggs are. She was still sitting, hugging her knees. Wow, she said. It's just . . . It's a sign, I think, Amy.

— A sign?

— Yes. Like someone wanted us to see that. Like the turtles chose us.

— I know! I said. I feel like that, too!

I was amazed that Mom had also felt it. And I felt even more amazed the next day, when we got talking to that hippy mom, and she told us that she and her son sat perfectly still, further down the beach, till 3 a.m., and they didn't see anything at all. And they were with guides whom they had paid to find them!

But that was the next day, and it might as well have been a lifetime away. For the moment, Mom and I just sat on the beach together in the moonlight and the starlight.

— Hmm, Mom said in her vague, distracted voice. So beautiful.

— Yes, I said.

— I mean, it's like they were telling me something, she said. Like they were telling me to hold on.

— To hold on?

She coughed.

— Ignore me, Amy, she said. That was lovely, that's all. I'm glad we got to share that moment.

She always sounded very American when she said things like that. She reached out and held my hand, then we got up and our legs were stiff, so maybe we'd been sitting even longer than I'd thought. And we walked back to the hotel.

The next day, we did tell the Turtle Watch people where to find the eggs, and they happened to have some baby turtles that had just hatched and were ready to go in the water. So we went with them to watch all these little things crawling into the sea, swimming away, to where most of them would die. When I saw the baby turtles, so tiny, I thought, each one of those had been inside an egg. And the eggs were inside a bigger turtle. It made my head spin: turtles in turtles, like a Russian doll that went on for ever.

And that was amazing, too.

But it was the earlier thing that I remembered, After. It was the way Mom said the turtle was telling her to hold on, and what that must have meant.

So, yes. That was the only sign. A turtle, laying its eggs.

That's not quite what I mean, though.

For the first time, Dad seemed suspicious of where I was going in the evenings. We must have been in Somali waters a week, at least. I was trying to leave the cinema room after sunset. We had just had soup, made by Felipe using tins from the stores, and toasted bread from the freezer. The pirates had taken a lot of our tins, though, to go with their pasta, and I knew we were getting low on plenty of stuff – I knew it from the looks between Dad and the crew, even though none of them had said anything.

— Where are you going? he asked. Why don't you stay and play Scrabble with us, Amy-bear?

— I need air, I said, which was a lie, but was also, obviously, true – we all need air.

— Oh, come on, said the stepmother, to my surprise. It's no good playing without you on my team. Your dad and Damian are too good.

And so I ended up playing one game with them to keep them happy, and, under the circumstances, it was actually kind of fun. The stepmother and I beat Dad and Damian, while Tony read some book about Magellan.

Outside, when I finally got out, there were clouds for once, obscuring the stars.

Farouz was already there, standing at the rail, blowing smoke out over the water. When he saw me, he turned and smiled.

— Hostage Three, he said.

— Pirate, I said.

He grinned. He beckoned me over to where he was standing. Below him, the sea was burning blue.

— Phosphorescence, I breathed. I'd seen it before, but now it was even brighter, like alcohol on fire.

— Pretty, isn't it? he said. Then he touched one of my piercings, the one in the side of my eyebrow. Does this hurt? he asked.

— What, now?

— Yes.

I tapped the silver ball where it protruded from my flesh. I hadn't really thought about it since I'd been kicked out of school.

— No, I said. It hurt when they were done. And in the sun, sometimes, because the metal gets hot. But not now.

— Oh. And what do they mean? He was looking curiously at the rod through my eyebrow, the stud in my nose, the ball below my lip.

— What do they mean? I said dumbly.

— Yes. That is what I asked you.

— I don't know, I said. Don't people do things like this in Africa? I've seen TV programmes. Women with stretched necks, big dangling earlobes, massive sticks pushed through their skin.

He gave me a look that was half-tender, half-patronising.

— In Africa? he said. Africa is big.

Of course it is, I thought, feeling super-stupid. Some African tribes did that kind of thing, but that didn't mean people in Somalia did it, too.

— So you don't know what they mean? he asked, looking at my nose stud now.

— They don't mean anything really.

Farouz threw his cigarette into the sea; it flashed red above the blue glow of the water, then fizzled out and was gone.

— Then why do you have them? he asked. Does your father like them?

I laughed.

— He's never said anything about them, I said. I guess not, I suppose.

Farouz looked at me hard, then.

— You do this to your face, and your father says nothing?

I nodded slowly.

— Strange father.

I said nothing.

We were walking back to the sunloungers when we heard a footstep inside the door to the deck. Instantly, Farouz melted into the shadow under the overhang of the bridge, leaving me standing there alone.

Mohammed opened the door and saw me standing there. He leered at me, came out on to the deck, walked towards me. I was shivering the whole time, even though it was hot, even though I knew Farouz was there. But then what could Farouz do to protect me? Would he even want to protect me?

Mohammed stopped, too close to me, beyond the invisible barrier that people usually respect, that keeps a safe distance between bodies. He stared at me for a moment. Then, abruptly, he put his hands into the pockets of my jeans. I froze, terrified. His fingers searched around inside, curling, like some terrible, many-limbed creature. Then he pulled the pockets, turned them inside out. An old cinema ticket fell out on to the deck, and a five-pence coin. He pulled his hands away.

— I look watch, he said.

I was shaking. I turned to go back inside, but he stopped me cold – not with a touch, exactly, but just with an inflection of his body, an accent to his stance.

— Soon you die, he said. He drew his finger across his throat, miming a cut. Like animal.

— I'm sorry?

— We get money, he said. But we kill anyway. Ahmed has decided.

— I'd like to go back inside now, I said. Otherwise I will start to scream very loudly.

I knew about the fines, of course. I hoped they might scare him, even if only a little bit, that the idea of being docked thousands of dollars just for touching me might put him off.

Mohammed snorted.

— OK, OK, he said. He turned and made for the door. As he went through it, he looked back at me. He made that throat-slitting gesture again. You all die, he said. You, your father, your mother. You all die soon.

He was wrong, she wasn't my mother, but I didn't correct him.

When Mohammed was gone, Farouz resolved out of the darkness, became physical again. He came over to me.

— It's not true, he said.

161

His body was a warm presence close to me, making my skin tingle.

— No? I said.

He made a *tsk* kind of sound, accompanied by a complicated hand gesture that no one in London would make.

— We don't kill, he said.

— You said you did, I told him. When you first came aboard. You were filming on your phone and you recorded a message for the – I caught myself in time – ship's owners, saying you would kill us if your demands weren't met.

— That was for show, he said. And anyway, I didn't know you then.

— Right, I said, wishing I could believe him.

— We would never hurt you, he insisted.

I was hanging back from him.

— What if they refuse to pay, the company that owns the yacht? What if you don't get any money?

— We always get the money.

— And if you don't?

— We always do.

I sighed.

— What if you don't this time?

He hesitated.

He still hesitated.

Oh god, I thought. He's not going to answer the question.

That was when the machine gun fire started, from somewhere behind us, unbelievably loud in the still night.

There was gunfire, too, when Farouz lost his parents, though he didn't tell me about it till later.

What happened was, the rebels were clearing out his district in Mogadishu. This was 1991, so Farouz was a little boy. It turned out he was a lot older than I thought he was at first. It wasn't the only thing I got wrong when it came to him.

In Mogadishu, fighting had been going on for months in the outskirts of the city, and now it had reached the quiet quarter where his family lived. Farouz remembered trees lining their avenue. A view of the sea, distant but gleaming, the white tower of a minaret rising above it.

Farouz's father was a professor. His mother taught English at a high school. When the gunmen came, both parents were completely unprepared. Farouz told me, a mixture of admiration and disappointment in his voice, that his father actually went to the door and tried to reason with them. He told them that he was just a professor, that his wife was –

And that was when the guns fired, a rattling explosion in the confines of the house. Farouz was eight at the time, which made him twenty-five when I met him – older than I'd thought, but it was too late by then, I was already half in love with him. His brother was ten. They were sitting on the stairs, so they saw their father fall back into the hallway, jerking, bleeding, and then their mother come running, screaming, to kneel by his side, and the soldiers shot her, too. Farouz said he saw her head burst – like a watermelon, a red watermelon.

Then Abdirashid made a decision that saved their lives. He

grabbed Farouz by the hand and quickly dragged him up the stairs. Instead of hesitating, he pulled him through to the back room, opened the window and made his little brother jump out on to the bushes of the garden below. And then he followed. They were both scratched and cut, their legs sore, but neither of them broke anything, and they rolled through the bush before getting to their feet and running.

The men shot at them, but missed in the dark night. Farouz and Abdirashid jumped the fence to the next garden, and the next, and then they were on the street. Farouz could smell blood and gunpowder and grass, damp grass that had soaked his feet with dew. They kept close to the houses, creeping through the suburbs of the capital city, avoiding the street-lights that were left. They passed rebel soldiers advancing, tanks, jeeps. The government forces by this point had completely abandoned their district – that's what Abdirashid told Farouz afterwards, anyway.

They walked past houses, then, after a while, past ware-houses and factories. Finally, the sea breathing darkly and hugely to their east, they emerged from the city on to the main north road. There, they merged into a river of refugees, just a tiny tributary of two little boys joining the general flood. There were thousands fleeing the city on foot. Coming the other way, still, were rebel soldiers, and Farouz said that on occasion they would shoot the people walking away for no reason, just for fun. He and his brother were so scared by then that they barely flinched when this happened – they just figured that Allah would either protect them, or not.

The hardest part came when they left the city behind and entered the countryside, which was really just desert and scrub. That was when things got seriously dangerous.

They saw old men give up and sit down in the road to die.

On the second day, they saw a mother burying her baby in the thin dry soil – and it wasn't the last time they saw that. Now Farouz was so scared that he envied these dead babies: they were safe under the earth, tucked in by their mothers.

They also saw people prey on the weak – not just rebel soldiers, but also people from the villages they passed, who couldn't resist the lure of the women, the few belongings being carried, the money.

Farouz and his brother had just passed a group of huts when the men found them. They were walking through a clump of trees, shadows dappling the ground, birds calling, and these guys stepped out. Farouz didn't know if they were soldiers or what. They had guns, though.

Farouz doesn't remember what the men said, or what his brother said back to them. But he does remember what Abdirashid told him after the conversation with the men was over.

His older brother took hold of his shoulders and said:

— Little brother, you must stay here while I go away with these men for a while, and not come after me, no matter what you hear, OK? You have to keep very still.

— No, said Farouz. I don't want you to leave. You stay with me.

— I'm sorry, said his brother. But you must stay here for a while. You will be safe. If you move, I'll know. And then something bad will happen and I will die and you will be alone.

He turned to the men, and Farouz remembers this bit. It has been burned into his mind. Abdirashid said:

— You don't touch my little brother. And one more thing. I would like a knife. To keep.

One of the men, who was holding a machete, laughed.

— A knife?

— Yes. For protection.

— Protection from who?

— From people like you, said Abdirashid, all bold.

The man kind of shook his head, as if he couldn't believe what he was hearing. He took a small sharp knife out of his pocket, a hunting knife.

— Like this?

— Yes, said Abdirashid. Like that.

— Forget this, said another of the men. This one was missing his front teeth – Farouz always remembered that, too. Let's just do it, then kill them. They are dead, anyway, on this road.

Machete-man got angry.

— No. The boy has a deal. Then he turned to Farouz. Remember what your brother did for you. He is a brave little man. Don't forget that.

And I guess that's why Farouz remembered, because the guy told him he should.

After that, the men took Abdirashid away to the other side of the trees, where Farouz couldn't see them. And Farouz heard his brother screaming, of course he did, but he didn't move, because his brother had told him to keep still, that Abdirashid would be killed if Farouz stepped away from the patch of shadow, the shade of the tree, where he was standing.

If he crossed that dark line, he would lose his brother.

So he stood there, very still, while his brother's cries rang out, making the birds flee the trees.

Sometime later, Abdirashid came back, without the men. Farouz could see that his brother was crying, but he was holding a knife, too, the one the man had taken from his pocket and shown them. For a moment, Farouz was afraid his brother was going to do something stupid with that knife – there was a kind of crazy look in his eyes, like their father used to get when he had been drinking too much – but he put the blade in his pocket.

What else happened on the way to Galkayo? Abdirashid found water – Farouz told me that once, as we were watching the stars. He followed the tracks of hyenas until he came to a watering hole, and he and Farouz drank till their stomachs hurt. That water probably saved their lives. They heard afterwards that many of the refugees who left Mogadishu did not survive because of humble thirst.

Another time Abdirashid, instead of heading back to the road, got Farouz to hide in the undergrowth until night fell. Abdirashid, meanwhile, climbed into the lower branch of a tree a little distance away.

— When an animal comes near you, burst out, he said. If the animal is between you and me, then run towards me. That will drive it to where I am.

Farouz waited for what felt like hours. He was crouching, and his feet went to sleep, but he didn't dare move to get rid of the pins and needles in case he showed any of the night creatures where he was. Finally, when there were tears on his cheeks, and he felt like he couldn't stay there any longer, a hyena came padding across the hard, cracked mud in front of him, heading for the water.

You had to be desperate to want to eat a hyena.

And Farouz wanted to eat it.

He jumped out, but his legs cramped up, and he stumbled and fell. He thought Abdirashid would be angry with him, except the hyena ran in the right direction by itself, and Farouz's brother dropped from the tree, knife blade flashing in the moonlit gloom.

So Abdirashid was the boy who killed a hyena, when all the old stories were about hyenas stealing children. He skinned it and built a fire and, even though the flesh was disgusting, that probably saved their lives, too.

Later, Abdirashid became another boy. The boy who hung out with pirates, even though he wasn't one himself. Who started to drink and take drugs, because Galkayo had an economy for these things now, now that there were pirates, with Western money taken from Western ships.

He became lost, that's how Farouz put it. Like his body might still have been there, yet his mind was gone.

But that's not how Farouz remembered him. Farouz remembered Abdirashid going away with those men, winning that knife, killing that hyena.

That's why Farouz needed the fifty thousand dollars.

So he could pay his brother back.

Because, really, he could never pay his brother back.

We ran down the walkway to the back of the yacht, neither of us speaking. Guns were still going off – why I was running towards them I didn't know, but Farouz was, and it didn't occur to me not to go with him.

Dad, I thought. I even, weirdly, thought about the step-mother, hoped she hadn't been shot. Fear was a fish, squirming in my stomach.

But when we got there, I could see that none of the passengers was involved. The pirates – Ahmed, Mohammed and a couple of others whose names I didn't know – were kneeling on the rear deck, firing out to sea. At first I couldn't make out what they were shooting at, but then a blaze of muzzle-flare came from the darkness out there, and I spotted a little boat, bobbing on the waves. Whoever was out there fired again and again.

Farouz yanked my head back. He pushed me against the side of the boat, then took his pistol and levelled it out to sea, started firing. He was, like, one pace away from me. If I said that the noise was loud, you wouldn't understand. Partly that's because films are always lying to you, showing people firing guns and then talking to each other – probably because if they showed the truth, that after you've fired a pistol or one has gone off near you, you can't hear anything, not even the sound of your own voice, it would really limit the amount of dialogue films have.

But this is the truth: the noise was like the colour of whiteness, filling my head and my ears. I tried to shout out to ask Farouz what was going on, but my own voice was gone, was nothing but a buzzing far away.

I saw one of the pirates on the deck go down, without a scream, just suddenly, like someone had kicked his legs out from under him. Blood spurted from his head, then began pooling on the ground where he lay.

Farouz kept firing. I couldn't take my eyes off him. The way he was shooting that gun it was obvious he had done it before. And his face had gone kind of blank, like a shop window dummy. It scared me. It was like he was a different person. A dangerous person.

A pirate.

The world kept being gone, kept being just a roaring *kccch-hhhhhh* sound, like an untuned radio. Then there was a dull *crump* behind that sound, percussion underneath it, and fire bloomed from the little boat out there on the dark water, lighting up the whole scene for just a second: the patch of shining sea between us and the little boat, the men silhouetted by flame, like a photo negative, and then –

Like a light being switched off, an instant darkness.

This blackness reverberated, the image of the burning men still lingering against my retinas, like ghosts.

The other boat must have exploded, I realised. The outboard motor, packed with diesel, was probably hit by a bullet, maybe even from Farouz's gun.

Our pirates – I was already starting to think of them as our pirates – lowered their guns. They moved to the man on the ground, touched him with their toes. Farouz seemed to have forgotten about me. He went forward, began speaking to Ahmed, who was looking down at the dead man with a look that, to me, mingled sadness with irritation. How Farouz could hear anything to have a conversation, I had no idea. But he didn't turn to look at me, so I guessed that he no longer knew I was there, or that he was expecting me to disappear, so no one would know we had been together. I took one last look at the blood, spreading in the light of the deck lamp, streaming in red filaments between the boards of the deck, and then I turned around and crept back to the front of the boat, and from there back inside.

— Where have you been? Dad said, when I got back to the cinema room – at least, his lips did. I could still only hear that dead radio-wave fuzz. What's happening? he asked. His hands were tight on my shoulders.

— Listening to music, I said. I waved my iPod. The pirates had some kind of fight with some guys on another boat. Nothing for us to worry about.

— Why are you shouting? said the stepmother.

I didn't realise I had been. I hadn't heard a single word I'd said.

— They were from the North Coast Guard, said Farouz, the next day.

We were talking under our breath, while one of the pirates fed hay to the goats, and Dad and the stepmother played Scrabble in the dining room. We had to talk quietly. I mean, Farouz could lose everything, getting too close to me. I could lose everything, getting too close to him. I'd seen him shoot at people, and he hadn't even hesitated. I felt like, I don't know, like if I was whispering it was almost like I wasn't talking to him.

Like it was safer.

— They were other pirates? I said.

— Coast guard, yes.

— But . . . you're on the same side, aren't you?

He laughed.

— No. We are the South Central. They are the North. They don't like us. We have one hundred and forty boats. Nearly a thousand men. Money, from our sponsor. They have less. So sometimes they try to take the ships we capture.

I remembered him talking about his sponsor before, though I hadn't got him to explain what it meant.

— Your sponsor? I asked. Amir?

— Yes. Amir.

— What does it mean, sponsor?

— He is a coast guard who made a lot of money – three million from a Greek container ship. Now he takes that money and invests in others. This is how it works.

As he was talking, a couple of the other pirates were loading the dead man, who had been wrapped in sheets from the

173

yacht – I could see the logo of the *Daisy May* embroidered on them – into one of the small boats. It was even harder to keep track of the number of pirates now that we had moved to Eyl, as they shuttled to and from the yacht, bringing reinforcements and supplies from the beach. I had the impression they were doing shifts, like it was a job. I suppose it was. The only ones who stayed on the yacht all the time were Ahmed, Farouz and Mohammed.

— What about him? I asked, pointing to the body.

— His family will receive a hundred thousand dollars, said Farouz. When we get our ransom.

— What? Seriously?

— Yes, of course. Compensation.

— But . . . how often do people die? Pirates, I mean? I didn't dare ask about hostages.

— Not often. Sometimes they fall in the water. Not many can swim. Sometimes – not often – the navy kill them.

— The British navy?

— I don't know. Or the American. Once, they took two boys, friends of mine, who got too close to a destroyer. They floated them back to us, just off the coast, in white wooden boxes. On one end they had written *HEAD* in red letters, in English. I don't know how they expected us to read that. I mean, I could, but no one else can read English in my crew.

— That's awful, I said.

— Yes. Well, at least they gave back the bodies. That way the families can have their compensation.

— Of a hundred thousand dollars.

— Yes.

The little boat unmoored from the yacht then, and began to chug towards the beach, the body inside it. I leaned closer to Farouz.

— So, I said, nervous. How much . . . I mean, what do you expect to get from us? You, personally?

— I need to free my brother. That's fifty thousand.

— And you think you'll get more than that?

— I hope so. I mean, this yacht, it's a dream for us. So many people on board, which is the really valuable thing. The last mission I was on, we took a container ship. They run those things with a skeleton crew. Once the ransom was split, my share was small. This . . . this is my chance.

— This is my *life*, I said.

Farouz turned away.

At the same time, I thought, oh no. These pirates want a lot of money. And I knew how much my dad loved money. I knew he wouldn't want to part with it. I felt worried again, so I asked Farouz the question he hadn't had a chance to answer before, when the guns went off and interrupted us.

— What happens if my – if the company who own the yacht won't pay?

He looked back at me again. Paused.

— We will continue to hold you, he said at last. For a year, maybe. This costs a lot, in goats and water. If it goes on too long, the sponsor will get angry at his money being wasted, and Ahmed will order us to kill you.

— Oh my god, I said. And if he orders you, will you . . .

Farouz didn't answer. He just looked down, frowning.

Oh god, oh god, oh god. You know those balls, like Magic 8 Balls, where one ball floats inside another one, in liquid, so when you turn it, the ball inside moves independently? That's what my mind felt like, like it had come unattached from the sides of my head.

— Are you serious? I asked.

— My brother . . .

— Oh god, I said. Oh god.

I got up and stumbled into the yacht, down the corridor to the cinema room. I felt floaty, dizzy. Farouz didn't come after me, but Dad stepped out of nowhere, blocking my way.

— I saw you talking to that boy, he said. Did he upset you?

— What? Yes. I mean, no.

— Amy, said Dad. I don't know what you were doing last night, but I don't think you were listening to music. I don't want you talking to him any more. OK? You could have got shot.

— Jesus, Dad.

He raised his hands, offended.

— I'm looking after you!

— Yeah? I'm seventeen! And for your information, I'm not interested in Farouz. This was true then. I pretty much hated Farouz at that moment.

— *Farouz?* said Dad.

— I mean, that guy.

176

Dad's face set, like plaster drying.

— Listen, he said. You cannot imagine how dangerous this situation is already, without you getting involved in some crush.

— I can't imagine? There are men with guns all around us, Dad.

— Point taken, he said. The thing is, Amy, these men are pirates. They're ruthless.

— Please, I said. They were fishermen, did you know that? Then, after their government fell, Western ships started coming into their waters and stealing their fish. That was when they began arming themselves.

— What? said Dad. Who told you that?

I didn't answer.

— It was him, wasn't it? That was what he told you. Bit bloody convenient, isn't it, making out that they're Robin Hood?

— Well, they're not exactly rolling in it! Ahmed doesn't have goddamn aspirin for his kids.

— OK, Dad said. His face softened for a second. I'll admit their situation may not be totally black and white. But you don't have to fraternise with them. You may want to get yourself killed, but don't get everyone else killed, too.

— I don't want to get myself killed, I said.

He looked at me.

— Don't you?

I hesitated, thinking of Mom. Was that it? Was I doing the same thing as her? Did I have some kind of death wish? I remembered a counsellor telling me that if one of your parents kills themselves, you're six times more likely to do it yourself. I think it was meant to be some kind of warning to look after myself, but I got it. That is, I got why people did it if their parents had. I mean, that's the only way to see them again, right? It's like following someone who gets on a bus. You get on the bus, too.

Only, no, I knew for a fact that I didn't want to die, because when Farouz wouldn't answer me, about whether he would kill me, I'd been scared. I wouldn't be scared if I had a death wish.

— I don't want to die, I said.

Dad paused.

— Right, he said, his voice gentler. Sorry, Amy. I am, really. I just . . . I worry about you and that boy. He's a lot older than you. You think that doesn't matter, but it does. Also, I don't know if you've noticed, but he's a fucking *pirate*.

— I don't think it doesn't matter, I said. I don't think anything.

— No, he said. That's the problem.

Anger popped in me like a jack-in-the-box.

— You don't want me to embarrass you, that's all, just like with failing my A level.

— What?

— Your daughter, the daughter of James Fields, fraternising, as you put it, with a pirate. You couldn't stand that, could you?

— So you're saying you and him –

— No! I'm not. I'm saying that's what you're thinking.

— I'm not thinking anything about it, he said. I told you – I worry about you, that's all.

— Because you can't stand the idea of me being with someone poor, and black.

Dad's eyes went wide.

— You really think that? he asked.

I wasn't sure. Actually, I hadn't even thought of the fact that Farouz was black, or dark-skinned at least. I mean, I really hadn't been aware of it, so it was kind of a surprise to hear myself say it. I guess I just wanted to shock Dad. Still, it was too late to back out now, so I said:

— Why not? It's the truth, isn't it?

Dad sighed.

— Believe it or not, I'm concerned about your happiness. If I were you, I'd ask myself: if this guy wasn't a pirate, if there wasn't something exciting about that, would I be interested? If he was an electrician, say, back home, or a banker, would the same frisson be there?

— I told you, there's no frisson.

— OK, fine, yes. But just . . . think about what I said, OK, Amy-bear?

His voice made my shoulders slump, and I didn't want to fight any more.

— OK, OK, I said.

He held his arms out, awkwardly, fractionally too late.

I shook my head, turned and walked back the way I'd come.

— Amy! said Dad.

— What?

— Nothing, he said. Nothing.

I should have stopped and listened to him, of course. I should have, but I didn't.

The wooden boat pulled up to our diving platform, and the man stepped off – dressed, improbably, in a suit with a tie. How he could wear that in this heat, I don't know. I was sweating constantly in shorts and a T-shirt, baking in the unmoving air.

It must have been about ten days after we got to the Somali coast.

— What the hell? said Dad.

He and the stepmother were playing – and I realise the irony of this – Battleships on the rear deck, under the sun canopy. That my father was spending all this time playing games was surprising. Still, I suppose there was competition involved, and Dad gets competition; he understands it. Games aren't jokes: they go somewhere; they involve action; some-one wins.

It was another brutally hot day, the heat haze so thick over the scrubby hills of the coast that it was like the rock and sand were on fire.

The man in the suit approached us. He was clean-shaven, about forty, with a thin, wiry frame, and he was carrying an equally thin, black briefcase. Ahmed was beside him, smiling.

— Nyesh, said the man, holding out a hand. I am the lawyer.

— The . . . lawyer? For us?

— No! He laughed. For these men. For Ahmed.

— I don't understand, said Dad.

Ahmed sighed, beckoned over Farouz, who came over, scowling. I hadn't spoken to him since two days before, when

181

he'd basically told me by omission that he'd put a bullet in my head if Ahmed told him to. He talked rapidly to Nyesh for a minute or so.

— This is how it works, said Farouz. I come on board at the start, as a translator. Now the lawyer has come so that we can negotiate.

— You will find me very reasonable, the man in the suit said, with a wolfish smile. His accent was almost as good as Farouz's. I understand the owners of the yacht know that you have been taken captive? A video was taken and emailed to them, yes?

Dad nodded.

— And the navy, too?

This time Farouz inclined his head.

— Yes. A helicopter came. And they called the yacht once.

— OK, good, good, said Nyesh. But you have refused all attempts at contact since then? Good. Right. I think, then, we'd better make some phone calls of our own.

We sat in the dining room, at the big table. Tony, who could walk around on his own now, came, too. He was the voice of the company, at least as far as the pirates were concerned. He introduced himself to Nyesh as our guide.

— Fine, said Nyesh. In that case you will speak. It is better if I do not talk to them directly. It makes things . . .

— Tense, supplied Farouz.

— Yes, tense.

— Tell me what you want, and I will tell them. Tony held the satellite phone in his hand.

Nyesh nodded.

— We want five million dollars.

Dad spluttered on the water he was drinking, spraying the table. Tony just raised an eyebrow.

— That's a lot of money, he said.

— We have an investor, said the lawyer apologetically. We must pay a dividend.

The sponsor, I thought. Amir. It was strange that I knew these things, but couldn't mention them to anyone else, because I knew them from Farouz.

This was Dad's territory, and now he turned on Nyesh.

— Are you fucking serious? he asked. This isn't some FTSE 100 company you're running here. We're being held by illiterates who bring goats on to our yacht! You're all fucking pirates!

Nyesh didn't blink. He just lifted up his briefcase, slid it on to the table and flicked the metal tabs to open it. He took out a sheaf of papers.

— I am the accountant as well as the lawyer, he said. These are the accounts of the South Central Coast Guard.

I saw columns of numbers on the papers, his finger tracing them.

— We take this very seriously, Mr Fields. Yes, there are illiterates in the operation, but there is no other industry in Puntland. Much as I would love to move to London and exercise my profession there, I cannot. And so I, too, and others like me, become pirates. Do you see?

— This is absurd, said Dad.

— Please, said Tony. Let's all calm down. He indicated Dad with his hand, then turned to Nyesh. Can I have a moment with my colleague? he asked.

Nyesh shrugged.

Tony drew Dad aside and they had a whispered conversation. We all just sat there waiting for them. Then they returned to the table.

— We can call our employers, Tony said. Five million dollars does sound a little expensive, though. The last private yacht that was taken, they paid 3.5 –

Nyesh shrugged.

— Inflation, he said. Make the phone call.

So, while Dad glared at everyone, Tony dialled a number. Immediately the bank – or whoever it was – answered.

— Yes, yes, we're all safe, said Tony, in response to a question from the other end. I was wounded in the leg, yes, but I'm better now. Uh-huh. Yes, I'm in the yacht in the dining room with three of the pirates. The others are mostly on guard outside, two on –

Smart, I thought. But at exactly the same time as I thought it, Ahmed raised a hand and Farouz lifted his pistol, pointed it at Tony's head.

— Ah, sorry, said Tony. I mean, the pirates have their demands. That is, I am to put their demands to you. Oh, OK. Hang on. He turned to Nyesh. Do you have a pen? Paper?

Nyesh handed them over and Tony wrote down a number, then he hung up the phone. There is a negotiator aboard a Royal Navy vessel that is heading towards our coordinates, he said. We are to call him.

— Fine, said Nyesh.

Tony dialled the new number. The guy must have been expecting the call because there was no greeting.

— Yes, said Tony, we have their demands. Yes, that's right. Yes. Five million dollars. No. Five million. Right, OK. He turned to Nyesh. They want two days.

Nyesh shook his head.

— They have twenty-four hours.

Later that day, they made us come out on to the deck.

I was watching a film in my room, I don't know where everyone else was. Mohammed came to get me. When he entered the room he gave me a kind of sickly smile, then he pointed his gun at me.

— Out, he said. On deck. There will be a die.

I stared at him. Everything below my pelvis disappeared, and my stomach fell through space.

— I'm sorry?

— A die. On deck.

— A death?

— Yes. Now.

Oh, Jesus, oh, Jesus, I thought. I remembered him mock-slitting his throat, telling me we would die like animals. I tried to push past him, to rush, but he gripped my arm. It was like being held by a bear. I stood very still, the skin of my arm smarting.

— Where is watch? he asked. You have? He was too close and his breath was sour against my face.

— Watch? I don't know what –

He raised his other hand, as if he were going to hit me, then he scowled and lowered it again. Mohammed might be the son of someone important, I realised, but Ahmed was still chief. He could get fined for striking me.

But what if a fine wasn't enough to –

He dug his fingers even further into my arm and took a deep breath. Then he leaned in close, and as he did so, his hand, the one he had been about to hit me with, brushed against my chest, sending a shiver of horror across my skin.

An awful, awful thought occurred to me then, appalling as eyes outside your window in the dead of night. I'd only worried about him hitting me.

What if he . . .

I mean, we were alone. He was a strong man. I was a girl. There would be nothing I could do, nothing to stop him. He had a gun! I felt like a mouse in a trap, like I could spin around and run in circles, but wouldn't go anywhere. I felt like energy was blazing inside me, even though I stood very still. It was like I was a furnace, bolted to the floor and roaring inside with flame.

I thought, I have to do something. Mohammed leered at me and I saw the khat in his mouth. On an instinct, I pointed to it.

— Can I taste some? I said. Some khat?

Mohammed looked mystified.

— Taste?

— Try.

— Try?

I took a breath. I mimed chewing, pointed to his mouth again, then to me, to show what I wanted.

He gave a surprised laugh, then reached into his pocket. He took out a cloth bag, from which he drew a little handful of leaves. He gave them to me.

— There, he said. Try.

I packed the leaves into my mouth and started chewing.

Oh, fuck.

It was awful – it tasted bitter, and kind of hurt my cheeks and tongue. It was astringent, too, pulling my mouth inwards, as if my cheeks and tongue wanted to fold themselves around it, bury it, stop me tasting it. But I smiled at him.

— Hmm, I said. Good.

Mohammed shook his head in disbelief, but the moment of terrible tension between us was gone.

— Come, he said. Outside.

Then he dragged me out of the room.

Out on deck, in the light, the pirates were gathered, all apart from Nyesh. He had returned to the beach on the same boat he arrived on, like some kind of commuter, in his suit, going to and from work.

Standing there, held fast by Ahmed and another pirate, was one of the goats. Ahmed had a knife in his hand. Mohammed turned to me and grinned, then winked.

— They're going to kill it, said the stepmother.

The goat, I thought. The goddamn goat. It's only the goddamn goat. I suppose we had run out of tinned food, so it was time to move on to the living supplies.

As the men prepared, I surreptitiously spat out the khat.

They did it on the diving platform – so that they could hose the blood down into the sea, I realised afterwards. Two of the men held the beast upside down by the rear legs. The muscles in their arms stood out, trembling.

Ahmed had a big knife. It looked shiny and new, so I figured it must be from the galley. I thought he was going to be the one to kill the creature, but then he walked over to Farouz and handed him the knife. Farouz nodded. He went up to the goat, which was strangely still, hanging there. He knelt by it and whispered something.

I watched him carefully. This was Farouz, who'd been gentle, who'd told me stories, and he was kneeling by the goat with a big knife in his hand. Then he put the blade to its throat and made a very deliberate, very precise sawing motion. I saw the muscles tense in his arm, the veins visible.

Blood gushed.

The stepmother screamed, but the goat didn't. It twisted, eyes bulging, mouth opening and closing. Every time I thought there must be no more blood inside it, the red stream kept coming, pooling on the deck at Ahmed's feet, running in the cracks between the wood, like the blood of the pirate who got shot, making a hard wet sound as it continued to drip from the goat's throat.

So much blood. I could smell it, too – an iron smell, one of those smells that seems so familiar, the smell of large amounts of blood, even though you have never come across it before. As if all those wars and battles and slaughtered animals, through all of human history, have embedded in us a memory that we're not even aware of. As if I, you, all people, know the smell of death, the same way we know to close our eyes when something flies towards our faces.

Farouz killed the goat, I thought. Ahmed asked him to, and he did.

Would he kill me the same way? Would he just saw through

my throat, the muscles in his arms, his tendons, his bones, working together to end my life?

Eventually, the goat stopped moving. I didn't feel sick, exactly, but I felt dizzy, like the yacht was rocking more than normal. This was partly the lingering effect of the khat, I think. I was feeling a kind of unpleasant buzz, like when you drink too much coffee.

The sun was a white-hot ball in the sky above, pale and blazing. It must have been two hundred degrees. As always, the sun was in one spot in the sky, but the light seemed to be coming from everywhere, levelling the world, making it shadowless and without depth. Everything – the dinghy and the lifeboat, the scuba equipment, the goat that Ahmed was beginning to carve up, even as he waved us back inside – looked flat, drained, colourless.

— You OK, Amy-bear? said Dad, taking me by the arm. Come on, let's get you inside.

I staggered into the shade with him. In the corridor, things popped back into existence – the paintings on the wall, the fire extinguisher – and the world was three-dimensional again.

— I'm not eating that, said the stepmother.

— Want to bet? said Dad.

I couldn't finish my film. Hours later, they called us out on to the deck again. All the blood had been cleaned up, so you wouldn't know a goat had died there. Except . . . I took a breath. The goat's head was lying on its side, staring up at the evening stars, its throat cut raggedly from its body, the white shaft of the spine sticking out.

The pirates laughed when they saw me staring at it. They had this gas-fired stove, with an enormous, scratched metal pot on it. One of the men – Yusuf, I think his name was – was stirring the stuff in the pot with a big spoon.

Ahmed gestured for us to sit. He had a stack of bowls next to him, which he handed to Yusuf to fill. Yusuf poured stew into the bowls, then started handing them out to the pirates, Farouz last, because he was the youngest, I guess. They passed them around until all the pirates had some.

Then I noticed there were no more bowls – it seemed like we weren't getting any. We, the hostages, I mean. Maybe the stepmother was in luck after all. Maybe she'd get her wish and starve to death.

Ahmed took a piece of meat from his bowl, with his bare fingers, and ate it. Juice ran down his chin.

— We are the lion! he said. We eat all.

Dad and the stepmother looked at him blankly. I suppose I did, too.

— The lion! he said. We are the lion. What you say?

Dad kind of straightened up, the way he does when he's not happy with a waiter.

— We don't understand, he said slowly.

Ahmed scowled, spat on the wooden floor. He waved at Farouz and said something in his own language. Farouz nodded.

— Ahmed is saying that we are taking the lion's share, he said.

— So you'll have more than us, is that it? asked Dad. He looked annoyed, and I hoped he wouldn't say anything stupid. He was so used to getting his own way.

— No, said Farouz. We will have all of it. The whole goat. That is the lion's share.

— What? said the stepmother, who had obviously forgotten about not eating the goat. I didn't blame her. It smelled really good, actually. Like a curry, only different.

Ahmed said something else irritably.

Farouz did a sort of *calm down* gesture.

— Ahmed wants me to explain, he said. We have a story about the jungle beasts, you see. They had killed an animal, a gazelle, and all of them were gathered together to share it. The lion is the king of the beasts, so he asked the hyena to divide the gazelle fairly. The hyena said, we'll give half to the lion, then the rest of it we will divide between ourselves.

— I'm sorry, but can we sit down now? interrupted Dad.

All the pirates were eating, and we were just standing, listening.

— Hostage One, shut up, said Ahmed. Listen Farouz.

— So the lion reached out with his big paw, said Farouz, and struck the hyena's head, tearing off his jaw. The hyena limped away, screaming. The lion turned to the fox. You divide the gazelle, he said. The fox thought for a moment – the fox was not a fool, you see. We'll divide it in two, he said. One half will go to the lion and the other half will go to the lion, too, said the fox quickly. The lion got all the meat, so he was happy, and that was the end of it. So you see, Ahmed is saying that we are the lion. You are the other beasts. I am sorry.

— We don't get any food? asked the stepmother, sounding disappointed.

Ahmed nodded in agreement.

— Good, he said, good. Now you understand.

— But – began Dad.

— No, said Ahmed. He waved his hand to indicate the yacht. You people, you are always the lion. Now it is us instead. He lowered his eyes to his bowl, as if we didn't exist any more.

Dad turned to walk back inside, and the stepmother turned, too.

At that moment, Ahmed burst out laughing. He laughed until tears came to his eyes. Then he reached behind him and brought out another stack of bowls.

— Sit, sit, he said, when he had stopped laughing. Eat. We are generous, forgive joke. Maybe we not lion. Maybe we fox.

At the negotiating table, Nyesh spread out some papers. He was wearing a different tie today, I noticed. Red. The last one had been blue.

Ahmed said he didn't have painkillers for his children. In a place like that, a man with two ties must be rich. Nyesh must also, I suddenly realised, come above Ahmed in the hierarchy. I suppose I'd been thinking of Ahmed as the ultimate leader, which was stupid, considering how big Farouz had told me the organisation was.

Speaking of Farouz, he was sitting opposite, studiously avoiding looking at me.

Well, good, I thought. We're back to normal now. He's a pirate. I'm a captive. I'm Hostage Three. I could tell on him, tell Ahmed he touched me, touched my hand, and that would be a thousand dollar fine for him.

No, I thought. Maybe that would stop him bailing out his brother. I wouldn't want that.

Outside, through the sliding doors to the rear deck, we could all see the outline of the navy destroyer that had turned up in the night, silently pulling up and then dropping anchor, a mile or so out to sea, arriving like a ghost. I expected one of the pirates to say something about it, but they barely gave it a glance, even Nyesh, when he came aboard from his little commuter boat.

The satellite phone on the table rang. Nyesh gestured for Tony to answer it.

Tony put the receiver to his ear, listened for a moment.

— I understand, he said. All right. He turned to Nyesh. Five million is too much, he said. They will pay three.

— You have to be kid– started the stepmother.

— It's OK, Sarah, said Dad. Just let Tony –

— Shut up! said Nyesh. Everyone. He took a pistol from his pocket, swung it till the barrel was pointing at the stepmother's head. OK. It's five million. Or I shoot this woman.

Tony spoke urgently into the phone, explained the situation. Then he turned white. Oh no, I thought. This isn't good. He put his hand over the mouthpiece.

— They say you won't shoot, Tony said to Nyesh. His voice was a little unsteady. They say if you do, you'll get nothing. The hostages are your only bargaining chip. You don't care about the yacht.

Nyesh grinned.

— Ha, he said. But we can keep hostages for years here. The navy can't board. We have too many guns. He paused. 4.5 million, he said.

Tony relayed that and then listened.

— Four million, he said after a moment.

— OK, said Nyesh. Four million. We will work out a game plan for the handover. We want to do it in two days' time.

— That's too soon, said Tony. We need time to pull together the funds, to –

— No, you don't, said Nyesh. You have two days. Your company will have appointed a broker already, and the navy are just outside that porthole. Don't make the mistake of thinking that we have not done this before.

— Two days, Tony said into the phone. He waited a moment. Right. He looked into Nyesh's eyes. OK, he said.

Tony stayed with Nyesh to work out the handover. The rest of us were dismissed.

My memory of days and time is fuzzy, but I know for a fact it was that day that Farouz disappeared. I know because we'd just been told we might be free in two days, and straight after that Farouz was gone, and I remember thinking: what if I don't ever see him again?

And then I remember thinking: Amy, what the fuck are you doing? You asked him if he'd shoot you and he didn't answer. This is taking the whole bad boy thing to the next level.

Still, it did freak me out when he vanished. He was there, strutting around the deck in the afternoon, and then in the evening I realised I hadn't seen him for hours. I didn't see the little boat go missing, but I did notice when I was out on deck that the diving platform had one less boat tied to it.

The thing was, he *never* went to shore. The others did, the soldiers, as he called them. But Farouz was an officer. He was one of the leaders, the translator, and he didn't have to ferry stuff to and from the yacht.

I bumped into Ahmed on my way back inside.

— Has Farouz gone to shore? I asked.

— Don't know, Ahmed said. He shrugged.

I looked him in the eyes, but his glance wouldn't hold; it went away from me and to the sea, like butter sliding across a pan. Then he made a kind of coughing noise and walked off.

The fuck? He was lying, obviously. But why?

Well, there wasn't much I could do about it. Anyway, I was angry with Farouz, I reminded myself. Only, what if something had happened to him? Was that why Ahmed was acting so weird?

Sitting in the cinema room, I thought up explanations:

A) Farouz had fallen overboard and drowned and been eaten by sharks.
B) He had won some kind of Somali lottery and had gone off to Egypt to start a new life.
C) He had got a job as a general dogsbody on a rich person's yacht and was now sailing around the world.
D) Or, you know, someone had just killed him.

No, I wasn't going to go there. He had left on some kind of errand, that must be it. But why hadn't he told me he was going somewhere? He didn't owe me anything. I knew that.

But still.

I sat there worrying, as the sun disappeared and darkness fell over the water. The stepmother asked me what was wrong, but I ignored her.

Outside the porthole in my cabin, the sea was tapping against the hull, over and over, unstoppable. As if it was

The next day, when I went out on the deck for breakfast, Farouz was there. As soon as I saw him my heart gave a jolt. He was slicing up watermelon, crouching there, large as life.

When he looked up, I gasped.

There was a cut running from his ear to his eyebrow, as if someone had tried to slash out his eye and missed. His other cheek was bruised and his lip was split. I almost went over there immediately, almost called out to ask what had happened, but I checked myself. There were other people around.

Instead I forced myself to sit down and take a piece of watermelon, and wait for no one else to be near. I felt pulled in two different directions: I wanted time to rush past so I could talk to him; at the same time I wished he hadn't come back. I wanted to know, and I didn't want to know. What if he'd got into a fight with other pirates? What if he'd killed someone?

But I guess I was too stupid, then, to heed my own warning systems.

Eventually we were more or less alone. I walked over to him, pretending to ask him for more watermelon.

— What happened? I asked. Where did you go?

— Nowhere, he said.

Then he started to walk away.

I stood there silently for a moment. I couldn't believe he'd just said that – it was such an obvious, ridiculous lie. A teenager's lie, and I'd know, because I'm a teenager. And a liar sometimes, but mostly to myself.

— Wait, I said, when my tongue had loosened in my mouth.
Don't you just walk . . .

But he was gone.

So you can imagine I wasn't in the best mood when I went to
the cinema room after dinner that night.

That made it even more of a surprise, what happened next.

I opened the door, and there was just blackness on the other
side. I reached for the light switch, but then someone struck
a match; I heard the *tsch* of it, and a flame jumped into being,
conjuring my dad's face out of the dark, his cupped hands.

Then the flame moved, and a candle appeared, a big
candle . . . stuck into a cake.

Happy birthday to you, they started singing.

More matches were flared, and people materialised out of
the gloom, holding candles. I could see now that they were
the yacht's emergency candles – even the one in the cake,
looking absurdly big in what was quite a small, dark cake.

— Is that . . . chocolate? I asked, when everyone had
stopped singing.

It was just the crew and my family – no pirates to be seen.

— Yes, Amy-bear, said my dad. Happy birthday.

— It's the sixth of October? I said.

— Well, yes, he said. Obviously.

— Wow, I said. Wow. So I'm eighteen.

And then I burst into tears.

*

I calmed down, of course, and I ate some of the cake. It was lovely, actually. I mean, it was sort of saggy in the middle and it didn't quite taste like chocolate should, but it was pretty good, considering the circumstances.

It seemed odd, somehow, that it was just us hostages there, but I guess it would be more odd to have pirates at your birthday party. Everyone was a little bit hysterical. Tony made some joke about the emergency candles and how we didn't really need them any more, and everyone laughed much more than they should have. The stepmother gave me a kiss on the cheek and I didn't even mind.

— Charades! said Tony. Come on, everybody.

— You start, said Dad. We'll just be a second.

He took me aside, and then fidgeted with his hands.

— I don't . . . he started. I mean, I did . . . That is to say . . .

— You don't have a present? I said. I meant it to sound flippant and funny, because why should he have a present for me when we were being held captive by pirates, but I obviously got the tone wrong, because he looked stricken.

— No, I did, he said. I had a present. But now I think maybe it wasn't a very good present. It was just some jewellery. Expensive jewellery. I don't know. It seems stupid now.

— Oh yes, I said. I smiled. Don't, whatever you do, give me expensive jewellery. How awful.

— Um, he said. Right, well, yes, if you want it, then of course I can get it. I hid it in my room, I can –

— Dad, I'm joking, I said. You're right. I don't need it.

— Oh, good! he said. Then he flushed. I mean, I'll get you

another present, when we get home. Something better. When we get back, just tell me what you want and I'll get it for you. Anything at all.

— I'll hold you to that, I said.

And he smiled back.

Then Tony was calling us over, and the moment was broken.

We all played charades, and it was a little island of silliness despite the drama of everything. Damian, it turned out, was very good – he should have been an actor. Dad, predictably, was terrible. Seeing him flapping around, doing *One Flew over the Cuckoo's Nest*, is kind of tattooed indelibly into my memory.

I was on my way back from the toilet, before going to sleep, when I bumped into the stepmother.

— It was nice to see you and your dad before, she said. You know, talking to each other like that.

— Er, yeah, I said. Right.

— He loves you very much, Amy.

I raised my eyebrows.

— I know, I said.

— Do you? He paid for the cake, you know that?

— What do you mean, paid for the cake? I frowned. It's not like there are any bakeries round here.

I hadn't even thought about the cake. I guess I'd just figured that there was some kind of cake mix on board.

— Eggs, said the stepmother. You need eggs for a cake. And milk.

A possibility, a likelihood, was starting to form in my

mind, like a house being revealed by the sweep of a car's headlights.

— You mean he paid the pirates to get some eggs?

— Yes. He had five thousand dollars hidden in a shoe or something. He gave it to Ahmed, and Ahmed sent that boy, the one –

— Farouz, I said. My head was a chorus of clicking, of gears falling into place.

— Yes, the one who speaks such good English. He went off to the shore and he came back with eggs. God only knows what he had to do to get them – he had bruises all over.

— Jesus, I said.

— That's how much your dad loves you, said the stepmother. He wanted you to have a cake.

— OK, I said. I swallowed. Thank you for telling me.

It was a struggle to say those words, believe me. And even more so because the stepmother was obviously so thrilled about it; delight was rising off her like fairy dust.

— You're welcome, Amy, she said.

And she turned and went back into the cinema room.

But listen, this is what an ungrateful bitch I was to my dad. She was right: it was nice what he had done. But I was mainly thinking of Farouz. I was thinking of how he'd gone to get stuff for my cake and he'd got himself hurt.

It made my stomach ache.

So, yes, in the end, you could say I deserved everything I got.

*

I felt weird the next day. I was eighteen. I was an adult. It was meant to be a big deal, one of those birthdays you never forget. Of course, I wouldn't ever forget mine, but that was hardly for the right reasons.

I couldn't really settle anywhere, and I couldn't very well go and talk to Farouz, ask him why fetching eggs had got him those cuts and bruises. In the end, I retreated to my room and listened to music for a bit – we were still allowed to go in our cabins, but not to sleep in them. My heart wasn't in it, though.

Then I saw a gleam of wood out of the corner of my eye.

It was my violin. The pirates must have taken it out of its case, then realised it wasn't anything of use, because it was lying sort of half in and half out of the velvet padding, in my wardrobe, which was open a crack.

I went over to the wardrobe, opened it. Then I picked up the violin.

— You play? said a voice from behind me.

I turned around, but I already knew it was Farouz.

— You shouldn't be here, I said. My dad doesn't want me talking to you.

I don't know why I said that, because it wasn't like I cared what my dad thought. But I wanted to hurt Farouz, like he'd hurt me by scaring me, and I figured that boys are scared of girls' dads; it's something that's got to be true everywhere, and that includes Somalia.

Of course, at the same time, I wanted him to stay. It was like I was my own worst enemy.

— Your father is speaking with Ahmed, on the bridge, he said.

I sighed and put down the violin.

— I hear you helped with my birthday cake, I said.

— A little bit, he said with a shrug. Your father paid.

— Well, I'm glad you did, I said. It was good. Thank you.

— That was not my doing, he said. Your stepmother made it.

— Oh, I said. She did?

I hadn't even thought about who made it – the spoiled little rich girl strikes again. But if someone had asked me, I'd have said Felipe.

— Yes, said Farouz. It seemed very important to her.

I blinked.

— Oh, I said again, like some kind of stuck record. Weird that we still use that analogy; I mean, I've never even used a record player.

— Are you all right? said Farouz. You seem far . . . distant.

— We say, you look like you're a million miles away, I said.

— Ah, thank you, said Farouz. You look like you're a million miles away, then.

— I suppose I am, I said.

I reached up and touched my face where his cut was on his own.

— What happened to you?

— Nothing, he said.

— You're joking, right?

— That other coast-guard group, he said. They saw me. He

raised his shoulders. There was a fight. But it was OK, no one had guns. And I had some friends there.

Get the fuck out of here, said a voice in my head. Get away from him. He's dangerous.

But I didn't.

He walked over to where I'd put down my violin.

— Do you play? he asked.

From his tone, it was clear that the whole conversation about his face was over.

— No, I said. Not any more.

— I play the oud, said Farouz.

— The . . . ood?

— It's a stringed instrument. Like a guitar, a bit. Or a lyre. It has a fat belly. You pluck the strings, but you can slap the belly, too, make percussion.

I was surprised Farouz knew a word like lyre.

— I'm surprised you know a word like lyre, I said.

— My father taught music, said Farouz. At university.

— Oh, I said. I knew his father was a professor, but hadn't realised what he'd taught.

— He played me the oud, said Farouz, when I was born. In Islam, the father is supposed to say a prayer to the baby. It is meant to be the first thing the baby hears, the first thing their father tells them. But my father, he played me an old song on the oud.

— That's nice, I said.

— Yes. But my mother was furious! She said, music is not a prayer. My father stood up straight, next to my crib. He said, yes, music is a prayer. It is the greatest prayer of all. He used to tell this story often.

I smiled, imagining the scene, thinking how weird it was, the way that stories could do that. I had never met his parents, I didn't know what they looked like, but in my head there was a picture – of a crib, a man and woman arguing, but maybe with a bit of affection in their anger – all of it something I wasn't there to see. Something Farouz never saw, either, only heard about from his parents, a story of his birth.

— My father loved the oud, said Farouz. It is a very old instrument. Though there are young people using it, too. There is a guy in London who does amazing things. We watch him on YouTube. You may have heard him. Aar Maanta?

— Sorry. I shook my head.

— Well, maybe I will play you one of his songs sometime, said Farouz. I didn't play for years after my brother and I left Mogadishu, of course.

There was a tone in his voice I hadn't heard before – wistful, I guess you would call it.

— Losing my oud, it was the worst thing, after losing my parents.

— But you have one now?

— Yes, he said. It was the first thing I bought after my first mission. My share was small, then, but enough to buy an oud. He looked at me. Why don't you play any more? he asked.

I shrugged. I didn't want to explain how there was a Before

and an After, and the violin belonged to Before. I mean, I'd told him about my mother, you know that. And he'd lost his parents, *I* knew that. So he was the perfect person to understand why I couldn't play that violin, why even just looking at it made me think of my mom, and how unbearable that was.

But how do you explain a feeling like that? You can't. I don't think I could explain it even now. If you know what I'm talking about anyway, if you've lived it yourself, then I'm sorry.

I won't explain how my mom's suicide changed me. All I'll say about it is this one thing, and then maybe you'll see, just a little bit.

This was maybe three weeks After. I was in the shopping mall in Kingston. It's one of those ones with lifts like glass cabins, so when you're going up and down you can see all the shopfronts on all the levels.

I was going down. And then, there at the bottom, by KFC, on the WH Smith side, I saw her, in her green-flowered summer dress – waiting for me, I guess, waiting for me to get down in the lift. I wanted the lift to hurry up, so I pressed the ground-floor button again. But then we stopped on level one for a woman with a pushchair, a curly-haired toddler crying inside it, to get in. I turned back and, for a second, the woman below, by KFC, was still my mom.

And then she turned around, two decades' and several skin-tones' worth of Not My Mom, not to mention the tattoo of little *stars* on her neck.

What happened to me was this. Right in front of the woman with the pushchair, my legs buckled, like someone had cut the what? – the tendons? the ligaments? – in them, and I fell to my knees in the middle of a glass-sided lift in the middle of a shopping mall containing approximately eighty per cent of the population of Kingston, which was where I went to school.

This makes me sound like a moron, but that was the first time I realised – I mean, really, really realised – that Mom was dead. That only happened once. But maybe it gives you an idea.

That full realisation, it might just happen once, but the loss happens every day. You see, when someone dies, you think: that's it, the bad thing has happened. And the idea is, you grieve it, and then you move on. But it doesn't work like that. I knew my mom all my life, it goes by definition. I remember her – I remember weekends, and holidays, and birthdays, and trips to the cinema, and digging for worms in the garden. Anything I see can remind me of her if I'm not careful, can call up some image or movie of her in my mind. Even the smell of her.

So you see, it's not that she died once. She dies over and over again every day. A person isn't just a head and a body and legs and arms. They reach out in space and time, and spill into possessions, bank accounts, email addresses, memories. A person is too big to fit into the word *dead*. The legs go, the head, the flesh. But the other stuff stays. A person is too big not to remind you of themselves, all the time, when you come across something they owned, something they gave you, or someone who calls up because they didn't know they were dead.

All of this was going through my mind, as I stood there with the violin in my hand, and also how I was still furious with Farouz over him practically telling me that he would shoot me if he had to. And then it crossed my mind that, really, what else was he going to do? Farouz was a pirate. Aside from anything else, it was his job, his livelihood. But also, his brother was still alive, and Farouz had the power to free him. If I had a chance to get my mom back, wouldn't I take it? Wouldn't I do anything to make it happen?

Maybe we weren't so different, Farouz and I.

And also . . .

And also, was it actually so hard to explain to him why I didn't play any more? I put the violin back down.

— My mother used to love it when I played, I said. She's dead, so now I don't play.

There – it was as easy as that.

— I understand, said Farouz.

And you know what? I was looking in his eyes, and I thought he did understand.

I went over to him. There was a porthole in my cabin, and you could see the navy vessel through it, dark and low in the water, bristling with guns.

— Aren't you scared? I asked. Of them? I hooked a thumb at the porthole.

— The navy? No. Are you kidding?

210

— But it's the navy! They have helicopters, rockets, massive guns . . .

— And if they shoot those massive guns they kill you, too. We say in Somalia: dabaggaalle ar diley ma aragteen.

— What?

— It means, the squirrel beats the lion. We are not afraid of the big ship. We are the squirrel.

— Ahmed said you were the fox.

— Oh no, said Farouz. We are the squirrel. We are small and the navy are big, but we always win.

— What's special about the squirrel? I asked, but Farouz made a dismissive gesture, like it wasn't important.

— I will tell you, he said. Another time.

I was still watching the navy ship, wondering what they were thinking over there, wondering whether they were listening in on the negotiations. I guessed so. I guessed they were probably going to help with the handover.

— How much will you get? I asked. Of the four million, I mean. How is it divided?

— The sponsor gets thirty per cent, he said. The hijackers fifty per cent. So that's shared between me, Ahmed, Mohammed, the other men who took the boat. Ahmed and Mohammed, a bit more than the others. Ahmed is Officer One, and Mohammed is Officer Two. Me, too, because I'm the translator. The man with the bazooka? He's Technical Military. He will take down a helicopter if it tries to attack. He has already killed three people. So he gets more, too. All of this is being worked out in detail now by Nyesh and

211

Ahmed. Then the guards who have done shifts from the shore, they get twenty per cent between them.

— What about Nyesh?

— He is on a salary from our sponsor. He doesn't take any risks in the hijacking, but he does all the accounts. He is paid a lot. Bonuses, too.

— So . . . wait. There were, what, ten of you who hijacked the yacht?

— Nine, since one died.

— So it's four million divided in half, divided by nine, give or take . . . Shit. That's a lot.

— Yes, said Farouz. Minus fifty thousand for my brother. That is all that matters to me, my brother.

— I know, I said, hoping that I believed it; deep down, thinking that I believed it.

— Well . . . he said.

— What?

— Also you.

— Also me what? I looked at him blankly.

He touched my hand, and electricity sparked. I could almost see it, a blue arc.

— You matter to me, too, he said.

— Oh, I said. My voice sounded very small, like it was a frightened little person inside me who was speaking.

— You asked me before, what I would do if Ahmed asked me to kill you. This is what I would do: I would kill him first.

— The other pirates would shoot you, I said.

— So? he answered. I would rather die than hurt you.

212

I stared at him.

— That's a bit over the top, isn't it? I asked.

— I am a pirate, he said. And then he smiled.

I smiled back at him. I stepped forward to give him a kiss on the cheek, on impulse, but I misstepped and tripped. He caught me. I was struck by how strong his arms were, how he smelled of sand and petrol, and sunshine. Suddenly our faces were very close together, and the waves were a rhythmical tapping on the hull, and the stars outside the porthole were gleaming.

And then, just when I thought Farouz was going to step away, he kissed me, his arms folding around me, pulling me in.

How can I describe that kiss?

It was like . . .

It was like I was a device – a TV, say – that had never been plugged in before, and now I was plugged in, connected, and electricity was coursing through me, and I realised: oh, this is what I am for; I light up with shining pictures; I glow. It was like my body found its purpose, and it scared me a bit, though at the same time everything was just his arms, his lips. Before this, it was like I hadn't been breathing, just sucking bits of air into my lungs.

Farouz pulled away for a moment.

— This is a thousand dollar fine, he says. If I get caught.

— Ha, I said. Count yourself lucky. If my dad saw us, he'd fricking kill me.

Farouz smiled weakly.

— You are surrounded by danger on all sides, he said.

He said it in a joking way, and when he did, I laughed. But it was only afterwards, lying in the cinema room, trying to sleep with the tingle of his mouth still on mine, that I replayed what he said in my head. The thing was, he was right.

I *was* in danger. All the time. And what if, by making friends with Farouz, or whatever it was we were doing, I was making things much worse?

— We've coordinated this handover plan with the bank and the navy, Tony said, as he sat at the negotiating table two days later. And the pirates are on board with it.

He didn't seem to be aware of the irony of using that expression on a yacht boarded by pirates. He spread out a document on the coffee table in the cinema room.

— I want all of you to study this, he said. Anything goes wrong with this, we're all screwed.

The plan was written in English and Somali. It had been emailed by the navy to the yacht. Tony had been allowed to open it when the satellite link came on at 6 p.m., but only with Farouz looking over his shoulder, making sure he didn't send any emails back.

My dad looked through it first, then it went to the stepmother, then to Damian, then to me. Felipe winked at me – we were always the last.

Finally it came to me, and I glanced down it. I couldn't believe how detailed it was.

INITIAL SITUATION

Nine Somalis and six passengers aboard the yacht Daisy May. *Royal Naval vessel HMS* Endeavour *at anchor 150 metres away.*

All communication to take place on VHF channel 16.

GO PLAN

SUBMITTED BY JERRY CHRISTOPHER, NEGOTIATOR FOR GOLDBLATT BANK, ABOARD HMS ENDEAVOUR. *RATIFIED BY ALL PARTIES.*

1) At 6 a.m. HMS Endeavour *will give the GO signal on VHF channel 16.*

2) All passengers will report to the rear deck. For purposes of clarity, that is Mr James Fields, Mrs Sarah Fields, Miss Amy Fields, Mr Damian Lacey, Mr Tony Purdue and Mr Felipe Santos. HMS Endeavour *will confirm the presence of all passengers.*

3) Helicopter will leave HMS Endeavour *and fly to a point 200 metres to the east of the* Daisy May. *Helicopter will be weapons cold.*

4) Three Somalis will leave the Daisy May *aboard a dinghy, carrying a portable VHF unit tuned to channel 16. They will navigate to a point below the helicopter.*

5) The helicopter will drop bags containing two million US dollars in cash. Somalis to recover the bags from the water and count to verify the full amount is present. They will then confirm by VHF to the Daisy May *that they are in possession of half the ransom.*

6) All Somalis will disembark the Daisy May, *leaving the passengers aboard, and get into their own remaining dinghies and wooden boats.*

7) The helicopter will then drop the remaining two million US dollars. The Somalis below the helicopter will confirm receipt of the full amount of the ransom, and instigate retreat from the theatre of operation.

8) All Somalis will repair to the coast in their vessels, to be verified by HMS Endeavour *by helicopter.*

9) End of exchange.

At the bottom of the list was a warning:

Note: it is absolutely imperative that this plan is followed to the letter by all passengers and hostage-takers. Any deviation could result in danger of death to either side. During the entire exchange, the six named passengers MUST remain on the rear deck of the Daisy May.

Jesus, I thought. These guys weren't messing around. I wondered if people back home knew about this, if we were on the news, if Esme and Carrie were watching. When the helicopter flew overhead, I'd assumed it was the military casing us out, but what if they were taking pictures, too? There was something surreal about the idea of people back in London, or New York, following this whole thing on the TV.

Interesting, too, I thought, how they talked in the plan about *Somalis*. Not pirates. Maybe because they didn't want to cause offence in an already tense situation. Maybe they knew all about the coast guard stuff that Farouz had told me. Or maybe they just wanted to make it sound more like a war.

Just then, there was a bang as the door flew open. Ahmed came storming in, Mohammed behind him, grinning. Farouz followed.

— Deal is off, said Ahmed.

— What? said Tony. But we agreed that –

Ahmed raised his gun, and Tony shut up. The pirates' leader turned to Dad.

— You own boat, he said.

— I don't know what –

BOOM. Ahmed fired, and my ears rang. A puff of plaster dust burst from the wall. I have to stop being around when guns go off, I thought.

— Farouz read emails, said Ahmed. He inclined his head to Farouz.

— It's true, Farouz said, his head lowered, not meeting my eyes. I was checking the go plan, he said. I saw some other messages and realised that Hostage One was not just a passenger. This is his yacht.

I stared at him in disbelief. Traitor, I thought. Meet my eyes, traitor. Look me in the bloody eyes.

I couldn't believe he had done this to us, had sold us out like this. And for what? A bigger share?

— Oh my god, Mr Fields, said Felipe. You did not tell you owned the yacht? Why didn't you tell them that?

— Be quiet, Felipe, said Tony.

— Sorry, sir, said Felipe, looking at Dad. Then he turned to Tony. But I don't understand. Why did Mr Fields not say?

— Because otherwise Mr Fields would end up paying out a fortune, obviously! shouted Tony.

— Why the fuck I care about that? Felipe asked, his anger suddenly driving out his grammar and his politeness. I want my family! I want home!

— So does Mr Fields! shouted Tony.

— Yes! But he pay for me to work. Is because of him I'm here. He should pay for me to be free, too!

My head was going back and forth, following this argument like someone at a tennis match. Actually, I couldn't fault Felipe's logic.

— Shut up! said Damian. None of this is helping.

— Yes, shut up, said Ahmed. Deal is now ten million dollars. There is no negotiate.

Well done, Farouz, I thought. You've more than doubled your share.

Tony turned to Ahmed.

— You can't do this. We had a deal. The navy are right there. They will come for us and they will save us –

Ahmed lifted his gun again.

— They lion, we squirrel, he said.

Tony looked confused, but I knew what he was saying. I

knew exactly what he was saying because Farouz had told me the story.

Farouz. Before, the name had seemed like a sigh in the mouth; now it was a cold wind inside me. I could say, *I felt betrayed*, but those are just words, and words alone can't express how I felt. It was like I was one of those Lego people made of three parts, and someone had come along and taken out the middle bit, had taken out my body, so I was just legs and a head and, in between, this whirling nothing of wind and air.

I knew, now, where Farouz's loyalty lay. And it didn't lie with me. When I looked at him and his glance caught mine before sliding away, I thought that I might faint.

There was a triumphant expression on Mohammed's malicious face.

— The navy can fuck, he said eloquently.

Tony seemed to understand that.

You don't know Farouz's voice.
And there is no way I could describe it to you,
its tone, its timbre.
But this is how I hear it, when I close my eyes at night.

This is how he tells me stories.

Once, there was a lion that had gone mad. It lived among the trees by the watering hole, so none of the other animals could drink. If they went near, the lion killed them, and many of his kills he wouldn't even eat, as if he were a hyena or a fox instead of the king of the beasts. The other animals didn't know what to do: the lion was powerful, so strong that no one could stand against him.

Then one day the camel, who had not drunk for five years, because camels rarely need water, became too thirsty to bear. She went carefully down to the water, but the lion heard this, and fell on her and devoured her.

The other beasts were shocked. They loved Camel, and couldn't believe she was gone. They asked who would rid the land of the mad lion.

— I will, said the squirrel.

The other beasts laughed, the hyena loudest of all.

— Don't be ridiculous, said the fox.

— You are puny, said the hippo. You are small. You will be killed.

— I am small, said the squirrel. So I will win. What will you give me if I do?

The turtle giggled.

— If you win, we will make you king of the beasts, she said.

— Very well, said the squirrel.

He went away from the other beasts, feeling very angry, but he knew what to do. He went to his hut and took out a ball of grease, which he put on a rock to soften in the sun. Then, when it was warm enough, he took the grease and rubbed it all over himself, all over his fur.

Finally, he began to walk to the watering hole. He didn't try to hide or to climb the trees. He just strolled towards the water, out in the open.

The lion saw the squirrel coming and his mad eyes rolled. He leaped at the little creature, roaring, and squashed it to death.

Or so he thought. For the lion didn't see or feel that the greasy squirrel had slipped out from under his paw and rolled away. As the lion roared again in triumph, the squirrel leaped up and into his mouth. Then he scurried down the lion's throat and into the mad king's belly.

Meanwhile, the rest of the beasts had arrived, having heard the ruckus, and stood at a safe distance.

— Oh dear, said the hyena, seeing the lion roaring his victory. The squirrel is dead.

— What a surprise, said the turtle.

But even as they spoke, the squirrel was running around inside the lion, biting, scratching.

As the beasts watched, the lion's eyes began to roll even more than usual. Then they froze, the whites showing, and the lion toppled down on to the grass. The squirrel emerged from the lion's mouth, hopped on to its head and did a little dance, all covered in blood.

— All hail the king, he said, before licking himself clean.

*

After the deal was called off, Tony and Dad spent a lot of time in the dining room with Ahmed and Nyesh, trying to restart negotiations. That meant I found it difficult to avoid the stepmother, which made for a whole festival of fun, I can tell you.

She came up to me when it was our shower time in the morning.

— Amy, she said. She'd lowered her voice into that I'm-going-to-tell-you-a-secret tone.

— What? I said, and I was annoyed to hear that I'd done it, too, just because she had, my voice in the corridor like a stage whisper. It's like a spell – if you whisper to someone they have to whisper back.

— I've got my period. She pointed down, like I couldn't understand words or something.

I stared at her for a moment.

— Oh, I said. Right.

She touched my arm.

— I can't talk to your dad about it, she said.

I could see what she was doing, see the bond she was trying to create, and all it did was make me cringe.

— I suppose not, I said, though I didn't really think so – I mean, aren't you supposed to be able to talk to your husband about anything?

— The thing is, she went on, I don't have any stuff.

— You didn't bring anything?

— Of course I brought some, she said a bit testily. I don't know what happened, though. The pirates must have taken it.

— Really?

— Yes, god knows why.

I looked at her. I didn't know if she was making it up to give us something to talk about, something girly, but it wasn't like I could say no.

— Don't worry, I said. I have some tampons in my cabin.

On the way, Ahmed stopped us. We were allowed in our cabins in the day, but the pirates always got suspicious if they saw two of us in there together, like we might be plotting something.

— We need . . . woman supplies, I said to him. I pointed to my cabin.

His face spoke embarrassment and understanding. He waved us onwards with his gun.

In the cabin, the stepmother put them in her pocket.

— Thanks, Amy, she said. You're a lifesaver. Now if you can just get me some herbal tea, a romcom and some aspirin . . .

— There are painkillers in the medicine cabinet, I said, pretending like she wasn't trying to do some creepy rapport thing. I'm sure Ahmed will let you have some.

I left her, and as soon as I left her, she left my thoughts.

There wasn't much spare room in my thoughts; there was too much of someone else in there.

What I thought about: Farouz. Only Farouz. I hated him, and at the same time I couldn't get him out of my head, couldn't get my thoughts to stop turning to him, like he was the North Star and my mind was a compass. It's like being ill, I realised then, having a crush on someone, being in love with someone, whatever. It changes the shapes and colours of absolutely everything; makes the world feel different, swollen.

I did speak to him a couple of times over those three days while the new deal was being done. I had to. I mean, it's not like we could totally blank each other on that little yacht. People would have noticed. And when I did speak to him, or when I saw him, it seemed like he was as angry as me, because he would suddenly blow up, not at me directly, but at nothing in particular.

— They've used all the fucking sugar! he would say, as I was passing in the corridor. Animals.

Or:

— That bloody bastard Mohammed!

— I hate this yacht, he said, kicking the pump for the shower as I walked past on the way to the toilet.

I think this was his way of telling me he wasn't happy about the situation, either. Like his feelings were at all comparable. I mean, what he'd done, the way he'd revealed us – informing Ahmed how Dad and Tony had lied – could have got us killed. He had put us in real danger – even more than before, that is – and he was going around acting like it was some kind of an argument of entitlement instead of him being selfish. He kind of smouldered constantly, and at the same time seemed to take up less room. He withdrew into himself, made himself smaller, harder and somehow more flammable, too, like trees get compacted by rock and time into coal.

Meanwhile, Damian was stalking the corridors, beaming, as if he was some kind of see-saw person with Farouz, and because one of them was bad-tempered, it made the other one tip up into happiness. I knew what it was: he could see what was happening with me and Farouz, and he liked it, because he hated the idea of a connection between us.

I thought, is he protecting me, like a dutiful captain, or does he just fancy me? Maybe it was a bit of both.

That second morning, when Farouz kicked the shower, Tony and Dad came into the cinema room, all excited because they had swiped a portable VHF that one of the pirates had left lying around. They said they'd managed to raise the navy on it, and had agreed a private channel. Tony admitted he wasn't sure what good it would do, though – there was still no way the navy would take the risk of an attack, not with us on board. But it was comforting to think that there was a potential link with the outside world, a link the pirates didn't know about. The navy had given them news from Tony and Damian and Felipe's families: they were well; they were thinking of them.

Esme and Carrie had set up a Facebook tribute page for me, apparently, which had, like, a hundred thousand fans. I thought that was a bit morbid – I mean, that's what people do for their dead friends.

I spent the day with Felipe on the deck. At first, I came out and he tried to look away, to not catch my eye. I got it, I really did. His life was at stake, but it was Dad's money that would get us all freed if things went well. It meant that Felipe wasn't in control, yet shouldn't he have a say in things?

I walked over to him, so that he had to look up at me.

— Dad and Tony, they don't mean to be dicks, I said.

Felipe did a surprised laugh.

— I didn't say they were, he said.

— No. But you were angry, and you had every right to be. They should tell you what's going on.

— Yes, he said thoughtfully. But not just them. Damian, also. Everyone. You.

— Me? I said, shocked.

— You went to the negotiation table. I was not there. You did not say anything.

I started to open my mouth, then closed it again.

— Sorry, I said.

— It's OK, he replied. It's just circumstances. Too close. Too small. People start to lose their shit.

Now it was my turn to do a surprised laugh. After that, the tension was broken, and Felipe motioned for me to sit down next to him.

It was nice – I hadn't spoken to him much before, but he turned out to be a lovely guy. He had a wife back home in London, and a baby. Nine months old. He showed me pictures from his wallet. I felt ashamed that I hadn't known.

— She's beautiful, I said, meaning his wife, meaning the baby, too. She had curly hair, these enormous black eyes and a wide smile, revealing two teeth at the bottom.

233

— Yes, he said. We were trying for many years. She is our blessing. When she was born . . . I used to think it was stupid when people said, I would die for you. Now I understand. When they put her in my arms, I felt I could levitate if I wanted to, or step in front of a bus for her, no problem.

When he touched the picture of his baby, I felt something constrict around my throat. I couldn't explain it – it was just his finger on a photo, but there was something about it. I felt the love in it, and I heard it in his voice when he told me that she'd just started crawling, but could only do it backward. How, when he used to Skype his wife at 6 p.m. when the internet came on, the baby, Melissa, would smile when she heard his voice. Of course, he hadn't been able to do that since the pirates took over.

— I am not afraid to die, said Felipe. But I am afraid to leave her without a father. I should be there to protect her. His voice cracked, and horror rushed out of the crack and into me.

My dad loved me like that once, I thought. My dad showed my photo to people and spoke with pride about my crawling.

— Sorry, said Felipe. Other people's babies are boring. He put away the photo.

— No, they're not, I said.

I asked him lots of questions about Melissa, and he answered, and as he did so he smiled properly for the first time since we'd been taken hostage, talking about her.

— She knows so many words, he said, so many already. It is like a miracle. Not to say them – she can only say Dada. But when I read with her, I hold the book, and she turns the pages. And when I say, where is the ball, she points, she finds the ball. Where is the sun, where is the cat, the same. She is clever, not like me. She will go far in life.

He turned away from me for a moment, did something with his hands, with his eyes.

— I – I started to say, but then I closed my mouth and just put my hand on his shoulder.

He turned to me and smiled, and, for just a second, I understood a bit of what Dad must have felt when I said I was going to work in a bar. I wanted to think that he would be embarrassed if I did that. But what if he really did just want me to do what would make me happy? For a moment, I felt like there was a violin in my hands, felt the weight and smoothness of it, and the waves lapping against the hull were suddenly in counterpoint, were suddenly playing Bach.

I shook my head slightly to dislodge these thoughts. The air was strained, so I cracked my knuckles.

— She *will* go far, I said to Felipe. And you will be there to see her do it. Besides, you've gone far yourself.

— I'm a cook, he said.

I held his eyes, winked.

— A cook in *Somalia*, I said.

Felipe laughed.

— Yes, he said. It is a long way to have come.

We were looking down at the sea by the diving platform, when one of the younger pirates came over. My guts clenched, thinking something was wrong. But he sort of shyly sidled closer to us and pointed to the box in which the diving stuff was stored, with the masks and snorkels, too.

— Can I lend? he asked. He pointed to a snorkel.

— You want to borrow that? I mimed swimming. You want to swim with it?

— Please, he said. He sounded very young. He had a thin covering of stubble, dark eyes. He was quite handsome, actually.

— You like snorkelling? asked Felipe, sounding surprised.

— Yes. But we don't have . . . He pointed to the snorkel again. These.

— What about Ahmed? I asked.

The pirate looked at the other guard on duty, who nodded.

— Ahmed busy, he said.

Then Felipe turned to me with a strange sort of smile.

— You want to go snorkelling, Amy? he said.

— We can't go with them, I said.

— Of course we can, said Felipe. He turned to the guard. Hey, Jamal, he said. He pointed to the snorkelling stuff. We come, too?

The guard grinned.

— OK, Felipe.

For a moment I was speechless.

— What the – I started.

— Coffee, said Felipe. I make it for them. Properly. And pasta.

Ah. Now he mentioned it, I wondered when was the last time I'd seen the pirates with their gross big pot of food.

Felipe was cooking for them, that was why. He was cooking for them, and he was cooking for us.

— Does Dad know? I said. Damian? Tony?

Felipe put a finger to his lips.

— They have power and money, he said. I have food. Maybe the pirates will remember my food, and they won't want to kill me.

I smiled, looking at the sea.

— Come on, said Felipe. Come snorkelling.

I thought of when Dad and the stepmother asked me to go snorkelling in the Red Sea, and how I said no and listened to music instead. I discovered that when I thought of the person who did that, it was like I was beginning to picture a different girl. Not me, just someone who looked like me. A doppelgänger, isn't that the word?

Then I thought, hey, all of us might be about to die on this yacht. We might never see home again. This was meant to be a holiday. So I went over to the box with Felipe and we took out three sets of snorkelling gear, the flippers, too – the pirate didn't know the purpose of them, but he picked it up quick when we showed him.

We sat at the end of the diving platform and tumbled in. The water was like a blessing, like an embrace. It was warmer than the air, silky, and a strange thought crossed my mind when I entered it, which was that I understood, in that moment, what baptism was all about. Oh good, I thought. At least if I die I'll have had this.

We were close to shore, so there were coral reefs right by

the yacht. We swam over them for what felt like hours, just drifting, watching all the colours, the fish, all of them teeming around us, some of them nibbling at my fingers when I held them out.

After a while, the guards swapped over, exchanged the snorkelling gear they were using, but I didn't really pay attention to that. The fact that they were guards, that one of them had to stay on deck at all times, a gun in his hand, seemed colossally irrelevant.

At one point, I felt something touch me on the leg, and Felipe gestured up with his thumb, for me to break water. When I did, he pointed down the beach.

— There's a turtle, he said, over there.

Then he went under again. I followed him, his flippers making explosions of bubbles in the water ahead of me, shimmering in the light, constellations. The colours of the coral below me, the little black and white fish darting, the parrotfish constantly gulping, it was all amazing. But when we hit the end of the reef and it sloped away steeply below us, the water suddenly darker and colder, fading to black in the near distance, that was when my breath stopped in my lungs, snorkel or no snorkel.

There, seeming to hang suspended in the water ahead of us, was a giant turtle. Its flippers were moving gently, and it was sort of drifting, its head higher than its tail. I don't know if it was feeding or what. It was beautiful. It was like a visitation from something that didn't belong in our world, a message, like on that beach in Mexico. From something sacred.

Then, with a very slow kick of its rear flipper, it began to turn, before swimming gracefully out into the blackness, and finally disappearing.

I broke the surface, and so did Felipe.

— Wow, I said. Which seemed like kind of a ridiculous understatement, but what else can you say?

— Yeah, said Felipe. Wow.

That was the good part of that second day. The bad part was that I was thinking about Farouz all the time, about how I'd thought he understood me, thought there was something real between us, and now he'd sold us down the river by revealing that it was Dad who had all the money. It made me furious.

At the time, though, I was just angry – not hurt.

That was about to change.

I was lying there that night, with my eyes closed, waiting to fall asleep. Dad and the stepmother were whispering to each other, revoltingly, in the dark. Tony was muttering to himself.

Then, adding to their soft voices, a beat, and music.

I sat up. I could make out Tony in the gloom, doing the same.

— What's that? asked Dad.

— Music, said Tony, with his talent for stating the obvious.

— Live music, I said.

I could tell – the sound has a different tone, a different fullness, when it's coming from instruments in real time.

— Let's check it out, said Tony.

I'll say one thing for Tony – he was brave. Getting shot didn't slow him down at all – he was like a Duracell bunny. And he was happy to sit at that negotiating table, staring down the pirates, just like he was happy to investigate anything weird.

— I'm staying here, said the stepmother.

— Of course you are, said Tony.

And he could have meant that she would be mad to come, that she'd be safer here, or it could have been a dig at her, at her cowardice. I thought it was the latter, but the way he said it, the ambiguity remained, so it wasn't like my dad could call him on it. That made me like Tony even more.

— I'm coming, I said. Because I already had an idea of what I was listening to and I wanted to make sure, even though there was a knot in the pit of my stomach.

Tony opened the door, and Dad and I followed him, after he peered down the corridor and saw that there was no guard. Damian would have come, too, I'm sure, but he was asleep, and snoring loudly.

The music was coming from the rear of the yacht – the stern, I think it's called? So we turned that way and crept along. We probably didn't need to – it wasn't like the pirates were going to hear us. In the dining room, we stopped and looked out of the portholes on to the rear deck, where the deck lights were on. An incongruous image flickered into life in my head: busybodies on an English street, peering out from between their curtains to see what their neighbours are up to.

Outside, there was a party going on. Bottles from the bar – some clear, some dark – were lying around on the deck.

— I thought Muslims didn't drink, said Dad.

— I bet they're not meant to chew that khat stuff, either, said Tony.

But I wasn't listening to Dad and Tony – I was watching Farouz.

He was sitting on an upturned crate of some kind and his oud was in his hands. The way he was holding it, it was like it was alive, like a baby, or a lover. It looked how he'd said, a bit like a banjo or a guitar, only with a fat belly and a thin neck.

His eyes were closed. His hands were moving very fast, but also softly. Not carefully, though – more . . . instinctively. Like he couldn't hit the wrong notes even if he wanted to because the oud was part of him.

He's good, was my stupid thought, a thought floating on all the anger and jealousy and pain.

Most of the other pirates were drumming, smacking their palms on whatever was to hand – coffee cans, the deck, their knees. Ahmed, though, was singing, his voice running over the music like water over a stream-bed, clear, flowing. Looking at him, you wouldn't have thought a sound like that could come out of him – it was like opening an Argos box and finding a Tiffany's ring inside.

Dad and Tony were whispering to each other, but I was watching and listening to the music. It was amazing. The scale was different from Western stuff – pentatonic, in a minor key, laid over complicated rhythms. It was a bit like blues, I thought, and then I told myself I was being dumb, because of course blues came from music like this in the first place, created by African slaves, its rhythms hummed low by work gangs in America, then sung out a hundred years later. There didn't seem to be a structure of verse and chorus – it was more like a free-flowing improvisation around set melodies, which reminded me of jazz.

And all the time, Farouz's fingers were moving over the strings of his instrument so fast, like the articulated parts of a programmed machine. It might sound strange, but that was the thing that really hurt me.

I had thought that Farouz, I don't know, needed me in some way. That he was a bit like me, that he didn't belong with the others. But here he was, smiling, playing his oud, while Ahmed sang, and if you wanted to create a scene that showed the concept of belonging, you couldn't do much better than the one I was looking at. There was an open bottle of what looked like whisky at Farouz's feet, the pirates were laughing, and there was such an atmosphere of bonhomie, of happiness rising from all of them, so thick you could almost see it, like mist.

I couldn't tear my eyes off him.

You're not like me, I realised with a painful jolt. You are one of them, even if you're smart. Even if you're sensitive. You have a family, and they're sitting with you on that deck. You have a place. You have your music.

And also: you lied to me. You made me feel like you were someone different, like you had to do this to save your brother, though maybe that was true, a little bit.

Looking at Farouz, his oud in his hand in the warm night air, I understood something I'd been trying to deny to myself: he loved this life. He loved being a pirate.

I hated him in that moment. Really, really hated him.

One of the pirates turned, as if to look at us, and Dad grabbed my arm, pulling me down. We stayed like that, breathing hard, crouching below the porthole. We were just waiting for the music to stop, for footsteps to come. The pirates had been drinking – might they lose control in a situation like that? Might someone get killed? That was what we were all thinking.

But the music didn't stop. In fact, it swelled, got louder, more raucous, spiralling out into the night.

If those northern coast guards turned up now, I thought, they could kill them all and take the yacht in minutes. Part of me even wished they would.

Tony was doing some kind of counting thing with his fingers, moving them around, as if remembering the positions of things.

— There's an AK lying by the door, he said. If we could –

— No, Dad whispered back.

— They're drunk, said Tony, and I realised that this was why he had wanted to sneak out and see what was happening. They won't be expecting it.

— I said no, Dad said. Are you mad? The kid still has his gun on his waist. The others can grab theirs, too.

This was true: the pirates were drinking, but their guns were lying beside them, within reach. I'd noticed that.

— We could take them, Tony said sullenly.

— We could, said Dad. But we would get killed, guaranteed.

— Amy can go back to the cinema room, and then –

— NO, said Dad, breaking out of his whisper, so that I flinched, thinking the pirates must have heard. In his voice was the old authority I'd heard when he was on work calls, on his BlackBerry. It was the trick of a charming person – the sudden shift into power, into fierceness, that shocks the other person into backing down.

And it worked – Tony held up his hands.

— It was only an idea, he said.

The next morning, I went to my cabin. I was trying to watch a DVD, but I couldn't concentrate. I kept turning to look at the violin, lying there in the wardrobe. I remembered what Farouz had said about it, and suddenly I wanted to hurt him or hurt the violin, or whatever was closest.

I picked up the instrument and walked down the corridor to the front deck, because generally people hung out on the rear one, and that was where the pirates ate the endless rounds of pasta that I now knew Felipe cooked for them. The sun was rising over the Indian Ocean, huge over the ever-shifting sea. On the other side of the yacht was the shore. It was weird how we were so close and so far away at the same time. It was just there, Somalia, almost within touching distance. The sun visited it every evening, lowered itself into the land, and then left again in the morning, but I had never set foot on it.

As I watched, a camel wandered past. A camel! I'd seen a couple of them from the yacht, like we were on some kind of really weird and slightly sick safari tour.

I watched until the camel disappeared behind a dune, then I just stood there. I thought of the sky camel, Farouz pointing out the stars. Then my mind went empty. I looked at this gnarled tree that stood near the shoreline. Every day, that tree was there, just being. It was strange how you got used to things like that. I mean, even now, I can picture that tree. I can safely say that if the whole world got blasted to smithereens by some alien invasion, and I was floating through space on some bit of rock and that tree floated past me, I would recognise it instantly.

But, as far as I knew, I would never touch it.

So I stood there for a while, thinking dumb thoughts like that. I was pretty much alone, though I could see a guard above me, in the bridge. There were always guards around, of course.

I looked down at the water and I thought about the turtle. I hefted the violin in my hand. It felt heavy and light at the same time. It felt, even after all these months of not playing it, like something special. Like an offering.

I held the violin out over the sea and got ready to drop it.

— Don't do that, said Farouz from behind me.

I turned my head.

— Why not? I asked. It doesn't matter anyway. And don't act like you care.

— I'm sorry, he said. I have upset you again. I'm sorry.

— You're *sorry*? This is our *lives*. We could die.

— No. Your father will have to pay more money. That is all.

— Oh, that's all, is it? I asked, my voice dripping bitterness. So you'll just get an extra million or so, right? Poor you.

I didn't tell him about watching him play the oud, about how left out it had made me feel, about how it had made me realise he didn't need me. I knew it would sound crazy and jealous, and that would give him an extra advantage.

Farouz took a step back. He raised his hands, seemed about to say something, but then Ahmed's voice came from inside, calling his name.

— Farouz! Farouz!

— Oh, yeah, I said. You should go to your boss. Go and see what he wants, make sure he's OK. Same way you went and told him about my dad.

Farouz sighed.

— You lied, too, he said. About the owners of the yacht.

— It's not the same! I said. You took us hostage. And then, just when I was liking you again, you told your fucking boss – who's in charge of a load of men with guns, including, oh, YOU – that my dad had lied to him.

— I had to, he said.

— Oh, you had to. For your precious brother.

He blew out a thin stream of smoke.

— No. It was Ahmed. I was checking the computer, to get the go plan that the navy were sending. He saw the word *owner*. He reads enough English to know that word. He made me translate the rest.

— And you did it.

— Of course I did it! What do you expect?

I hugged my knees up to my chest.

— It's just coincidence that this way you get more money? I said.

— This way I get to stay alive, he said, more angry than I had ever heard him. What happens if I lie when I translate? What happens if Ahmed asks Nyesh to read the email instead? I don't get fined. I die.

— Oh, I said, my voice all small.

— Please, said Farouz, just don't throw the violin, OK? I will explain everything. You will understand, I promise. Meet me here tonight, where I told you about the stars. About the camel. OK?

— I can't, I said. My dad.

— You can sneak, he said. When he's asleep. It will be all right, I promise.

I was feeling so angry with him, but there was something about the way he said this, about his grey eyes in the morning light, and even though I wanted to tell him what to do with himself and his promises, I didn't. I just nodded instead. I trusted him.

I was an idiot. Not because I shouldn't have trusted him. Not because of that at all. But because of what happened afterwards.

If I hadn't nodded, if I'd sworn at him, if I'd dropped the violin in the ocean and walked away without looking back, maybe things would have been different.

Maybe nobody would have had to die.

My dad was snoring, the stepmother curled up on his shoulder. They were holding hands, which was disgusting. It was bad enough having the stepmother around all the time, like in our house in London, but it was another thing having her, my mom's usurper, in the same room cuddled up with my dad at night.

Tony was on the sofa, breathing heavily.

I got up from the armchair I was sitting on, moving gingerly. I took one step, then held my breath, looked around.

Dad snored on.

The room was dark as there was only one lamp on, in the corner, where Felipe had been reading a magazine. He was sleeping now, too. I crept towards the door, avoiding the obstacles on the floor – the discarded clothes, Damian stretched out on some sofa cushions, face down. I felt clumsy, but my bare feet were silent over the plush carpet.

It felt like a mile, the length of the cinema room, when really it was probably only twenty steps. I kept turning around, convinced I'd heard my dad sitting up. If he did, I'd say I was going to the toilet.

I put my hand on the silver doorknob and turned it. There was a barely audible squeak, and I whipped my head round again.

No one moved.

I pulled the door ever so slowly.

Creak.

Shit. I froze, holding the door still. I listened. My dad had stopped snoring. I watched the shape of him in the gloom.

Then, a sort of ratcheting sound, and the snoring started again. I felt breath rush back into my lungs, sudden, and hard as an attack.

Gritting my teeth, I opened the door a little further, then twisted myself through it, remembering to hold it as it closed to stop it slamming.

When I got out on the deck, the stars were out, of course. It was like there were never any clouds, never any rain. How the hell did anything grow here? I could understand why Farouz said that all Somali stories were about hunger. Even the squirrel and the lion – because the lion ate the squirrel, didn't it?

I sat down on a sunlounger. I'd dressed in the dark, but I had on an All Saints top I loved and a vintage 50s skirt I got on Brick Lane. Foolish of me to dress up, I know, and weird when I was still so angry, but go figure.

I didn't have long to wait for Farouz to come out. I knew the sound of his footsteps by then, the particular pace of his walk. I was seriously hoping that no one was going to wake up to go to the loo or something, and realise I was gone. I wasn't worried about the pirates. Most of the guards, Ahmed and Farouz excepted, were usually high on khat, or drunk, or wired from drinking that terrible coffee and sugar mixture they seemed addicted to.

So I was on my own, and then Farouz appeared, his hello when he saw me low and slow, so as not to alert anyone, and I wasn't on my own any more.

Farouz sat down on the sunlounger next to mine. His face

was wreathed in smoke, as usual. He was toying with his gun. He started to say something, stopped, started again.

— I . . . I have told Ahmed that I will take the same share as before, he said eventually.

— What? I said, shocked. Why?

— For you.

I looked at him. I could feel something inside me, some hardness, softening, like stale bread in water.

— Won't Ahmed wonder why? I asked.

— Perhaps. Farouz made an equivocal gesture with his hand. He just knows I don't want any extra money. Ahmed is . . . he is not a bad man. He has children, a wife.

— I know, I said.

— Also . . . Farouz said hesitantly. I think Ahmed suspects that I like you.

A silence.

— You like me?

I couldn't be sure, but I think he blushed.

— Maybe, he said. And you?

— I don't know. There's someone I like. He's good-looking. Sweet. But there's a problem, you see.

— Oh?

— Yes. He's a pirate.

Farouz edged on to my sunlounger.

— Coast guard, he said.

— And that's another problem, I said with a laugh. There's this language barrier. He doesn't speak very good English, so –

He poked me, gently, on the arm.

— Hey!

Then he said something in Somali that sounded like a curse.

— I forgot, he said. I got you a present, for your birthday. I was going to give it to you before, in your cabin, but . . . Well, I was distracted.

I thought of that kiss: yes, he had been distracted. I had been, too.

— Anyway, he said. Here. He reached into his pocket and placed something in my hand. It was cool and compact, smooth.

I looked down at it, a very simple wooden box, about the size of a jewellery box. For a moment I thought, no, he couldn't have, could he? I mean, he's a –

And then I thought, stupid Amy. He could have stolen some earrings from anywhere. A ring.

So my veins were running a bit cold when I opened it. I was all prepared to be polite, but I already felt offended, like, did he really think some damn stolen jewellery was going to make me happy?

But it wasn't jewellery.

I didn't see inside the box properly at first, just had an impression of something heaped and multiple and glinting.

Then –

— Sand, I said.

He smiled.

— From Somalia, he said. I got it when I went for the eggs, from the beach. So that you have some of my country to carry with you, even if you never go yourself. Even when –

253

I held up a hand to stop him saying it, to stop him talking about when we would be saying goodbye.

I held the glittering sand in its box in my palm, then closed the lid and squeezed my hand tight around it.

— Thank you, I said.

He touched my hand with the box inside it.

— You are welcome, he said.

I loosened my fingers and held his hand, too, stopped him withdrawing it.

— It's cold, I said.

— It is, he replied.

We were very close together now. I could feel the heat from his body.

On his face, the bruises had barely faded. And the hard muscles of his arms were just there, in front of me. Muscles that were made for hitting people, for . . .

No.

I closed my eyes. Dad was wrong and the stepmother was wrong: I wasn't self-destructive, and I didn't have a death wish. I knew it most fiercely in that moment – not because I *wasn't* scared, but because I *was* excited. I wanted to live. I wanted to experience everything.

— Are you OK? said Farouz.

— Yes, I said.

I put a hand on the back of his neck, felt the shifting bulk of his muscle. It was like it rose to meet my hand, fitting itself there, in the curve of my palm, the way my violin used to sit perfectly in the compass of my touch.

I think Farouz would have liked to go further, but I wasn't ready for it, and he respected that. I appreciated that. Some people would probably say it was Stockhausen syndrome, or whatever it's called, where people fall in love with their captors, but really he was very gentle.

I hadn't done much of this kind of stuff before. I mean, I know: the piercings, and the smoking and the clubbing, right? So you might think, well . . . But you would be wrong.

I'd only ever kissed one boy, Travis, by the time I left New York. He tasted of onion bagel, and his glasses caught in my hair, so we had to disentangle him afterwards. Since then, nothing. I think the English boys were scared of me, or they hated me, I don't know.

Most of the time we didn't even kiss, me and Farouz. We just snuggled up, held each other's hands. If someone else was telling me this I'd want to puke, but there you go. We're all hypocrites.

So, we sat there, wrapped around each other. It was like we were in our own little world inside the real world, like one Russian doll inside another, everything just warmth and the stars, and the sound of the sea lapping at the hull of the yacht.

— Our country was made this way, said Farouz. Our language.

His fingers were interlaced with mine, brown and white.

— I'm sorry?

— An Arab man and a Somali woman, a long time ago, he said. Pale and dark, only the other way around. The man was called Darod, which means *stranger* in Somali, so I guess that wasn't his real name. The woman was Dombiro. The man, he was thrown from a ship and he swam to the beach, near here.

— Why was he thrown from a ship?

— He was the youngest prince, and had many older brothers. He came from Al-Hejaz, from Arabia. When his father died, the other princes told him he would be exiled to stop him from competing for the throne. And that is what they planned, but instead the captain of the ship threw him overboard, and took his belongings and his money. At first, Darod was very afraid. This land he found himself in was hot, hotter than Arabia. And there were none of the trees and the birds he was used to. Only bushes and dust. He could find no shelter from the burning sun, and feared that he would die. He knew that to drink seawater could drive him mad. Farouz pointed to the land. Imagine washing up on that beach alone, he said.

I looked at Somalia, an even blacker outline in the darkness.

— Scary, I said.

— Yes. But it was all right, because when he crawled up the beach and into Somalia, Dombiro found him. She was a beautiful woman of the Dir clan, tall and with long, loose limbs, large dark eyes, long hair like the night, falling around her face. She was the chieftain's daughter, as he was a prince. He was Arab and she was African; they spoke no words in common. But when their eyes met, something happened, some music in the air. She sheltered him in an oasis, brought him water to drink and figs to eat, which were *beirda* in her language, and *tinata* in his.

— And they fell in love?

— And they fell in love. And he taught her about Mohammed, while she taught him how to live on the arid land and raise cattle there. She taught him to find water for her goats, which she was tending. He taught her writing, culture, religion. She taught him how to dig a well, how to find berries safe to eat, how to recognise the tracks of a hyena, where to cut a goat's throat – not to kill it, but to get a little blood for mixing with milk for strength.

— Yuck, I said.

— You would not say that if you were starving. I told you –

— All your stories are stories of hunger. I know. I rolled my eyes at him.

— You are a good student, he said condescendingly. Like Darod.

— I'm Darod, in this story? I should be Dombiro, the beautiful girl.

— No. You are the pale stranger who knows nothing about surviving in our land.

— OK, yes. Fair enough.

— At first, Farouz went on, Dombiro's family were not pleased to see Darod when she finally showed him to them, after keeping him in the oasis for many months. But eventually they welcomed him, as is the Somali way. He never returned to Al-Hejaz. And their descendants are the people of Puntland, to this very day.

— That's lovely, I said.

I liked that idea – that they had come from different cultures, but fallen in love all the same.

— Yes, he said. It is probably not true. But it is nice.

— A lot of things are like that, I said.

— Yes, he replied.

Farouz fell silent then, and I did, too.

I looked up at the stars sparkling above us. I remembered Mom talking about black holes, and supernovas, and how there were a hundred billion stars in our galaxy and a hundred billion galaxies, and how that should have made her feel small, but it didn't – it made everything seem more meaningful.

I didn't know what she meant then, but now I did.

I also remembered, as I lay there in Farouz's hard arms, Mom telling me about the music of the spheres. It's an old idea from philosophy. It was Pythagoras who came up with it first. He knew that there was a mathematics behind music. Take an octave: every time you go up an octave, all you're really doing is doubling the frequency of the note. Middle C is 261 hertz, or 261 vibrations a second. The next C up on the keyboard, or fretboard or whatever, is 522 hertz. Even chords are in harmony; they go up in mathematical steps. If you want a major chord, the ratio of the frequencies is 4:5:6.

But Pythagoras thought it didn't stop with music. He saw the planets, spinning around in their orbits, and he noticed what he thought were some regularities in their distance. He decided that the spaces between the planets in the solar system must be like notes in a chord, must be following some kind of grand harmony. That planets must make notes by spinning, and together a symphony; that if you could stand in the right place, if your ear was big enough, you would hear their music.

Oh, Mom, I thought, remembering how she told me this on a cold November evening on the loneliest beach in North America, looking up at the stars. How she got excited and made lots of gestures to try to explain what she was talking about, spreading her hands for the distance between the stars, dancing around to show their spinning. How she babbled as she tried to convey how exciting it was, even if it was wrong, the idea that the stars and music were somehow the same.

I miss you so much, I thought.

Suddenly, lying there with Farouz, I didn't mind so much that Mom said *stardust* like that in her note to me. Now it was OK. I was thinking about what she said, about all things being linked, about us all being stardust, and I wasn't angry about it like I was before. I was thinking about the music of the spheres, too. Because I loved that idea, I really did. And I knew why she loved it.

Because things might be meant to happen.

Because an order might exist, under the chaos.

Because the universe might be playing a tune.

This is what I was thinking, when there came the sound of footsteps leading up to the door on to the deck.

Someone was coming out.

And I was in Farouz's arms.

Heart racing, I tried to move away – but not quick enough, as Mohammed opened the door and stepped outside.

For a moment, he stayed completely still, looking at us, then a smirk began to spread across his face. Very slowly, very deliberately, he closed the door behind him.

— Ah. Hostage Three is . . . whore, he said.

Farouz jumped to his feet, but Mohammed pushed him back down. He said something to him in their language, something contemptuous.

Oh god, this is worse than a fine, I thought. This isn't just a thousand dollars.

I started to run towards the door.

Mohammed grabbed my top and it tore, so he grabbed my arm instead and spun me back towards him, yanking the breath from me. He clasped my hand in his. His other hand held his AK-47; I could feel the coldness of the metal against my back. He shook his head: no. I didn't try to run again. His hand moved up my arm. Then his fingers splayed and he stroked my skin. It seemed to contract at his touch, shrivelling away from him – the sensation of him brushing against me was like sloe berries in the mouth.

He barked something at Farouz.

Farouz shook his head.

Mohammed shouted and his spittle landed on my face.

A hardness came over Farouz's expression.

— He says since you have already been touched by a coast guard, it will do no harm for another to touch you, said Farouz in a blank voice.

— No, I said.

Mohammed laughed.

— You not die, he said. He tapped his head. I not idiot. We want money.

— Farouz! I said. Farouz, please . . .

— I am sorry, said Farouz. I am sorry. His voice was hollow, scooped out, like an eaten avocado.

— Yes. Good. Now, said Mohammed, with his sour voice, his black-stained khat-teeth, his fat revolting tongue. Now, quiet.

He was close to me, his breath a physical thing, leaping out from his mouth.

The yacht tilted on some awful secret axis that I had never known was there. I found myself praying, silently, even though I had not prayed for years and years, and I wasn't even sure how any more.

Mohammed undid his belt buckle. He unbuttoned my All Saints top.

He put his gun down.

He pushed me down,

down,

down,

on to the sunlounger.

I've told you about the sound when a gun goes off next to you. But I can't describe the feeling of it – the feeling of a man looming over you one moment, scarred face lowering down, unstoppable, and then half his face is gone, blown away in bloody rags, and his body falls on to you, meaty, heavy, and his blood is hot on your face, and somewhere behind all that, like lightning becoming thunder, a crack loud enough to be the world breaking.

Energy, violence, heat, and, to begin with, no sound at all.

It's a bit like a heavy blankness, a bit like this:

(

).

Followed by a boom that shakes your inner ears – only you have to imagine that all of it is red, blood-red, and weighs a hundred kilos.

Then I screamed.

There was sticky stuff in my hair, a smell of burning, of cordite, I guess, and my head felt like it had been inside a big bell when someone struck it. I scrabbled at Mohammed's leaden corpse, trying to get it off me, still screaming for all I knew, for all I could hear. My leg was trapped – oh god, my leg was trapped – but then it popped out, and I kind of half-fell, half-crawled off the sunlounger on to the deck. I realised I could taste blood in my mouth, metallic, and I thought for a moment I had bitten my tongue, before it hit me that this was Mohammed's blood, his blood, in my *mouth*.

Farouz's hand was holding his pistol, and it was smoking from the barrel. I didn't realise they actually did that. He was standing in, like, a lozenge of light from one of the portholes, and there was a smile, or what looked like a smile, on his face.

He shot him, I thought dumbly.

I glanced at him again, and his smile was gone. Maybe I imagined it, I thought. Yes, I must have imagined it. He saved me, yes, and that meant killing Mohammed. And I was sure he hadn't enjoyed it.

Wasn't I?

When the yacht had stopped spinning enough for me to get to my knees and look up, Farouz was already dressed. I didn't understand how he had done that already. There was a look almost of surprise on his face. I started to button up my top, but he shook his head.

— No, he said. This looks better. The tears, too. His voice came at me like underwater speech.

With trembling fingers, he took a pack of cigarettes from his pocket, then a lighter. He lit a cigarette. I watched the whole sequence, like it was the only thing I had ever seen. The tap of the packet. The cigarette falling out into the other hand, the faint *pop* when the lighter thrust out its little flame. The first deep drag, right down into the lungs, the smoke drifting out again through his nostrils.

— Jesus, I said, looking at the dead man.

— No, said Farouz, his face not moving, save for the wisps of smoke still curling from his nose. That is Mohammed.

I kind of half-laughed, but at the same time, I didn't know if I would ever be able to stand up again.

— You were alone out here. He tried to rape you, said Farouz, as if explaining something to a child. It was lucky I came out for a cigarette.

— He . . . Right, I said, yes, as I understood that Farouz was creating our cover story.

That was it, that was all the time we had to prepare, because then Ahmed appeared, a look – of what? terror? anger? – on his face. I could see him taking in the whole scene, his eyes flicking from Mohammed, his head haloed in blood, bits of brain and skull scattered on the sunlounger, to me, in my torn top, my hands clutching at myself, to hold myself together, to cover myself. And to Farouz, standing there with the gun.

— Did he . . . ? Ahmed began.

— No, said Farouz. I came in time. Then he added something in Somali.

Ahmed nodded. Even then, I don't know if he really believed it. In his face, there was no emotion at all. But what was he going to do? Secretly, he was probably pleased with the result. I'd seen him roll his eyes behind Mohammed's back. The man had been imposed on Ahmed by people with influence, that much was obvious. He came closer to me.

— Are you OK? Ahmed asked.

— No, I said truthfully.

— I mean, did he . . . hurt?

— No, I said.

— Good, good. You precious, said Ahmed's mouth. We do not want hurt.

Ahmed's eyes, though. His eyes said nothing at all.

— No, I said again. No, he didn't hurt me.

Ahmed nodded slowly.

— You don't speak now. With Farouz. Never alone. Understand?

Something gripped my throat, something with long thin fingers.

— Yes, I said in a low voice.

Ahmed raised his eyebrows at Farouz.

— Yes, OK, said Farouz.

I could hear shouting from inside – I guessed that the guards were stopping any of the passengers from coming out. Dad, I thought. Shit. Dad.

Ahmed looked into my eyes.

— Your father – he began.

— I understand, I said. Mohammed grabbed me. He threw me down on the sunlounger, and that was when Farouz shot him. Farouz never touched me. Mohammed tore my clothes.

Farouz was translating, just in case, but Ahmed didn't need it. He just put his hands together, like a prayer.

— Thank you, he said.

It sounded important.

It sounded like doing a deal.

Then, yes, Dad came out on deck, and he hugged me, and examined me. There might have been other people, too, the stepmother, maybe. I don't know.

Only then did Dad see the stuff on my face, the man lying on the wood, blood pooling in the cracks, the way it had with the goat.

— What happened? he asked.

— I came outside, I said.

— Why?

— For a cigarette, I said. A flash of guilt passed through me. I was lying to him, saying something he wouldn't like, but it was so, so, so much less bad than the truth, which might just kill him. Looking at my dad's face, his grey hair and his crow's feet, while the image of Mohammed's body was still in my mind, made me feel a little sick.

— Jesus, Amy, he said. And then?

— Mohammed tried to –

— Mohammed?

— The one who took my watch.

— Oh, right. God, Amy. And . . . he . . . ?

— No. Farouz caught him in time.

— Shot him, said Dad blankly.

— Y-yeah, I said.

Dad turned to Farouz then. Dad looked shaky – I don't know if it was from fear, or the blood, or both.

— You did this? he asked, pointing to the body, the blood.

— Yes, said Farouz.

You know in films when robbers are breaking in somewhere, and they loop the CCTV footage from a camera so that they can walk down a corridor without being seen? And the reason the guards realise is that they see a glitch, someone

– a receptionist, say – flicking between sitting down and standing up, or whatever? That was what Dad looked like – one version of him was standing still, angry, and the other was taking a step towards Farouz.

Then he did take a step, and he shook Farouz's hand.

Farouz looked down, surprised.

— Thank you, said Dad.

— Ah. You're welcome, said Farouz.

I was only half-paying attention to this exchange because I was looking down at my hands. I guess I had been functioning on adrenalin up to this point, lost in the focused tunnel it made of the world, and now I was surprised to see that my hands were shaking. I mean properly shaking, like when it's incredibly cold, compulsively, involuntarily. I stared at them, like they belonged to someone else and were complying with that other person's nervous impulses, not mine.

Ahmed spoke in Somali.

— Mohammed dies a traitor, translated Farouz. A criminal. His family receive nothing.

— Oh. Er, good, said Dad. He turned to Ahmed. But what about my daughter? Your men are meant to be protecting us. You said it yourself. We are valuable. More valuable than the yacht.

When Farouz had finished interpreting, Ahmed made that sort of praying gesture again.

— I am sorry, he said.

— You realise, said Dad slowly, smiling to bring Ahmed into

Dad was angry with me on some level, but he seemed to accept my story about going out for a cigarette – or find it convenient to accept it, anyway. The stepmother tried to have a conversation with me about it, which I'm sure Dad put her up to, since he was still treading on eggshells around me. It was excruciating. She talked about How I Felt As A Woman, stuff like that.

I didn't know how I felt as a woman.

I didn't even know if there was a name for what I was feeling. I was terrified of Mohammed, but it wasn't quite fear, because he was already dead. I was scared, I suppose, of what could have happened, and at the same time I kept seeing, in my mind's eye, the crimson explosion of his head, the blossoming of gore, the wrong stillness of his body. I was shocked, I guess, but it was a complicated kind of shock.

Pretty much straight away, Nyesh and Ahmed summoned us to the dining room to talk about the money. Dad and Tony and Damian got up to go with them. I looked over at Felipe, sitting quietly in the corner.

— Take Felipe, I said.

— Sorry? said Damian, turning round.

— Felipe. He should go, too.

— But he's –

— He's a passenger on this yacht, I said. He deserves to be part of the conversation.

— Come on, Amy, said Tony. He's a cook.

— Yes, I said. And by leaving him here, you're making sure the pirates know that. You don't think they've thought carefully about who might be expendable, who they might shoot first?

Tony paused.

— Amy, said Felipe. This isn't –

I waved a hand at him.

— Think about it, I said to Tony. They didn't know Dad owned the yacht. They'll be worried they got other things wrong, too. It couldn't hurt to cause them some doubt.

— She's right, said Dad. How do they know he's not a trusted advisor of mine?

— Well, said Damian, they've got the manifest, for a start.

— True, said Dad. OK. Fine. They know he's a cook. But he can still come with us. It's his life, too.

I caught Dad's eye and nodded my thanks.

Damian beckoned to Felipe and he got up and joined them.

— You coming, too, Amy? said Damian.

— No, I said. I'll leave the money stuff to you big men.

I don't know why I said it so bitterly; I think I was still angry with him for lecturing me about Farouz.

— Fine, he said, and they left.

An hour later, they came back.

— Five million, said Dad. And we can do it soon. Tomorrow, possibly.

I was impressed, despite myself. Half off. We were also right back to where we had started.

— It was tricky, said Tony. Ahmed tried to argue that the whole thing with Mohammed shouldn't lower the ransom. He said it just showed the danger we were in, so all the more reason to pay up.

— Yes, said Dad. But then Felipe pointed out that if Mohammed had . . . had hurt you, Amy, then the navy might have come down on them like a ton of bricks, so five million was actually a good deal. That shut them up.

I looked at Felipe, and he looked back, and I smiled.

One day left, maybe. It was a weird feeling. I think all of us had it. Like it was Christmas tomorrow, but there was also a chance someone might cancel it. And a chance that it wasn't Christmas at all, but something terrible, like a funeral. I didn't know how I was going to feel about leaving the yacht, about going back to my life. It would be nice to not have the smoke everywhere, the gobbets of khat on the ground, the stink of coffee, the danger.

But . . .

There was Farouz. And he was the smoke everywhere, he was the danger, and I knew it was going to hurt when we said goodbye.

Out there in the public spaces of the yacht the next morning, Ahmed and Farouz looked on edge. I don't know if that was anxiety over the exchange, or them worrying about Mohammed's family coming back at them, the reprisals that might take place when they got back to shore. I noticed that once Mohammed's body left the yacht, there were no more shift changes, no more reinforcements from the land, almost as if they were afraid who might come aboard.

Finally, Tony announced that the exchange was going to take place at 6 a.m. the following day. Now it felt even more peculiar, the idea of going home. That things there had just kept on going in our absence – traffic lights changing, cars driving around, *Doctor Who* on a Saturday night. I'd thought that same thing when Mom died – how strange it was that the world kept on turning regardless. But now we were the ones who were gone, and that was even stranger. I didn't know how I felt about it. There was a part of me, odd as it might sound, that didn't want to leave, no matter what had happened to Mohammed, and even though there was a little voice in my head that kept whispering it was my fault that he was dead.

That night, I don't think any of us slept. We all sat up in the cinema room, playing a game, which was: *what's the first thing you're going to do when you get home?* For the stepmother, it was a bath. Felipe was going to hug his daughter and give her a kiss. Tony was going to get drunk. Damian was going to order steak and chips at his favourite restaurant. Dad was going to play golf.

And me?

I didn't know. Nothing came into my head, nothing at all. When I got home, I'd be safe. But there would be no Farouz, no school, and still no Mom. Only, everyone was still looking at me, waiting for me to play the game, so I said:

— Well, I guess I'll just catch up on TV.

Obviously that was the wrong thing to say because they all laughed, patronising, like I was an idiot.

After that, I went to the loo before going to bed – or trying to go to bed, anyway. As I was leaving the cinema room, Damian touched my arm.

— I'm sorry, he said. That whole thing with Farouz. I guess . . . I guess it was lucky he was there last night.

— Yes, I said.

— I was just trying to protect you, he said.

— I know. But I don't need two dads.

Damian cleared his throat.

— No, of course not. His cheeks were quite red, and I was glad because that told me what I had suspected anyway.

Yes, he'd been trying to protect me. But he fancied me a bit, too. I mean, I wasn't glad that he fancied me – it wasn't like that. But I was glad that he had a weakness. There was too much power on that yacht, too much control. I didn't want someone like Damian having any power over me, too.

— It's cool, I said. Don't worry about it.

I brushed past him.

As I came back into the room, the stepmother was waiting by the door.

— Everything OK with you and Damian? she asked.

— Er, yeah, I said. I thought quickly. I was just apologising, I said. For being a hard-ass about Felipe.

— You shouldn't apologise, she said. You think Damian and Tony don't know they're getting big bonuses if we get out of here alive? Damian's the captain and Tony's paid by the bank. If you think about it, Felipe's the only one who's really crew.

I looked over at him, sitting a little aside from everyone else, and I saw that it was true.

— Shit, I said.

— Don't worry about it, said the stepmother. You did what you could. And anyway, we're nearly out of here.

— Yeah, I said, but I think she could hear in my voice that I wasn't sure about it, and her face went all concerned, so before she could ask anything I went past her and lay on my bed of pillows on the floor.

You know when the world sort of shrinks to just the one thing you're looking at? For me that night, it was the halogen strip light in the ceiling that was flickering at one end. I lay there, my head hanging back, and stared at it the whole time, not sleeping. When you're waiting like that, it isn't like it's a long time. It's like, in some way, the waiting lasts for ever. Like there's a part of me, somewhere, that's still looking at that strip light. I would almost believe it's the rest of my life since that's a dream, a blink of the eye, and I'm *still* just looking at that light. It's hard to explain.

As I looked at the light, I thought and I thought about Farouz. Was I in love with him? I wasn't sure. I didn't know if it was possible to be in love with someone who had taken you hostage. Or maybe what I mean is, I knew it was probably quite easy to fall in love with someone who had taken you hostage. Because you got used to saying the things they wanted to hear, the things that would keep you alive. You got used to pleasing them, which meant you were always thinking about what they might think, about

275

what was in their minds, instead of what was in your own mind.

That looks a lot like love, from a certain angle.

I didn't like the idea of leaving the yacht, leaving him behind, never seeing him again.

I wanted to speak to him, I realised suddenly.

I wanted to see him, to say goodbye.

But I couldn't. My dad would never allow it, and now Ahmed would never allow it, either. I lay there, feeling like a clockwork toy whose handle has been wound, but it's being held down on a surface to stop it moving.

Then I thought of something.

— Dad, I said. Are you awake?

— Yes.

— Would you come to my room with me?

— What? Why?

— Well, I want to go to my room, but I guess that you'll worry about me, and so I'm saying come with me.

— Why do you want to go to your room now, though? he asked.

— You'll see, I said.

— What about the guards? said Dad.

— They won't care. It's the last night. And anyway, they still owe me.

— That's true, said Dad.

And sure enough, when we opened the door of the cinema room, it was Ahmed standing there. When we said we wanted to get something from my room, he just waved us past casually.

In my room, Dad sat down on the bed, while I went to the wardrobe. I took the Mulberry case on wheels and I unzipped it, took out my clothes.

I lifted out my violin case.

— Can we go outside? I asked Dad.

He held my eyes for a moment.

— OK, Amy-bear, he said.

Outside, the air was cool. Unconsciously, I led Dad to the rear deck, and I realised it was because I didn't want to be seeing Mohammed's invisible body, lying there on the front deck. Maybe, I thought, that's one meaning of the word *ghost*. Mohammed might not be there any more, his blood and brains might not be there, but if I went out on that wooden floor, I would see them, I knew it.

Up above, the sky was scattered with stars. I could see the Camel and the Pleiades, the dusty streak of the Milky Way.

The sunlounger, when I sat down, was damp. I felt the dew seeping into my trousers.

I took my violin out of its case, felt its wooden smoothness in my hands. It was warm, almost like it was alive, which I know is a super-stupid thing to think, but I thought it anyway. The bow almost jumped into my hand, wanting to be held, but I made myself put the bow down and apply some rosin to the strings, because the violin hadn't been played for a long time and I didn't want to hurt it.

Then, very gently, I laid the bow on the strings. There was sound waiting to come out – I could almost hear it – but I needed to move the bow if I wanted to release it. Did I want to do that?

277

I hesitated.

Then, slowly, I started to draw the bow. I hovered on the notes, listening to the tuning, adjusting the pegs. The warmth and the moisture at sea hadn't done the violin a lot of good, but it was still just about in tune once I got it right. Behind me, I heard Dad take a breath, but I didn't turn around.

I started to play, the music bright and clear, like spring water.

At first, I didn't know what I was playing, but then I realised: it was the *Chaconne*, Bach's *Chaconne*, the piece I was preparing for the Menuhin Competition, when Mom died, which I never got to play for her on stage. What was I thinking? Was I thinking that I was playing it for her? Because that would be an idiotic idea, of course.

Really, though, I was playing it for Farouz. I just hoped he was listening, and knew what I meant.

Anyway, I was still playing, and the sound was filling the deck, reaching out to Eyl beside us, to the stars. It was everywhere, surrounding me, in me, resonating in my ear canals, shivering along my skin. I let out a long, slow breath. It was like I'd been living with the screen turned to black and white, and now someone had switched the colour on.

Because I didn't just hear the music – I saw it. When you've played like I have, as long as I have, this is what happens – the notes that are in your head, in your memory, are there in front of you, just as present as the stars, superimposed on them. It's like you can see this whole architecture holding up the world, this skeleton, like you're looking at a building and can make out the beams, the stairways, the arches. So I was seeing the sunlounger, the life ring set into the side of the yacht, the moon sparkling on the sea, but also and at the same time I was seeing this:

And it was hanging in the air in front of me.

How did I live without this? I thought.

When I had finished, I put the violin back in its case.

— Beautiful, said Dad. Thank you.

He came over and gave me an awkward hug.

— Er, yeah, I said, realising that he thought I'd played for him.

— I've missed you, Amy-bear, he said.

That broke the magic. I pulled away.

— You're the one who's never around, I said.

A veil came down over his eyes.

— Uh-huh, he said. Come on. Back inside.

*

At dawn Ahmed and Farouz came and told us to get ready.

— Shower, said Ahmed. One time.

— One time? said Dad.

— One at a time, Farouz explained. So you're presentable, when you return to your people.

— Hostage One first, said Ahmed. Rest, stay here.

So we waited while Dad went and had a shower, then changed into new clothes that the pirates had brought for each of us. The stepmother followed, then Tony.

I went fourth. Ahmed pointed to the showers down the corridor, not the en suites, but the ones that were meant for the crew. I nodded and went in. There were two shower cubicles inside, and the door of one of them was slightly ajar. I frowned. Then the door opened, and Farouz stood there.

— Farouz! I said. Does Ahmed –

— Yes. I persuaded him. He is not happy.

I smiled.

— I didn't want to leave without saying goodbye, I said.

— No. I didn't want to, either, he said.

— I played for you last night. Did you hear?

— Yes, he said. I heard. Thank you.

He handed me a little piece of paper, folded.

— My email address, he said. When I go back to Galkayo . . . It will be complicated. Mohammed's family might be looking for me. But email me when you are home. I will try to reply.

— Should you go to Galkayo? I said. If it's dangerous?

— I have to. My brother.

A dull fear settled on me. I'd been thinking about myself,

about the risks, the exchange. I hadn't thought about Farouz being in danger when he left the yacht.

— Shower, he said. We can talk while you do. Otherwise you'll be too slow and your father will suspect.

He was right, I realised. As much as I wanted to look at his face, to memorise it – the mole on his right cheek, his long eyelashes – I went into the cubicle, undressed, turned on the water.

— I will come to England, he said, after, when –

— I'm sorry, I lied. I can't hear you.

I didn't want to deal with that. Farouz, in England? I didn't want to think about it in real, practical terms, didn't want to ruin the stupid impossible fantasy I had of him coming, of us having a life together; speaking about it might make it disappear, like a soap bubble going pop. To stop him talking about things that could never happen, I said:

— Tell me something. Tell me something about when you were young. Before the war.

— Which war? There are many wars.

— The one . . . when your parents died. Tell me something from before that.

This was probably the last time I was going to see him. I wanted something to take away with me, something that was just mine.

— All right, he said. I will tell you. But it is not a story about my parents. It is a story about Abdirashid.

He started to speak, and I closed my eyes as the water flowed over me.

*

281

Sometime soon after 6 a.m. we trooped out on to the deck, came out of the shadowed corridor into that total sunlight, blasting at us from all angles. It was early, the sun low, but the heat was already like a beating. It was already all around us, giving us no room for escape.

Farouz was out there, waiting. He caught my eye when I came out, then looked away. The navy destroyer had moved a little closer in the night, I saw – I guess to comply with the go plan. I could just make out tiny figures on its deck, watching us. Ahmed had his AK at the ready, his finger resting in the trigger guard. Everyone seemed nervous. Even Farouz was shifting from one foot to the other, tapping his thumb on his pistol. I guess, for them, this was when things could go really wrong.

I tried not to think about the logical consequence:

If things went wrong for them, it meant they would go wrong for us. And they were the ones with the guns.

Ahmed shepherded us with the barrel of his rifle, pointing us further down, to where the diving platform met the sea. We shuffled forward, giving him and Farouz the advantage of height. The sea was clapping against the deck: *clap, clap, clap.* The sun blared its heat, unchanging, like white noise. I don't know how long we stood there. After a certain time, Dad put his arm around me, and I smelled his sweat and thought about how far we had come from normal life, if my dad was smelling like that and not of Clinique.

Dad glanced at his watch. The pirates had never taken it because he had always been wearing it – which was unlucky for them, because it was a Patek, and probably worth nearly as much as the yacht.

— Six thirty already, he said. What the hell are they doing?

— Don't worry, said Tony, who was perched on the railing, scanning the sea. They're professionals. They'll stick to the plan.

There was no sign of any helicopter, though. We waited for ten minutes, twenty. That was when the navy dinghy appeared, scooting over the waves, getting closer and closer. This had nothing to do with the game plan – I didn't have a clue what they were playing at. It was like they were deliberately trying to antagonise the pirates, or maybe they just wanted a closer look. I don't know. All I knew was that the men on the dinghy were armed.

But you know how this played out – you have seen it already. Ahmed started to freak out and told the navy over VHF to back off, or he'd kill a hostage.

Even Dad lost it a bit.

— What the living fuck are they doing? he said to Tony.

— Relax, relax, said Tony, though there was sweat beading on his upper lip and his fingers were shaking. They're just testing. Testing, and getting a closer look.

— Shut up, said Ahmed reflexively.

And the dinghy kept coming.

That was when, with the VHF turned on so that the navy could hear, Ahmed told Farouz to point his gun at me, and kill me.

Farouz takes off the safety, and it makes that noise.

Click.

I close my eyes, and the sun is just as bright behind my eyelids, only it's red now, billowing, like clouds of blood in water. I listen to the waves, smell the salt of the sea.

I was scared before. I was. But it was, oh-this-is-frightening-but-kind-of-exciting-too. Now it's, OH-GOD-OH-GOD-I'M-GOING-TO-DIE-AND-THERE'S-NOTHING-I-CAN-DO-ABOUT-IT. Fear doesn't so much seize me as surround me, the way that a dark cloud breaks and the air all around is suddenly hail.

I'm actually going to die, right here and now. I'm thinking about how Farouz promised me that he wouldn't hurt me, that he would rather die himself, but I don't know if he will hold to that promise. I don't think he will. *I would rather die* is an easy thing to say, but it's a harder thing to do.

You might hope that I would have a more profound thought than that, but I don't. It's more a peculiar realisation – that this moment, the moment of my death, that has always seemed really abstract and far away, is actually NOW. I feel like that polo horse, waiting for the vet to come and give the injection.

Then I think, we'll be on the news for maybe a week. And then it'll be something else, some earthquake, some foot-baller having sex with a prostitute. And that will be it. In my head, I start to listen to Milstein's 1953 recording of the *Sonatas* and *Partitas*, trying to remember every note, every flourish.

Why have I not been playing my violin every day? I ask myself. Because, yes, there's a beauty in electronic music that's like echoes in space, but what Milstein told the world was that the violin has a voice, and it can sing. It's alive, that music; it's not just voices from the past, twisted and distorted over time. It's the sound of the human heart if you could hear what it wanted to say.

There's another soft metallic sound as Farouz starts to squeeze the trigger. My dad is suddenly shouting, my step-mother screaming – nothing comprehensible, just noise.

I take a deep breath . . .

And my dad stops shouting. I open my eyes and turn to see the navy dinghy retreating towards the destroyer. Ahmed is smiling.

— All OK, he says.

I stare at him. OK? Fucking OK? That's all he's going to say? I wonder if Farouz would have pulled the trigger, if he would have killed me. Or if he would have turned and shot Ahmed instead, like it would happen in a movie. Who knows? I'll never know, I realise.

— Sorry, Ahmed says. Sorry. Was just to make scare for navy. Not true.

Not true, I think. Not true.

— Jesus Christ, says my dad. I hope that was worth it for them, to get their closer look.

He hugs me tight and, for once, I don't mind.

— They know now that the pirates aren't messing around, says Tony.

— You would think, says the stepmother a little acidly, that they would have known that already.

My knees feel wobbly, like they're not sure they can keep me up any more.

Then, from the destroyer, comes a sort of pale, far-off whine, and we see the helicopter lift into the air. It banks and flies towards us, before stopping over the ocean to drop the money.

But Ahmed thumbs the VHF.

— No, he says, to the navy and the negotiator. No exchange.

— Sir, a voice comes back, this plan has been agreed by all parties. It can't –

— Quiet, says Ahmed.

He speaks quickly to Farouz, then throws him the VHF. Farouz takes over speaking.

— The plan was agreed, he says. But you were late. And the dinghy was not part of the plan. We now reject your plan.

— You won't get any more money, says the voice at the other end, a man of indeterminate age.

Farouz talks to Ahmed for a moment.

— OK, he says into the handset. But we will no longer let the hostages leave before we return to shore.

He takes his thumb off the VHF. Then he questions Ahmed, frowning, but Ahmed waves at him, insisting on something. Farouz nods reluctantly, presses the button again.

— We will take one of the hostages back to shore with us after we have the money, he says to the person on the other end. When we have safely reached the shore, they will return to you.

— Absolutely not, says the navy voice, crackling.

— It's OK, says Tony, coming closer. I'll go.

— No. Ahmed shakes his head. He points to me, Dad and the stepmother. One of them. One of owners.

— You're mad, says Tony.

— No. Ahmed looks offended. We want safe, that is all. He talks to Farouz for a while.

— As soon as we are on shore, says Farouz, the hostage will be put in a boat with a motor. They can then return to the yacht.

— Listen, all of you, says the navy. This is not acceptable. I repeat: this is not acceptable. No one is going to take the risk of –

Ahmed turns off the VHF. He points his gun at the three of us.

— Choose, he says. Choose one.

— This is crazy, says Dad. You can't really think one of us is going to go to the shore with you? To *Somalia*. I mean, what guarantee do we have that we'll come back safely?

— What guarantee do *we* have? says Farouz. That after we leave with the money, the navy won't come after us? They have dinghies, a helicopter, guns. This is our guarantee.

— I won't do it, says Dad. I won't risk my life like that. My daughter, my wife – they depend on me.

Farouz shrugs. He and Ahmed are still standing there, guns levelled at us. But for just a moment, Ahmed turns to look at the destroyer, and Farouz winks at me, to say he wouldn't have done it, I suppose, and for a split second I'm all happy because my – my what? my boyfriend? – didn't want to shoot me. I realise I'm being ridiculous. How do I know he wouldn't have done it? Just because he winked?

Winking afterwards is easy, so I don't meet his eye. I look down.

— You have the word of the navy, says Tony. The plan is in place. Let's stick to –

Ahmed points his gun at him, and Tony shuts up. The tension is like the sun – everywhere, pushing down on us. I can see sweat trickling down Farouz's temple. My dad's arm is stiff on my shoulders.

— Oh, screw it, says the stepmother. I'll do it.

I turn to her, surprised. Dad is staring at her, too.

— I'll do it, she repeats, to Ahmed this time. I'll go with you and the money. Just as long as we can get out of here.

— Are you insane? says Dad. Are you actually insane? If you think I'm going to let –

— You're my husband, says the stepmother. You're not my owner.

That makes Dad close his mouth for a moment, and I look into the stepmother's eyes.

— Why would you do that? I say to her. You could get killed.

— I don't think so. She holds my gaze. But if I do, you'll be safe.

— What? I say.

I didn't even think she liked me, but she's looking at me, and I can see something in her eyes that looks like affection. This is a weird moment. Suddenly I'm looking at her, and it seems to me now that her hardness is something thin and on the outside of her, like an eggshell.

Then she ices over again, and is just the stepmother.

— What? says Tony. No, this is not the plan. This is not the plan.

— The plan just changed, says the stepmother.

Suddenly, I feel really ashamed. It didn't even occur to me to volunteer, even to be with Farouz for a bit longer, and here's my stepmother, who's usually selfish and who complains about stuff, saying that she'll go with the pirates because she wants me to be *safe*.

— I forbid this! says Dad. I absolutely forbid it.

— The only way you can forbid it is if you go yourself, says the stepmother. She's looking right at him, challenging him.

Dad looks back for a minute, maybe. Then he drops his

eyes. He takes his arm away from me, and it feels like a good-bye, like a defeat.

— I can't go, he says. You know that. He glances at me as he says this.

Coward! I think, but the stepmother looks at him kindly, like she has only this moment worked something out.

— No, she says. Of course not. I understand.

— What? I say. He should go! He's the man.

The stepmother turns to me.

— Don't you get it? she says. He can't.

— He can, I say.

— No. You've already lost your mother.

— What? What's she got to do with anything?

— Think, Amy, says the stepmother. If something happens to your dad what happens to you?

I did think, and I got it. If something happened to him, then I would have no parents at all.

I stare at Dad.

— Is that true? I say.

He looks down.

— Is that true? I say again.

He doesn't answer.

Coward, I think again. But I don't even know if I mean it any more.

GO PLAN VERSION TWO

SUBMITTED BY JERRY CHRISTOPHER, NEGOTIATOR FOR GOLDBLATT BANK, ABOARD HMS ENDEAVOUR. *RATIFIED BY ALL PARTIES.*

1) At 3 p.m. Royal Navy ship HMS Endeavour *will give the GO signal on VHF channel 16.*

2) All passengers will report to the rear deck. HMS Endeavour *will confirm the presence of all passengers by long-range telescope. HMS* Endeavour *will give the exchange signal.*

3) Helicopter will leave HMS Endeavour *and fly to a point 200 metres to the east of the* Daisy May. *Helicopter will be weapons cold.*

4) Three Somalis will leave the Daisy May *aboard a dinghy, carrying a portable VHF unit also tuned to channel 16. They will navigate to a point below the helicopter.*

5) The helicopter will then drop bags containing three million US dollars in cash. The Somalis will recover the bags from the water and count to verify the full amount is present. They will then confirm by VHF to the Daisy May *that they are in possession of part one of the ransom.*

6) Mr James Fields, Miss Amy Fields and the crew will board a dinghy and repair to HMS Endeavour. *Once they are on board, HMS* Endeavour *will give the GO signal to the helicopter.*

7) The helicopter will drop the remaining two million US dollars. The Somalis will count and confirm to their colleagues that they are now in possession of the full ransom.

8) All the Somalis will leave the Daisy May *with Mrs Sarah Fields, who will accompany them to the shore. The Somalis below the helicopter will repair to the shore with the money.*

9) All Somalis, the money and Mrs Fields will reach the shore.

10) Mrs Fields will then get into a motor boat immediately and return to HMS Endeavour.

11) End of exchange.

Note: if any harm should come to Mrs Fields after delivery of the ransom, HMS Endeavour *will respond with EXTREME PREJUDICE.*

— Inshallah, you home soon, Ahmed says to me. Inshallah.

We are standing on the rear deck again, close to 3 p.m., waiting for the exchange signal.

— Inshallah? I ask.

— If Allah wills it, says Farouz.

Ahmed smiles at me.

— Don't smile, I say. You were going to shoot me last time.

— No! Ahmed shakes his head. Because Allah did not will it.

I look at him to try to work out if he is joking or not. But he is just smiling, his features unreadable.

I sigh, and turn away from him.

Again, the two of them are watching over us, guns at the ready. My stepmother – Sarah – and my dad are standing on opposite sides of the deck, watching each other, talking with their eyes. Felipe and Tony are just lounging on the wooden floor of the deck, as if they don't think this is even going to happen, as if they are just casual about it.

And again, the navy are keeping us waiting.

Then, finally, there is a crackle on the VHF that Ahmed is holding.

— We confirm visuals on the hostages, says a voice. We are go on the exchange. I repeat: we are go on the exchange.

Three pirates – and it hasn't escaped my notice that none of them is Ahmed or Farouz – pull away from the yacht, the outboard on their boat sputtering.

On the deck of the destroyer, a helicopter lofts into the air. It seems to hang there for a moment, then it swings towards us, a growing blackness in the sky, until it hovers over the sea between the *Daisy May* and the big navy ship. Soon the pirates' boat is underneath it, the sea around it flattened by the pressure of the helicopter's spinning blades. The sound of the helicopter is enormous in the stillness of the hot air, the whip-like *whoooom* of the rotor.

A shape drops from the helicopter and splashes down into the sea. A gym bag. And then another. One of the pirates leans over and hooks them out, pulling them into the boat. The helicopter hovers in place while the pirates open the bags.

A burst of static, and then Somali, comes over the VHF.

— OK, says Ahmed. OK. He turns to us. Three million, he says with a smile. Then he points to the yacht's own dinghy, which Tony put into the sea earlier. You can go.

And like that, the moment has come. I stare at the dinghy. I flick my eyes to Farouz and stare at him.

The dinghy.

Farouz.

The dinghy.

Farouz.

The dinghy is . . . freedom. Home. But what is at home? What if I want to stay, under this sun, with the sand and scrub of Eyl just over there?

I turn to look at the shore. I watch as a four-by-four bounces over the dunes and pulls up by the discarded boats on the beach. Someone gets out and leans on the door, binoculars to their eyes. The pirates' contact on shore, I guess.

I think, couldn't I stay? Could I just jump off the yacht and make for the shore?

I've been in the water, when I snorkelled. It's warm. I could jump in there and swim, get in that four-by-four, let them drive me away . . .

— Amy, Dad says, pushing me forward. Come on.

I stumble, then walk. Someone is making me go. That's good – someone is taking the choice away from me. And yes, I'm aware of the irony.

Dad pauses before getting into the dinghy.

— You don't have to do this, he says to the stepmother.

— Yes, I do, she says back.

I notice that the sun has brought out freckles on her face, dusted them across her nose. It makes her look pretty.

Dad sighs and hesitates, then walks over to her. He gives her a kiss on the cheek.

— Thank you, he says. I love you for this.

She smiles wanly.

— You didn't love me before?

— Yes, he says.

And me? you ask. What do I do? Well, I don't walk over to her, but I do smile. And if you knew me, you would know that was a huge deal.

She smiles back, big, showing her white teeth.

— If you come Somalia, you call me, says Ahmed, breaking the spell. Surreally, absurdly, he hands Dad a piece of paper with his phone number written on it. I help you, I show you around. You come Puntland – is very beautiful.

Dad is dumbfounded.

— Er, thank you, he says. I think.

— Yes, thank you, Ahmed, I say.

I kind of get it, actually. This wasn't personal for him. It was a job. We had lots of money and he didn't have much at all. He was just redistributing wealth, like Miss Walker talked about in our economics classes.

Events tumble into one another. We are on the deck, then, for a split second, we are straddling the sea, one foot up and one foot down, then we are in the dinghy. The stepmother is still on the yacht with the pirates. Cooler air from the sea rises around us, cocooning us. Tony is there, Damian, Felipe. There are life jackets, but we don't put them on; the idea seems preposterous. We have a VHF and Tony says into it that we are leaving the yacht, that we are all safe.

Wait, I think. Then I say it out loud:

— Wait. Wait.

— What is it, Amy-bear? Dad asks.

I get up and climb back on to the yacht, wobbling a little, almost falling. All the time Dad is asking me what is going on. I go over to the stepmother.

— You go with Dad, I say. I'll do it. I'll be the collateral.

— Don't be ridiculous, says the stepmother. You're a child. You can't.

— I can, I say. In fact, it's safer for me. I am looking at Farouz as I say this.

— What? Why?

— You wouldn't understand. Just, please, go. Get in the boat. I will join you soon.

— What's going on? Tony shouts from the boat. What's the hold-up?

— Amy wants to go with them instead, says the stepmother. She wants to swap with me.

— That's out of the question, says Dad.

I push the stepmother towards the boat.

— Please, I say. Please. It's easier this way.

Eventually, she sort of stumbles on to the dinghy, leaving the yacht behind. Dad is red in the face now, spittle coming from his mouth.

— YOU COME BACK HERE, AMY FIELDS, he shouts.

— No, I say.

I don't move.

Then Dad starts to get out of the boat, but Tony stops him, and there's this whole ridiculous situation going on, until Ahmed shoots his gun in the air. Immediately the VHF spits into life as someone asks if everything is OK.

— Is fine, Ahmed says back to them.

— What's the delay? they ask.

Ahmed turns to us.

— Come on! he says. Who is stay? Who is go?

I plant my feet, hard, on the ground.

— I'm staying, I say.

— AMY FIELDS, DON'T EVEN THINK –

— Dad, I say softly. Please. I'll be OK, I promise. Just let me do this.

He looks at me long and slow.

— Please, I say again.

At the same time the navy are asking over and over what the hold-up is.

— We don't have time for this, says Tony.

Dad looks at him in horror.

— Seriously, this is jeopardising the whole operation, Tony continues. Make a decision, quickly.

Troops are running over there on the destroyer. We can all see them.

— Go, says Ahmed. Go.

— Come on, says Damian. We can't force her to stay on the dinghy.

Dad glares at him, but he doesn't say anything.

And that seems to settle the matter, because finally Tony starts the outboard and the little boat pulls away, leaving the yacht behind.

With me on it.

Alone with the pirates.

As we stand there on the deck watching the dinghy, with Dad and the stepmother and Damian and Tony and Felipe on it, as it pulls away from us and towards the navy vessel, a signal comes through on Ahmed's VHF. The three pirates have evidently received the rest of the ransom, because Ahmed nods and then indicates for us to get into the remaining two boats. We do; the swell of the sea takes us, cradles us. The motor starts up, and we accelerate over the waves; the sea-water sprays cool on my face.

Suddenly, the yacht, which had been our whole world, seems small as I look at it from the outside, and it's getting smaller. Suddenly, I can't believe we lived in that little thing for so long, and also, from the growing distance, it seems like it wasn't so long.

I'm going to Somalia, I think dumbly.

When we reach the beach, Ahmed points to my trainers.

— Take off, he says. Sand will eat them.

I pull the shoes off and jump barefoot out of the boat into the shallow water. I'm amazed by how hot it is, warmed by the sun. I walk up on to the sand, and it burns, making me yelp and cling to Farouz's arm. That's when I see Ahmed frown at me.

Further up, we come to where the four-by-four has stopped. Ahmed meets up with the three pirates from the helicopter rendezvous, who have come up on the beach in their wooden boat. He takes one black sports bag from them. He hands it through the window of the jeep to someone sitting in there – Amir, I guess, the sponsor. Then the wheels of the jeep bite the sand, flinging it into the air, as it guns away, reversing in a circle before racing off towards the dunes.

After that, two pickups approach, much more battered than the four-by-four. I figure these are the pirates' own vehicles. The men hoist up the bags and load one into each of the trucks.

Further inland, above the dunes, I can see the shacks on the lowlands of Eyl. I can just make out figures, watching from a distance, and the awnings of what might be little cafés, with plastic furniture in the dust outside them. There are dogs, too, milling around. There are no trees, except higher up in the mountains, which stretch up from the beach, just scrub.

I am in Somalia, I think. I am standing on Somalia.

A pirate gets into one of the pickup trucks and leaves the driver's door open. He beckons for the others.

Ahmed points to one of the boats that we just came in on.

— I show you motor, he says. Then you go.

— That's not necessary, I reply.

— What?

— I'm staying, I say. Here. With Farouz.

Farouz hears his name and looks over. When he sees the expression on Ahmed's face, he walks up to us.

— What's wrong? he says.

Ahmed rattles Somali at him.

Farouz clearly doesn't know whether to smile or furrow his brow. He kind of does both.

— It's not possible, he says.

— Of course it is, I say. I'm just not going back.

— Navy! Ahmed says, pointing to the destroyer. Navy!

— The navy will come after us, Farouz says to me.

— How? They're on a ship.

— They have a helicopter.

— They can't, can they? I say. This is Somali territory. They can't just fly over it without permission.

I have no idea if this is true, but it sounds true.

Farouz stops short. He turns to Ahmed, says something.

Ahmed throws up his hands, barks out a reply.

— If you stay here in Somalia, we will be . . . What is the word? When no one will speak to you?

— Pariahs?

— Is that the word? Yes, OK. We will be . . . pariahs. The other coast guard will hate us even more. Not harming hostages, that is how we survive. If we take you, we break the code. Others will suffer. And then the navy will come after us, when they do get permission, which they will, and –

— You're not harming me, I say. I'm coming of my own free will. I can tell them that. I can write to the news in England and tell them.

— The other pir–. I mean, the other coast guard will not care. They will say we are traitors to our own kind.

— Who cares? I say. You have millions of dollars now. You can do what you want.

That really makes him think. He obviously translates to Ahmed, because then Ahmed is nodding reluctantly. He can see my point.

304

We get in one of the pickups. The engine starts, then it pulls forward and accelerates. After so long on the yacht, I have forgotten motion like this – the sudden speed of it; the way it feels like it is the slingshot, but also the thing that it is firing.

After the pickups bounce up the dunes, we stop in Eyl for a while. The pirates are obviously nervous, more nervous than me, and keep hold of their guns the whole time. I guess this would be a good time for someone to swoop in and take the money, and the pirates are freaked out by the idea. I assume this is why they have two trucks, with the money divided between them – if one of the trucks gets hit, at least not all the money will be taken.

I don't know why I'm thinking so calmly about this idea. If one of the trucks gets hit, if my truck gets hit, I will be dead.

The pirates make a stop here because they have to pay some little storekeepers – I assume these are the people who supplied the cigarettes, the water, that kind of thing. Ahmed hands out bundles of money like it's Christmas. Mangy dogs follow us, as we go from shop to shop, Farouz's knuckles white on his pistol. Old men chew khat outside cafés, sitting in the shade. A blind beggar sits on his haunches, hands out.

Finally, we get back in the pickups and hit the dry road – well, it's more of a track, really. Some of the tension disappears. We head up into the hills, spewing brown dust behind us. There are white peaks of mountains in front and we drive towards them, snaking up into the highlands.

My dad is going to go ape-shit, I think. This is going to hurt

306

him so much, I know that. But somehow I can't bring myself to care. The truth is that Mom left me, but then Dad left me, too. And that's hard to forgive because my dad is still here. I mean, his body is like a shell being carted around by some impostor person, a hermit crab who took over when Mom died.

He has only himself to blame for this. That's what I tell myself, as the jeep cruises deeper into Somalia.

As we drive, as we cross the mountains on a hair-raising pass, the track becomes more and more like a road, until, when we come down the other side on to a plateau, it is practically a highway. Now we start to see other people, the occasional beat-up car, a man using a donkey to pull a cart. The desert stretches all around us, hazy with heat. I see a clump of trees in the distance, that I take to be an oasis.

I am in Somalia, I think again. In the desert. Driving to a place I only heard of the other day.

Galkayo, when we come to it from the desert hours later, is exactly as I imagined it. Low houses, most of them daubed with white to keep out the heat of the sun, with flat roofs, the occasional stork nesting up there. What does surprise me, though, is that in one district, as we drive through, there are the kinds of houses you'd see in California: columns by the front door, two or three floors high. One has a new Chevrolet parked outside, gleaming black; another, a silver Mercedes.

— Pirates? I ask Farouz.

— Yes, he says.

He is holding my hand. He has been holding my hand this

whole time we've been sitting in the back of the truck. There is no air conditioning, so I have the window wide open, the wind whipping in, making my hair fly.

— We will buy one like this, he says. Or we will leave. It is up to you.

We pass a swimming pool, blue as jewellery in the surrounding brownness of sand and dust.

— Let's buy one, I say. With a pool. We'll be like Darod and Dombiro in their oasis.

— OK, says Farouz.

Past the rich pirates' houses, we come to the single-storey dwellings. Here there are lots more people in the street, sitting on the ground for the most part. There are little shops, open to the air, with signs in a language I can't read. It's hard to tell what they sell, these shops. There are women carrying babies strapped to their bodies with cloth, and we pass several men with missing legs.

— The war, says Farouz.

— Which war? I say, because I know from talking to him that there have been several.

— Oh, I don't know, he says. There is always a war.

After maybe half an hour, Ahmed stops outside a particular shop – at least, I presume it's because of the shop that he has stopped, because he gets out of the pickup truck, goes inside, then reappears and jerks his head for us to follow. We get out, Farouz carrying one of the bags of money, one of the other pirates – Asiz, I think – carrying the bag from the other truck. Again, their fingers are on the triggers of their guns. I'm pretty overwhelmed at this point – by the heat, by the strong smells, by the animals bleating and chattering.

A couple of people watch us, watch me – the white girl with the Somali men – go in, and then we're in the cool darkness of the shop, surrounded by tins and packets of strange-looking food. I recognise the brand of pasta that the pirates were always eating, boiled for hours in their big pot at the front of the yacht.

A fat man emerges from the gloom and hugs Ahmed, then Farouz. He beckons us further into the shop, where we come out of shadows into a brightly lit room, like a living room, with a rug on the floor and a bare bulb hanging from the ceiling. The fat man withdraws respectfully.

Ahmed arranges the bags on a little table that stands on the rug. He starts to pull out bundles of money, consulting a sheet of paper that he has taken from his pocket. Pirates enter, go up to him, get their money and retreat out of the shop, nodding their gratitude. Some of them narrow their eyes when they see me – surprised to see me, I guess. A couple shoot questioning looks at Ahmed, but he waves them away.

Finally, there is only me and Farouz. Ahmed hands Farouz one the bags, with the remaining money in it. It's like a ransom in a movie, these big thick wads of cash.

It is a ransom, I remind myself. I'm basically stealing my dad's money. This makes me giggle, and Ahmed glares at me. He says something to Farouz.

— Ahmed says we must be careful, Farouz says. Mohammed's family will be looking for retribution.

This is a sobering thought, so I stop giggling. Farouz hefts the bag on to his shoulder, then hugs Ahmed – not one of those quick man-hugs that people in England do, but a proper embrace, affectionate. Then, to my surprise, Ahmed comes up to me, arms spread wide, and hugs me, too.

— Good luck, he says. You will need.

— Thank you, I say. Really.

And I mean it.

After that, we leave the shop. Farouz tucks his pistol inside his trousers, but I can still see it there. He leads me down some narrow, snaking streets, until we come to a shack with a corrugated iron door.

— This is your house?

— For now, yes.

We go inside. Farouz moves a chair from the corner of the room, a deep, soft one, from which stuffing is spilling. Under it is a board, which he moves to reveal a deep hole in the ground. Taking a couple of money bundles from the bag, he puts them in his pocket, then drops the bag into the hole.

— What do we do now? I ask him.

He kisses me.

— We free my brother. Then we do whatever we like, he says.

— That sounds good.

He winks.

— Maybe we will buy you a violin. And I will have my oud. We could play together.

— I'd like that, I say.

We leave the hut and follow the crazy, busy streets to the jail. As we leave Farouz's street, a monkey sitting on a rooftop screams at us.

I'm shocked when I see the prison. I mean, I was picturing a proper structure, with big walls, and men in towers with guns. This is just an open-fronted building, like a shop, with bars across the front and men inside, right there, visible from the street. Next door is a stall where a man is selling chickens; he takes them from the ceiling, where he has tied them upside down, by the feet. They are alive, their heads shaking, and when he grabs one, it kind of squeals and clucks. Then he puts it on a filthy board, running with blood, chops off its head and throws it straight into a bucket. The chicken bangs around in there, frantic, beating out a rhythm. When it stops, the man takes it out and hands it to whoever has bought it.

— Oh god, that's gross, I say.

Farouz raises his eyebrows.

— Before, I could never afford one of those, he says.

I notice then that the people queuing for the chickens don't look as ill, as dirty, as malnourished as a lot of the people I have seen here in Galkayo. I feel guilty then. So I turn back to the jail and pay more attention to that.

Farouz is walking the length of the bars, obviously looking for his brother. It's long, the prison – like, almost a city block in length. And the men are just displayed there. I can't get over it; it's more like a zoo than a prison.

Then Farouz stops, and there is a man in front of him, his hands on the bars, who looks a little like him, but older, more

hurt. He looks like Farouz would look if you took him somewhere, rubbed dirt on him, beat him up, made him drink a
bottle of vodka and threw him in a ditch.

— Abdirashid, he says.

— Farouz.

Then they speak to each other in Somali, their voices fitting
into each other's neatly, like matching jigsaw puzzle pieces,
finding the quiet moments in the other's speech. The effect is
compelling, like running water.

They speak for what seems quite a long time, then Farouz
spots a guard who has entered at the back of the giant open
cell that is the prison. He beckons him over.

The guard strolls to where we're standing, pushing
Abdirashid out of the way with a stick. He glowers at Farouz.
He is as big as an ox, with a mean expression. Farouz says
something to him, and the man obviously doesn't like it
because he scowls even deeper. Then Farouz takes one of the
wads of cash out of his pocket and hands it to the guard
through the bars. Just like that, casual as you please.

Smoothly, like a magician, the man slides it into his pocket.
Then he nods. He says something to me, laughs.

— What did he say? I ask.

— He said you brought me luck, says Farouz. He didn't
think I would get the money.

— So is he going to let your brother go? I ask.

Farouz puts a hand through the bars and squeezes his
brother's hand. His brother smiles, but there are tears in his
eyes, too.

— Yes, says Farouz. Yes, he is.

I look at him, then I look at his brother, so like him in his features, and I look back at Farouz again.

— Good, I say. I'm happy for you.

And I am. I'm so happy I could burst, like something sparkling, like a soap bubble on a sunny day, iridescent with petrol sheen, floating in the air, just before it pops into soft sound and spray.

No, that is not what happens.

But I imagine it afterwards.

I imagine it so many times, until it's a scene in my head, incredibly vivid.

A film.

That I can watch whenever I like.

This is the part that is true.

I am on the dinghy, leaving the yacht, and I do think, wait, and then I do say it.

— Wait. Wait, I say.

— What is it, Amy-bear? Dad asks.

And I do get out of the dinghy, and I do go to the step-mother and say:

— You go with Dad. I'll do it. I'll be the collateral.

— Don't be ridiculous, says the stepmother. You're a child. You can't.

— I can, I say. In fact, it's safer for me.

— What? Why?

— You wouldn't understand. Just, please, go. Get in the boat. I will join you soon.

All of this, too. All of this happens like I said.

— What's going on? Tony shouts from the boat. What's the hold-up?

— Amy wants to go with them instead, says the stepmother. She wants to swap with me.

— That's out of the question, says Dad.

I push the stepmother towards the boat.

— Please, I say. Please. It's easier this way.

And that . . .

That's where it stops going the way I said. That's the only part of what I've just told you that's true.

Dad doesn't just have a go at me and then leave it. Dad gets off the dinghy, comes up on to the deck and he shouts:

— YOU'RE COMING WITH ME, AMY FIELDS.

Then he puts his hands on my arms and he lifts me bodily into the air and hauls me over to the dinghy. He throws me in, and I land on the inflated rubber of the boat, but even so it's hard enough to knock the air out of my lungs. I lie there, staring up at Dad as he jumps into the boat beside me and says to Tony:

— Start the engine right now.

I am paralysed. I am incapable of movement.

Farouz is looking down at me, and I'm looking back at him, shock keeping my mouth shut when I should be protesting, should be doing something to overpower my dad, to get off the dinghy. I should be taking the stepmother's place and going with them, but instead I'm running away with my dad, and Tony and Damian and Felipe. I can't move, but it still feels like I'm running away.

Tony starts the engine and, like a reverse death scene, it coughs into life. He has a hand on the hull of the *Daisy May*, steadying us in the swell.

This is the moment, I think. This is the moment to say something to Farouz. But I don't, even though I can breathe again now, even though I could speak if I wanted to. I don't say anything.

The VHF sparks up.

— This is HMS *Endeavour*, come in. Is there a problem?

— No problem, Tony says into it. We're coming.

Ahmed raises a hand in a salute.

— Goodbye, he says.

— Goodbye, says Dad, automatically polite, so British that way.

I don't say anything, still.

I keep thinking there'll be more time. But here's a lesson I hope you don't ever have to learn: sometimes, there just isn't any more time.

Without any fanfare, Tony lets go of the hull, turns the throttle on the outboard and its death rattle, or life rattle or whatever, opens up into a full-throated roar as we ease off from the yacht.

Only then do I look up properly and see Farouz.

In full view of Ahmed, of the other guard on the deck, of the men on the destroyer, who must be watching everything, Farouz turns to face me full on, then he lifts his hand and he starts waving, waving, waving at me, not stopping, as I draw away, as the sea fills the gap between us. For one crazy moment I want to step out of the boat, to run across the waves to him – on some level in my mind I know I would have to swim, but I picture it as walking, walking on the water – and throw my arms around him.

But I don't, of course. I stay in the boat.

Then, just when he is shrinking to where I can't see his features any more, he puts his hand to his chest, covering his heart, and then he points it at me, hands me his heart, from all that distance away.

A strong arm helps me up on to the deck of HMS *Endeavour*. My overriding impression is of grey metal paint. There is a whole row of men and women in uniform, lined up on the deck, and when they see us they start clapping. The women are wearing white shirts and black ties, neat little caps. The men are wearing those sailor shirt things with the big lapels; it's like something out of the past.

I feel myself blush, my eyes sliding around, trying to find somewhere to look. We haven't done anything, I want to say. They didn't hurt us, not intentionally, anyway. They didn't treat us badly.

But I don't say anything, because they all look so proud that we're here, these people, and most of them not much older than me.

A man in a linen suit, not navy, steps forward to shake Dad's hand.

— Jerry, he says. Goldblatt Bank. I'm the negotiator whose voice you've been hearing. This here is Captain Campbell.

Captain Campbell is wearing his hat, his epaulettes, everything. He shakes Dad's hand, too.

— I apologise for the situation with the dinghy, he said. It's protocol to rattle the sabre a bit, see how the enemy reacts. But, still, I'm sorry.

Dad holds his eyes for a bit, but then he nods.

— That's OK, he says.

No, it's not, I think, but no one is listening to my thoughts.

— You've all been so brave, the captain says in a soft Scottish accent. So brave. He turns to Tony. And you're the one who was shot? Incredible.

— Just a flesh wound, says Tony.

— Well, says the captain. It's not entirely over yet, of course. But we have prepared cabins for you all. Showers. And a phone line to whoever you want to call.

Who do I want to call? I think. Esme? The idea is like calling an alien or a dolphin, some creature that could never understand. There's a pain in my chest, and I wonder if it's actually my heart breaking, if that's actually a thing that happens. It's an hour or so from sunset now, and already the stars are out, pale in the deepening sky.

I don't see the Plough.

I see the Camel.

And I see its missing tail.

Captain Campbell jerks his head at one of the crew, and then people move forward to hand us binoculars.

— We thought you would want to keep an eye on Mrs Fields, he says. Of course, we've got our eye on her, too. And our helicopter. We never would have agreed to this if we couldn't guarantee her safety.

— You had to agree to it, I'm a bit surprised to hear myself say.

— I'm sorry?

— You didn't exactly have a choice, did you? I say.

I don't know why I challenge him. I guess it makes me angry, this guy with his curly red hair poking out from under his hat – not that the colour of his hair is the problem – acting like he's all in control of this situation when he's not. It's the pirates who are in control, and they always have been.

— It's been a tense three weeks, says Dad. Please excuse her.

— Of course, says Captain Campbell. Of course. There's nothing to excuse.

I lift the binoculars to my eyes and watch as the helicopter drops the second batch of money. Again, the pirates hook it into the boat, count it. We hear Somali over the VHF that Tony is holding, and over Jerry's, too. Then, long moments later, we see the little boat leave the *Daisy May*, with Ahmed and the other pirates and the stepmother . . .

and Farouz . . .

and Farouz . . .

and Farouz aboard it. I look at those washed-out stars in the sky and I see his eyes. I smell the sea and I smell his skin.

Through the binoculars, I can see the boat quite well. I can see my stepmother hunched between Ahmed and Farouz, as the waves jog the hull. I can see as she gets smaller, heading for the coast. By the time they get there, the people I see get off on to the sand are just silhouettes, stick figures, but I think I can tell which one is the step-mother because she's taller. It's the Western food, Western standards of hygiene.

Oh god, I think. Oh god, Farouz. He's going back to that place, where his parents were killed, where his brother was . . . where bad things happened to his brother. Where Ahmed is grateful to take even some codeine and paracetamol to give to his kids.

But at least he'll free his brother, I think. Then maybe they can get out of there, get to Egypt. Maybe even . . . No, I can't let myself think it . . . Maybe even make it to England one day. To London.

Maybe even.

Some kind of discussion seems to be taking place on the beach between the stick figures.

— What's happening? asks Dad. What's going on? Why isn't she coming back?

— Airborne One, sitrep, says Captain Campbell, taking a VHF from his waist.

— This is Airborne One. Situation is, one of the pirates appears to be struggling with the hostage, sir –

Noise erupts around us.

— Er, no, scratch that, sir. Pirate is hugging her. Repeat: pirate is hugging her. Over.

Farouz, I think. I smile.

— Repeat that, Airborne One, says the captain. He sounds confused.

— Pirate was hugging the hostage, says the helicopter pilot. She is walking to the boat now . . . getting in . . . She's OK, sir. She's on her way. Wait.

A collective intake of breath.

— One of the pirates is . . . He's waving, sir. He's waving at her. Over.

— OK, Airborne One, says the captain, raising his eyebrows. Over and out.

I hug myself. I hug myself tight. Dad puts his arm around me, probably thinking that I am worried about the step-mother, which makes me feel a bit guilty – not a lot, but a bit.

Then we watch as the dot that is the stepmother's boat becomes a smudge, and then the smudge becomes a boat, miniature, and gradually gets bigger. I say *we* watch. I'm not watching, actually. Instead I'm watching Farouz, or the stick figure that I think is him.

The four-by-four that was already on the beach drives up to the pirates. Then, from the other end of the beach, two pick-up trucks arrive. They pull right up to the men who are standing just by the sea. I can make out the shapes of the money bags at their feet. The pirates hand one of the bags to someone in the four-by-four, through the window. The four-by-four reverses, spraying sand, and guns away. The sponsor, I think, Amir, getting his share.

After that, the pirates start to load the rest of the money into a truck. Farouz is with them, I think over and over, like an incantation in my head. Farouz is one of them. I strain to see if I can distinguish his shape, his profile, but I can't. It's too far and there's a heat haze, making all of them shimmer.

All of them shimmering now, not just him.

As they climb into the pickup trucks, I hear Captain Campbell beside me say four words in a calm voice, and instantly I know, instantly icicles are in my spine, pressing.

— Switch to channel 71, he says.

I turn to him. I'm moving slowly, like the air is not air any more, but glue. I have a cold, foreboding feeling, standing there on the hot deck. It's like when you're swimming in the sea and you cross some current, or the mouth of some invisible freshwater stream, and suddenly the warm seawater mingles with something that chills your skin.

He lifts his VHF to his mouth and says:

— This is Captain Campbell on channel 71. This is Captain Campbell. Go, go, go.

No, I think. No, please. Not channel 71.

I mean, it's not significant that it's channel 71. It could have been any channel. But I still know what it means. I know because it's a channel that is not 16, and 16 is the channel the pirates are using, the channel the pirates are monitoring. It could have been any channel, literally any channel between 1 and 100, and as long as it wasn't channel 16, that same ice would have put its fingers in my back and clawed me.

But somehow, already, I know that it will mean something to me. It will mean something to me for ever, whenever I'm on a flight with 71 in the name, whenever I dial 7 then 1 on my cell phone, just because it happens to be part of someone's number, whenever I grab a ticket at the baker's or the supermarket or whatever stupid irrelevant place back in the world called home, and the number comes up: 71.

Because the captain's voice is saying again:

— Airborne One, go, go, go.

And then the helicopter, which had been heading back to the destroyer, turns, hangs sideways in the air for a moment – the noise like a colossal heartbeat, the downrush of air forcing us into a crouch – and then it is moving towards the shore. The way the helicopter flies is fast, but it's slow, too, because I can feel what's happening; I heard it in that word, *go*, repeated three times, and I want it to stop.

It doesn't stop.

The helicopter is over the sand now, the pickup trucks rolling towards the dunes, as if they can see, as if they're animals with the shadow of a hawk over them. For an idiotic moment I think they might get away.

I see the muzzle-glare before I hear the helicopter's big gun firing. Again the word *lightning* flashes in my head, because it's the same, isn't it? The thunder doesn't reach you till after the release, till after the heavens strike down on the earth, which means that you always see the destruction before you hear it.

The bullets come out of the helicopter like streaks of yellow fire in the air, like those trails you see when you swish a sparkler in front of your eyes, smashing into one of the pickup trucks, which is driving away but, oh, so, so not quick enough. It is the truck Farouz got into, I know it – I saw his shape, his shoulders, before he slid into the back seat.

— The money, you fucking idiots! says Jerry, the negotiator. The money!

But no one is listening to him.

Flame billows out of the truck and it spins up into the air, black struts and side panels in a fireball, an X-ray, before crashing back down on the sand and stopping.

Then, and only then, I hear it. An explosion that seems to rock the destroyer on the sea, even though there is no swell, even at this distance.

Then the other truck is hit: it careers, tyres blown, then somersaults, rolls.

I feel Dad's arm fall away from my shoulder. I wonder if it is the last thing I will ever feel. There, on the shore, maybe, like, half a mile away, the pickup truck is going up in smoke, and I know that expression is a cliché – my English teacher, Mrs Arkwright, would mark me down for using it – but that is what's happening. The truck, Farouz, the money, it's all just pouring itself into the air, dissolving into this thick black smoke that is writhing and curling in the cruel hot empty white air over Somalia.

I remember Farouz, sucking in smoke, seeming to draw the stars from the sky and into his lungs, and think, now he's smoke himself, he's rising back up into the air.

It was a pickup truck, it was Farouz, it was money. Now it is just smoke and now –

Oh god, now I can smell it, lifted on the wind as a dark bird: a petrol smell, explosive, like when Mohammed was shot right over me. I guess you see the end, then you hear it, then the reek of it hits you.

Dad is saying something.

I don't listen. I can hardly see anything. I thought the world had changed its contours and its colours when Farouz came

I looked up through shimmering water at the disc of the sun above, watching it tremble and glow.

I was holding my breath, and I could hear the echoing hiss of the pool in my ears. The voices of my parents came to me from far away, from the other side of a barrier.

We were staying at our beach house on North Fork. Dad was up for the weekend, which I remember as being rare. I was maybe six or seven. I had chickenpox, and so I spent most of my time in the pool behind our house, swimming. It was when I was swimming that the itching went away, at least for a little while. Dad, that weekend, spent most of his time at the barbecue – that's how I picture him, anyway, hunched over the grill, the meat flaming and spitting. Fish, too, that he bought direct from the fishermen's market at Southold.

I was in the shallow end of the pool. I wasn't swimming, but I didn't want to get out, either, so I was messing around in the water. Then I discovered something amazing. I discovered that if I went under, held my breath, opened my eyes and turned to the sky, I could see the blueness and the fluffy clouds above through the lens of the water, making everything shimmer and dance. It was incredible – the glare of the sun on the water, the sparkle, the way the whole sky trembled and pulsed.

So I rolled on to my back, held my breath and deadened my limbs, so that I could float with my face just under the water, looking up. I could hold my breath quite a long time. It meant I could lie there for ages before I had to break the spell, and the surface.

The next thing I knew, there was something like iron wrapping itself around my arm, and I was jerked out of the water, thrown to the hard tiles, flopping like a fish. I screamed as my mom bent her head down, her fingers reaching for my mouth.

— Mom! I shouted.

— Oh, Amy, you –

And then she slapped me. It was the first and the only time that she ever hit me. I couldn't believe it. I lay there, on the damp hot tiles that surrounded the pool, staring up at her. She was wearing a sundress, blue with yellow flowers, and the dress was soaked, I saw now. Her eyes were big and terrified and terrifying, her face streaked with tears.

— What did I – I started.

— I thought you were *dead*, she shrieked. I had never heard anyone sound like this before; her voice was like an animal's, nothing human in it at all. Behind her, I saw Dad running up, late, as always. I thought you *drowned*, she shrieked.

— Oh, I said.

It was all I could think to say. And even then, even so young, I could see how stupid I'd been, how she had thought what she thought. A terrible shame opened its petals inside me, a dark, night flower, that has never really gone away since.

I did that, I thought. I made her cry. I did that.

Then she picked me up and hugged me. It hurt my chicken-pox, but I didn't say anything. I just let her hold me as she sobbed.

— Oh my Amy, she said, oh my Amy, over and over again,

like it was a prayer, like it was the thing that was keeping me alive.

I was just looking at the sky. I wanted to say to her, I didn't think. I didn't mean to scare you.

Later, as I was growing up, I always remembered that time, because of the searing horror I felt whenever I thought of it, that look on my mom's face that I never wanted to see again. This feeling of mine, it's called shame. There was embarrassment, too – something about the whole memory that made me shrivel up to think about it, the same way you might if you caught your parents having sex. I guess because I caught a glimpse of something private. I saw something I wasn't meant to see. I saw just how much my mother loved me, and it scared me senseless.

Is that what it would be like for me? I asked myself a thousand times. Is that how much I'll love my kids, how much it would hurt me if anything happened to one of them? It doesn't seem worth it, that kind of fear.

Mostly, though, it was after she killed herself that I thought about that summer and the time Mom pulled me out of the pool, wet and spluttering.

I thought:

If it hurt you so much, the idea that I had drowned, then why did you leave me? Why did you leave me on my own?

When I come to, there is commotion all around me on the deck of HMS *Endeavour*. Someone pulls me up into a sitting position, my back against the wall. I can see the sea and the sky, merging into one another. In my mind's eye I am still seeing Farouz, dying, the smoke of the pickup truck.

My father is saying something to me, and then he turns because there is some kind of activity over to his left. I crane my head. It is the stepmother, being helped up from the ladder. She smiles at me, one of those smiles that is sad and concerned at the same time. Her clothes are wet at the hems with seawater, from going on to the beach and back.

I'm still impressed at how brave she was, but she doesn't know that everything is over anyway, because Farouz is dead.

— What's wrong? she asks. What happened to Amy?

— We don't know, says Dad.

— Heatstroke, says Captain Campbell. Trauma. We have counsellors on board, and medicine, too. She'll be OK. We should just get her inside, get some Coke and some food into her. Then the doctors can –

— No, I say. No, I want to stay here.

— Amy, listen to the captain, says Dad. Go and –

— Let her be, says the stepmother.

Dad closes his mouth, surprised.

I ignore them both. I can see the beach from where I am. I can see the pickup, still burning.

But wait.

I can see something else, too. I can see that the helicopter has landed, and there are soldiers there. Some of them have

336

formed a kind of cordon, their guns pointed outwards, while others are dragging . . .

— Binoculars, I say.

— Amy, we –

— Binoculars!

Someone hands a pair to me. I hold them up to my face, twiddle the dial until the scene jumps into focus. The less burned pickup truck is there in front of my eyes – there is a man face down on its hood, his hands cuffed behind his back.

And the reason I called for the binoculars: there are other men being secured, too, being pushed towards the helicopter – and it looks from the direction of the movement like they're being dragged from where the pickup was burning. Again, though, the men are only silhouettes, all shimmering, indistinguishable from each other.

What if . . .

Hands tug at my arm, but I ignore them. I keep my eyes locked on the helicopter, as the captured Somali men are bundled into it. Then, as the armed men holding the cordon back up, the rotor starts up. The last men jump in, and it lifts into the air. There is a pop sound – *pop, pop, pop* – and I realise that someone is shooting at it, but the helicopter doesn't respond, it just flies back towards the ship.

What if . . .

I know where the helipad is, I saw it from the *Daisy May*. I jump up, dropping the binoculars, and start running. There is shouting from behind me. A sailor opens a door in front of me, and I veer around it, catching a glimpse of his startled face, my feet ringing on the metal of the deck. I pass doors and corridors, even an enormous gun, pointing out to sea.

The blue-black of metal walls reels past, giddily. That everywhere-sun is still out, printing my shadow on to the wall, on to the floor, as I run. Above me the antennae and dishes poke up into the sky.

— Amy, stop! my dad shouts from behind me.

I do not stop. I keep going until I get to the rear deck. There is a yellow cross on a hexagonal pad. The helicopter is descending on to it, vertical, like a giant bird. A guy is standing on the deck, with goggles and earphones on, waving two yellow sticks. I move forward, the air from its blades throwing my hair behind me like a stream of dark water, my eyes half-closed against the blast. It is warm on my skin, that air, like standing in front of an enormous hairdryer.

The helicopter door opens and the first of the soldiers – do you call them soldiers when they're on a ship? – jumps out. He ducks as he walks, hunched over, towards us. More follow him.

And then the pirates.

I see beards, I see headscarves. I see crazy clothing, Armani mixed with rags. The rotor begins to power down, but its down-blast is still powerful, stretching the faces of the men who get off, making them strange yet familiar, like sea creatures brought up from the ocean floor to lower pressure.

The first I recognise is Asiz, looking very small as he cowers under the force of the blasted air, even as the motor whines in diminuendo. He is only moving forward because there is a man poking a gun in his back. Another pirate I recognise – but whose name I don't know – follows, his hands restrained, all the pride and fight gone out of him. I notice that Asiz's clothes are burned, his hair singed.

Did he jump out of the pickup? I think. Did he get out before it blew up?

I don't see Ahmed. And I don't see . . .

No.

Suddenly, it seems there's a boulder on my chest, crushing it, stopping me from breathing.

I see Ahmed.

Hands close around my arms, and I am dragged backward, as he jumps from the helicopter.

He lands gracefully on the deck – as gracefully as is possible, with his hands tied behind his back. A uniformed guy is behind him, assault rifle in his hand, but Ahmed doesn't bend over like Asiz; he walks tall, his hair whipping in the down-draught, which disappears anyway as he steps off the big yellow X of the helipad and on to the main deck, the engine of the helicopter finally falling silent.

Dad turns me towards him, cupping his hand under my chin, worry in his eyes. I wrench my head away.

Ahmed. And that means, if Ahmed is alive . . .

If Ahmed is alive, then . . .

There is blood running from Ahmed's nose. And one side of his face is . . . what? Bubbling, and melting. Oh god, he's been burned, I realise. He was in the truck and he must have got out just in time, but not quick enough to stop the flames. His

T-shirt is charred, the shoulder of the fabric gone on one side, the flesh below black and awful.

Still, he smiles at me, as I stand there with my father holding me back.

I watch the helicopter, but no more men are coming out. Is that it? I think. What about Farouz?

Hope and fear fight, like snarling animals, in my chest. What if he got away?

Out of the corner of my eye, I see the captain step forward to take something from one of the soldiers. He brings it back and sets it on the ground, near where Dad is holding me. The negotiator, Jerry, is here, too, I realise. The captain pokes the black thing with his foot. For one terrible moment, I think it's the roasted corpse of a pirate, but then I see that it's a bag, a sports bag.

— Kevlar lining, he says to Jerry. We lost one, but there's two mil in there. Should keep the insurance company happy, huh?

Jerry shakes his head in wonder.

— Bastards, he says.

The captain raises an eyebrow.

— Well done, says Jerry in a slightly different tone. Well done.

All of this is happening, and I'm taking it in, but mainly I'm watching Ahmed. When I sense that my dad's attention is on the bag of money, I twist and pull away. I run towards Ahmed, as they march him to a grey metal door, a door Asiz has already gone through.

When I'm about a metre away, the soldier escorting Ahmed pushes around him and holds up a hand to stop me.

— I know you're angry, he says. But we have to follow the law. We can't hurt these –

— I don't want to hurt him, I say.

Behind the soldier, Ahmed is smiling – at least, half his mouth is. The other half is melting, and I feel like my heart will break if I keep having to look at his wounds.

— I don't understand, says the soldier. Please, miss, if you could back away –

— Amy, says Dad, coming up behind me. Amy, let them do their job.

I wrap my arms around myself to stop anyone touching me.

— What will happen to them? I ask. What will happen to the pirates?

The captain and Jerry have caught up with us, too, because it's Jerry who answers.

— They'll be tried according to international law, he says. They'll go to prison.

All this time, Ahmed isn't saying anything. He is just looking at me, his hands cuffed behind his back.

— How long for? I say.

— Life, probably, says Jerry, sounding satisfied with this, like it's a good outcome for the day.

Like beating a bunch of pirates with old guns, from a country where people have nothing, and then putting them in prison for ever is some kind of triumph for justice.

Even as Jerry is talking, the soldier is pushing Ahmed away, towards that door. I feel like if he goes through it into the shadows behind that cool blue metal, I will never see him again, and it will be too late, too late to find out about Farouz. His head is turned the whole time, though, and he is looking at me.

I take a deep breath.

— Farouz? I ask.

Ahmed keeps looking at me as he is dragged away. Then there is an expression of total sadness on his face, and I think, he loved him, and I know in my heart of hearts that I am already using the past tense and there is a reason for that.

Then Ahmed shakes his head, every movement like a physical blow to me, and he is gone into the ship.

In my head I see Farouz, standing on the deck of the *Daisy May*, waving at me, waving and waving. It seemed like the helicopter coming back with the captured men on board was like a ball springing back to the hand, but it wasn't; it was a ball bouncing once, dully, on carpet, before coming to a total and utter stop.

No, I think. Please don't leave me. Don't you leave me, too.

But it's too late.

THREE MONTHS LATER

Listen.

My name is Amy Fields, but the men called me Hostage Three.

You've probably read about me or seen that special on Channel 5 or something.

Maybe you thought I was some kind of heroine. Or maybe you thought I was a slut, a fuck-up – the girl with the piercings, the girl who lit a cigarette in her last exam. I get that, too.

You'd think it would be the slut thing that would upset me, but of the two options, people thinking I'm a heroine makes me the most sick. Because I am the furthest thing from that. I could have gone instead of the stepmother. I could have taken her place, then none of those men would have had to die. The helicopter never would have fired if I had been there on the beach.

So, yes. You've probably read about me or seen pictures of me or listened to people talking about me on the radio – maybe even Carrie or Esme, who seem to be the go-to girls for stories about me – but I haven't told anyone what really happened on the *Daisy May*.

Until now.

And yes, I have told you about the pirates. I have told you about me and Farouz. I've told you about the guns, and the times I thought I was going to die, and the time when people did die, the time when Farouz died, and he, who was always smoking, was smoke instead.

But there's something more important I've got to tell you, something I feel like I'm meant to tell you.

347

This is it:

I'm here to tell you that if you get broken, it's possible to put yourself back together. I'm here to tell you that if you get lost, it's possible that a light will come, dancing, on the horizon, to lead you home.

I know this sounds like something a vicar might say. Actually, no, it doesn't; they probably say things like, would you like some more tea, and, could you pass me that Battenberg.

But it does sound like something a preacher might say, one of those zealous guys you get on US TV, from the kind of states where my mom came from. Only, here's the difference: a preacher doesn't know for sure that god exists, or that Jesus died for our sins, or any of those things. But I do know what I'm talking about. I know for an absolute honest-to-goodness fact that life can kick you to pieces, break you into a thousand little shards, and that you can get up again and mend yourself.

I promise.

And maybe, by the time I'm finished, you will believe me.

After my interview at the Royal Academy of Music, I head home, sitting for nearly two hours on the tube and then the bus, not reading, not listening to anything, just watching the world move past me.

It's already after dusk as I walk across Ham Common to our house, and the stars are out. I look up and see the sky blazing – not as bright or as much of a multitude as in Somalia, but still beautiful. The Milky Way is a streak of stardust across the sky.

As I open our gate and follow the short gravel path to the front door, I think about how, if you look at a picture of the Milky Way, like the ones that the Hubble Space Telescope takes, it looks like someone has painted fire across the darkness. From down here we see the stars as clear things, sparkling, like ice or diamonds. But really they are burning.

While I'm turning my key in the door, I hear something from upstairs floating down through the window. For a moment I think it must be some kind of animal that has got into the house. But then I realise what it is: it's Dad, laughing. I'm startled. Dad doesn't laugh; it isn't his style. Laughing doesn't inform you or make you money or achieve anything. The thought of Dad laughing is like the thought of Dad reading fiction. And yet there he is again, laughing.

Sarah is doing that, I think. Sarah is making him laugh. I'm grateful for it – for her lightness, her silliness, the things I hated about her before, her little sweetnesses. Even my mom never managed to make my dad laugh, not really, and this strikes me as an important realisation. I am aware, all of a sudden, that if I'm not careful, my mom's untimely death will cause me to remember an ideal version of her, like some perfect specimen caught in amber.

She was not perfect.

She was my mom.

When I get inside, I stand at the bottom of the stairs.

— Dad, I call. Can I speak to you?

He comes downstairs on his own, and I guess Sarah has decided we need to talk alone. I'm grateful to her for that, too.

We go into the living room. I sit on the sofa, and he sits on the armchair in the window.

Then, slowly, my voice halting, I tell him everything.

When I'm finished, I look up at him. Dad looks like he's just found something unspeakable floating in his soup.

— What were you *thinking*? he says.

— I wasn't, I say. I wasn't thinking.

— Did you . . . ? he asks. He does this awful mime that I never want to see again, no matter how long I live.

Which I'm now hoping, by the way, will be a very long time – my life, I mean. I wondered – a hundred years ago, it seems like – if I was like my mom. If I really was self-destructive, like Sarah said, that night before she announced the trip. Now I know I'm not.

— Jesus, Dad, I say. No, OK? No, we didn't.

Something happens on Dad's face – it's like there are two hims, a sad one and a happier one, and they're struggling against each other.

— The boy, Farouz, says Dad. His voice is kind of strangled. You really felt something for him, didn't you?

— Yes, I say. Yes, I felt something.

— Oh, Amy, he says.

— Yes, I know, OK? You told me not to. I disobeyed you, so have a go at me. But not right now, please.

He gets up and comes and sits on the couch next to me, the leather one that Mom had made by some guy in Connecticut who took, like, a year to do it. His hand touches my arm.

— That's not what I meant, he said. I meant that I'm sorry. For you.

I stare at him.

— What? I say.

Now Dad looks hurt.

— Amy, he says. Do you think I don't care about you, or something?

— I think . . . I say. I think that . . . Mom was amazing, and she was hardly cold in her grave before you replaced her with someone else.

I sit a little straighter, startled. Even I wasn't expecting this to come out of my mouth.

Dad doesn't seem surprised, though. He just looks down at his hands.

— You're right, he says. Your mother was amazing. He pauses for quite a long time. Then he looks me right in the eye. But she left us, Amy, he says.

And there it is. I hug myself.

— I know, I say very quietly.

— You . . . he begins. I remember you saying that it was her right, if she was unhappy. And it was, of course, it was. But I think . . . by thinking that . . . by forgiving her so quickly . . . maybe you made yourself forget some things.

I blink, finding myself on the brink of tears.

— Maybe, I admit, even more quietly now. But my voice doesn't break, the tears don't come, even though my mind is churning, like waves in the sea.

See, there are things. Dad is right – there are some things.

There is, for example, the watch. I remember going into my dad's wallet, a week or so after my sixteenth birthday, to get some money for a night out. And in there, tucked into the bill fold compartment, was a credit card receipt for a Chanel watch, with a signature on it.

My dad's signature.

Was he with her, and they bought it together? Did he buy it, and she just decided to give it to me on her own, over breakfast? I don't know; I've never been able to ask him. And he never said anything, even though I saw the surprise flare in his eyes, like a match being struck, when he came home the next day from work and saw the watch on my wrist.

My mind flies to Mexico then. And this is the truth: Dad wasn't working that summer. His own mom, my Granny Fields, was dying. But my mom wouldn't stay in London with him, wouldn't go to the hospice.

She said:

— I'm only just coping. I can't deal with that shit.

She said:

— I need the sunshine, for my serotonin levels.

She said:

— If I don't go to Mexico, you may as well commit me here and now.

So she and I went to Mexico instead.

Sitting there with my dad, I realise for the first time that it is possible and allowable to believe two opposite things at exactly the same time:

I still love my mom. I still believe that she was entitled to her choice, that she answered her unhappiness, that she escaped from something terrible, that she had no other way out, and I can't blame her for it.

Also, I admit something else to myself.

I admit:

That I hate her for leaving me.

That I will never, ever forgive her.

I look at Dad, sitting beside me on the sofa, looking crumpled, like a worn suit. He had to live with her, too, I think. He has had to live without her as well. He probably hates her, or part of him does, even while he loves her, and that must be tearing him apart; I can imagine, because it's been tearing me apart, too.

And yet, even though none of this is OK, even though it's so not OK, what has happened, everything that has happened . . . Despite all that . . . I have a feeling, as I look at Dad sitting there. I have a feeling it might just, one day, be OK.

— I'm sorry, Amy-bear, he says. I fell in love. It happens. He touches my hair by my forehead, hooks it over my ear. I think you know that, he says gently.

— I know, I say. It isn't that. It's . . .

But no. I can't say what I want to say. My mouth closes on the words.

— It's what, Amy? he asks.

— It's that you left me, too, I say, the words coming out in a rush, as if I was trapping them in there all that time, like birds in my lungs, in my vocal cords, and now they've escaped.

— What do you –

— Work! I say. Trips. The office. Yes, she left me, she left us. But you left me, too. And you're *alive*.

Dad shrinks, like a balloon when you untwist the end.

— I know, he says. Of course, he continues, work isn't an issue any more.

— No, I say.

Out of the corner of my eye, I can see a family walking home across Ham Common. A mother, a father, two children, one of them swinging between their parents' hands. I'm lucky, I think. I'm so, so, so lucky. In my mind I am picturing those women Farouz told me about, even though I never saw them, the ones burying their babies by the side of the road, as they ran from Mogadishu.

— I need . . . I start to say, but I can't finish. It's too American, speaking about feelings like this, and I've been in London for years – it's atrophied some muscle in me, the one that

354

pushes sincere emotions out of your mouth and into the world. Or maybe it's just that there's too much now: Mom, Dad, Farouz ... There's too much hurt there, and if I start to let it out, what if it never stops?

— You need a parent, he says. You need comfort. You need security.

— Yes, I say.

— I'm sorry, he says. I'm so sorry. And I'm sorry about Farouz, too.

He sits still for quite a long time. Then he holds out his arm, and I incline my head a fraction, let him know it's OK – I'm still hugging myself, but, yes, maybe it's better to be hugged by someone else – and he puts his arm around me, holds me close.

— I thought of a present, I say. For my eighteenth.

— Yes? he says. Name it.

— Lunch. Once a week. And you're not allowed to cancel on me. Ever.

He finds my hand and shakes it.

— Deal, he says.

There's silence for a moment.

Then.

— Dad, I say. On the yacht, when Sarah wanted to go with the pirates ... Was that true, what she said? That you couldn't do it because you didn't want to leave me?

He doesn't answer for a moment.

Then ...

— Yes, he says.

And I know that it is the truth, that he wasn't scared, not for himself, anyway.

— Oh, I say.

— And the thing is, Amy, he says. The thing is that I'm here now.

— Yes, I say.

And it turns out that, actually, this is all that needs to be said.

I meet him a couple of weeks after my interview.

I've sent emails, using the address he gave me in the shower cubicle – loads of emails. I don't know why – it's a stupid thing to do, really. But I write to him anyway, tell him about my life.

And one day, to my total shock, I get a reply.

We talk back and forth a bit; his written English is not so good and it's tricky. But we get across the essentials, I tell him my side of the story, and then he says he's coming to London, and would I like to meet him? It's so out of the blue, it shocks me. Of course I want to meet him. But I'm scared, too, of what he might say, of what it might be like.

Dad, of all people, drives me to Richmond, to the tube. He's still not working at the moment. I haven't spoken to him about it again, him getting fired – we're not quite at that point yet. Still, things are much better, that much I can say, and it's only been three months since we left the *Daisy May*. Not perfect – I haven't totally forgiven him yet, not at all, and I don't think he's forgiven me, for growing up, for falling in love with the worst possible boy – but definitely better. Above all, however much Dad is judging me in his head, he doesn't say anything out loud.

That's my dad all over, it seems. My old dad – because suddenly it's like he's kicked out the hermit crab that was squatting in his body and come back to me, a little. He's paying for Ahmed's defence – his lawyer thinks that, with our character references, she can get his sentence commuted. Maybe get him back to Somalia before too long.

After he drops me off, telling me to be careful, I take the tube to Embankment, then cross the Thames on the amazing footbridge, London laid out like a diorama around me. We've arranged to meet at the London Eye, so I walk along the river till I get there.

I see him after maybe two minutes of looking. He's thinner, somehow weaker-seeming, a little paler, as if the English air has leached some of the colour out of him. There are different lines on his face, around his eyes. He is wearing an Arsenal cap. It makes me think of those parakeets in London and how long it will be before they belong.

I wave at him and he walks over to me.

— Amy, he says.

I shake his hand, which he is holding out in front of him, like an offering.

— Hello, I say.

— Is good to meet, he says. I'm sorry. My English not good.

— It's perfectly good, I say.

There is something with soft wings moving inside my stomach, and there is something hot and wet in my eyes, but I blink it back. I won't let myself cry. It's just – he's so like him. Older, of course, and harder somehow, like he's a version of Farouz that was left a little too long in a cupboard and has gone slightly stale. But still with those grey eyes, the long eyelashes.

— You look like him, I say.

He nods.

— But not so good, I think, he says with a wink.

I laugh, surprised.

Then Farouz's brother points to the Eye.

— We go? he says.

I wasn't really expecting this, hadn't planned for it, but I guess it makes sense. Actually, I've never been on it – when you live in a city you don't tend to do the touristy things.

— Yeah, OK, I say.

So we buy tickets and queue, then we enter one of the little round pods, and we're lofted slowly into the sky. I see the river elongate below us, Big Ben rising up, the city stretching out like a map, which is a stupid comparison, but I don't care, that's what it looks like. White clouds are sailing low over London.

— He speak of me? says Abdirashid, as we stand next to each other, looking out at the view.

We are near the apex of the circle. Around us, seagulls are wheeling, and we could almost be back on the sea. I wonder when there will be more seagulls in London than pigeons – when they will just be part of the city, belonging to it, at home.

— Yes, I say, which is the pure truth. He talked about you all the time.

Abdirashid is trembling, and I don't know if that's because of talking about his brother or drugs or what. I know from Farouz that he has not had a good life.

— Good thing? he says. Farouz say good thing?

— All good things, I say. He told me a story about a concert. As I say this I remember being under the shower, listening to Farouz telling it.

— Concert?

I mime playing an oud.

— Ah, says Abdirashid. Yes. He smiles.

— How . . . how did you get here? I ask. How did you get out of prison?

Abdirashid taps his pocket.

— A man bring money. A hundred thousand dollar. I pay for free. Then I know someone who sell passport.

— You got compensation? I say. For Farouz dying?

— Yes. From lawyer.

— Nyesh?

— Yes. Him. And then I am wanting leave. And I am checking Farouz email. And I get email from you. You speak to my brother, who is dead.

He says this in a kind of gentle questioning way, not like he's saying I'm crazy, but more like he's just curious. I nod.

— I knew he was dead, I say. But I thought . . . I don't know. I hoped he might be there, anyway.

— Me also, says Abdirashid. This why I check email.

It's a heavy moment, so to lighten it, I say in a kind of jolly breezy tone:

— It's a good job you knew his password.

Abdirashid looks embarrassed, though, and at first I think it's because he tricked his brother somehow, looked over his shoulder or something when he was logging into Hotmail.

But then he says:

— I always know Farouz password. Always the same.

— Oh, I say. OK.

— Is always my name. Abdirashid.

He looks down at his feet.

Whatever I was about to say, it stops in my throat, and it's like it's going to choke me. I'm about to cry, and I don't want to do that. Instead I watch a barge, crawling small through the silvery water below us. I think about love. I think about money, about compensation. I assume this is why Abdirashid touched his pocket, because there is still some cash in there left over from the hundred thousand. So Farouz was right – that kind of thing does happen. There's honour with the pirates, like he said. I'm so glad. I'm so glad that something has come out of Farouz's death, something positive. I can't say all this to Abdirashid – he wouldn't understand my English.

So, as the pod we're in arcs down towards the ground, I tell him, in as simple English as I can, about what happened on the yacht, how his brother died, the things that Farouz told me, the way I felt about him. Which is complicated – some part of me loved him but a big part of me was afraid of him, too; muscles are attractive things, but they pull triggers also, they slit throats. I did fancy him, obviously. And I felt sorry for him, for what had happened to him in his life. But is that the same thing as love? I don't think so.

I don't know if I make Abdirashid understand, but I don't think it matters, either. I am talking about Farouz, his brother, and that is the important thing.

When I have finished, he looks level at me for a while.

— I help you, he says. I have money.

This is so the most absurd thing I've ever heard that I literally don't know how to respond. Because, yes, he has money, but it's my dad's money or the bank's money, which more or less amounts to the same thing. And now the brother of one of the pirates who took us hostage, with guns, is trying to give it back to me!

— It's OK, I say. Don't worry. I don't need money, thank you. I'm resitting one of my A levels, then I'm going to college.

— A levels? College?

I make a show of playing the violin.

— To learn, I say. Learn more.

Abdirashid nods his understanding, looks out at the darkening sky above London. The stars are just starting to come out. He takes a cigarette packet from his pocket, flicks the bottom with a fingernail, and a cigarette jumps out into his fingers, like a magic trick. He lights it, then offers the pack to me.

— No, thanks, I say. I don't smoke.

And as I say it, I realise it's true.

Abdirashid opens his mouth to say something, then closes it again. Takes a moment.

— Farouz . . . was happy? he asks finally. Before . . . before he die?

I think of when I was lying in Farouz's arms, looking up at the sky, my body glowing.

I think of him laughing.

I think of him showing me the stars, the enthusiasm in his voice.

And I am glad, because this is an easy question to answer, and there are other questions he could have asked which would have been more difficult.

I take Abdirashid's hand.

— Yes, I say.

And it is something I can say with confidence. It is something I know. As I say it, as I say that word, *yes*, I feel like there is a weight that has been pressing down on Abdirashid's shoulders, and now it looks like at least some of it is gone; he is standing straighter already.

This is the thing: people think that magic doesn't exist, but it does, all the time. We use spells every day: the spell of forgiveness, the spell of thanks. Abdirashid put Farouz under a kind of spell. He saved his younger brother's life – he cast on him a spell of loyalty, which Farouz only shook off by dying, by saving Abdirashid in return. I think Abdirashid knows this, and it explains a lot of the weight that was pressing on his shoulders.

But I have just given him the spell of moving on, despite everything, and, more than anything, he seems grateful.

— Yes, I say again to Abdirashid. He was happy.

Water rushes and courses over me in the shower on the yacht, the morning of the handover.

— From before the war? Farouz says. A story of me and my brother?

— Yes, I say.

— OK. OK, I have one. This story happened before we left Mogadishu, he says. In 1990 maybe, or 1989. So I was six, I think.

I close my eyes, listening to Farouz speaking, to the long spell of his voice. Shampoo foams in my hands.

— We knew the rebels were coming, he says – even us children. But we tried not to know it. At my school, there was a concert. The orchestra played for the parents who were all in the audience, and the children who could play well also did solo pieces. I was one of those children. I mean, I didn't play that well. I was only six. But my father was a professor of music – he made me play from when I was small, so I was better than most children of that age, I suppose. Abdirashid, too, he was made to play the piano, but he was always more of a rebel; he had stopped already.

That day, at the concert, I was supposed to play some simple music on my oud. I don't even remember what, I was so young. Some folk song, I suppose.

But, Amy, I was scared. I did not want to play on that stage, on my own, in front of all those people. It was a hot day, I remember, and as we entered the hall I was sweating. My parents must have been with me, but I don't remember them. I mean, I don't see them when I picture this event. I only see Abdirashid.

What happened was that I left my family in the seats and joined the other children on stage. We played a few things, which was fine, because I was with other people. Then a girl stood up with her clarinet, and walked to the microphone at the front of the stage. I listened to her, but all I could hear was my heart thumping in my chest. My hands would not stay still.

Eventually, the time came when I was meant to get up myself. But I could not move. I was hot, sweating, but I was also frozen, like a piece of meat, hard and still. The teacher was telling me that I had to go to the microphone, but I couldn't do it. The stage lights were blazing, it seemed like, cooking me in that seat, and there was nothing I could do about it. Usually, when I held my oud, it was like it was alive, like it was shaping itself to fit my body, not the other way around. Now it was a dead weight in my hands.

I was aware of all those people out there, waiting for me to play, though I couldn't see them because of the lighting, and I felt afraid, as afraid as if they had gathered to see me killed, not to see me play my instrument.

That was when Abdirashid left the audience and climbed up on to the stage. He walked over to me, took my hand and helped me to stand up. Then he led me to the microphone.

OK? he said to me, not in a hurry, just calm and gentle, even though so many people were watching. We were standing in a circle of light. It was impossible to see the audience, but I could sense them out there, breathing, the way the sea respires at night, invisible.

No, I told him. I want you to stay.

There was a music stand in front of the microphone, and someone had already put on it my sheets. Abdirashid nodded at me, then he took the music off the stand and held it out, so that I could read it. He smiled at me for me to start.

But we had not seen the teacher, who had come up beside us. She always wore a headscarf, this teacher, and was always glaring under it.

You cannot be here, she said to Abdirashid. This is a Year Two concert. Persons from other school years cannot stand on the stage.

Abdirashid did not flinch or blink. He held out the music on his flat palms. I am not a person, he said to her. I am a music stand.

On the yacht, in our time, Farouz pauses, and is silent.

The shower is a rushing in my ears.

— Are you still there? I say.

— Yes, says Farouz.

— What happened after that? What did the teacher say?

— I do not know, says Farouz. I must have played the piece, I suppose. I just remember Abdirashid telling the teacher he was a music stand, staying with me on that stage, in that circle of light.

I close my eyes, as Farouz tells me this, as the shower washes over me. My senses merge: his words are all over me; the water is talking.

Suddenly, there is a prickling feeling in my head. It's like pins and needles in my mind – it's like there's something inside me, some emotion, that I have been sitting on for months, curled under me like a forgotten limb, dead, and now it is coming back to life, blood pouring into it, hot like tears.

And the thing that is making it come back to life is Farouz, and the idea of leaving him behind.

Don't leave me, I think – stupidly, because, in fact, it's me who's going to leave, and there's no way it could be any other way.

And then real tears start to spill out, merging with the water, merging with the words from Farouz's mouth. And I'm surprised because I never cry, never even did when Mom died, but there I am pouring tears, just absolutely pouring them, like a container that is overflowing.

— Are you OK? asks Farouz.

— Yeah, yeah, I say. Just got some water in my mouth.

Which must be pretty unconvincing when there I am sobbing, but he doesn't ask again.

I think, we won't ever see each other again after today.

But it's OK, it's all right.

Because I have his stories, little pieces of him, and they are inside my mind, and I will be able to remember them whenever I like. It's the same with my mom, I realise, just as the hot water begins to run out, and my skin tingles with the cold. I have my memories of her, and I can put them next to Farouz, in my mind, and take them out whenever I like and look at them.

Mom and Farouz, they will be my hostages. I will carry them around inside me, secretly, and never let them go, and only ever keep them safe.

My mom was wrong, and then I was wrong, I think.

I turn off the water and stand there, steaming.

My mom was wrong when she said we would meet again in the stars. We don't even have to wait that long. She's here, inside me.

I was wrong when I thought that because so many things reminded me of her, it would be like she was always dying, over and over again. It's the opposite, really, I realise now. She wasn't just a body – she was a person, spreading out in time, into bank accounts and email addresses and a thousand holidays and Christmases, spreading into my mind; and because I saw her nearly every day before she died, all those days are stored inside me, all those images, and they will never, ever go away.

Everything that has happened is still happening, and will always happen, over and over.

These, then . . .

These are just three:

On a stage, in a circle of light, a boy is holding out his hands to his brother, and will always be holding them out, and on those hands is music.

In the middle of Richmond Park, my mother is laughing, and will always be laughing, at a table that shouldn't be there.

On the deck of a luxury yacht, Farouz is standing, and will always be standing, breathing in the stars.

This, then . . .

This, finally, is the end.

And . . .

At the same time . . .

It will never be the end.